THE WOMAN NEXT DOOR

Cass Green is the pseudonym of Caroline Green, an award-winning author of fiction for young people. Her first novel, *Dark Ride* won the RoNA Young Adult Book of the Year and the Waverton Good Read Award. *Cracks* and *Hold Your Breath* garnered rave reviews and were shortlisted for eleven awards between them. She is the Writer in Residence at East Barnet School and teaches Writing for Children at City University. Caroline has been a journalist for over twenty years and has written for many broadsheet newspapers and glossy magazines. *The Woman Next Door* is her first novel for adults.

 @CassGreenWriter

THE WOMAN NEXT DOOR

CASS GREEN

HARPER

This novel is entirely a work of fiction.
The names, characters and incidents portrayed in it are
the work of the author's imagination. Any resemblance to
actual persons, living or dead, events or localities is
entirely coincidental.

Harper
An imprint of HarperCollins*Publishers*
1 London Bridge Street
London SE1 9GF

www.harpercollins.co.uk

This paperback edition 2016
4

First published in Great Britain by
HarperCollins*Publishers* 2016

A catalogue record for this book is
available from the British Library

ISBN: 9780008203566

Set in Minion by Palimpsest Book Production Limited, Falkirk, Stirlingshire

Find out more about HarperCollins and the environment at
www.harpercollins.co.uk/green

For my Dad, George Green
1927–2014
Much missed.

PART ONE

HESTER

Cough, sniff, sigh.

Sniff, sigh, cough.

And so it goes on.

Mary, at the next terminal, is a veritable one-person orchestra of bodily sounds. It must be something to do with her size. She's constantly spilling out of herself, like there's someone bigger trapped inside.

She's not the only person I'm finding distracting today. The old chap opposite, Jacky, I think he's called, apparently believes an Adult Education course on Essential Computer Skills – in a *library* – is a suitable place to eat his lunchtime sandwiches. I can clearly hear the click of his jaw as he masticates bread, cheese, and pickle. The reason I know so much about the sandwich is because he is scattering a confetti of the contents over the keyboard.

You would think that his advanced years would have brought a little more wisdom about this sort of thing. He is possibly like many of the elderly and doesn't really give a stuff anymore what others think. I quite envy that.

I clear my throat and turn my attention back to the screen, where I 'scroll' down the pages of the *Mail Online*. It's all depressing: stories about immigration; teenagers heading off to join ISIS; and politicians telling the usual fibs.

But I enjoy knowing the correct word for what I am doing. I am now a woman who 'scrolls', 'downloads', and 'surfs the web', among other things.

Oh yes, Terry, you didn't think I had it in me, did you?

The point is: I will no longer feel inadequate when I see people tapping away at computers, as though they belong to yet another club I am excluded from. I can do this now, too. Although heaven knows whether I really shall bother.

I look around the library, glancing at the big clock to see how much of the session is left. A couple of teenagers across the way have managed to cover a whole table with their belongings and, like the old man, are openly eating lunch. One of them has some sort of fast food and the fatty, savoury smell tickles my nose and makes my tummy give a little growl. I would never eat anything like that, but breakfast does seem a long time ago.

I think about lunch – a ham sandwich perhaps, or an omelette – and picture my kitchen. Bertie will be a big scruffy comma in his bed, gently snoring. The clock will tick with a dull *thunk*, which has always been a little too loud. Or maybe there just aren't enough other noises to balance it out?

This sort of thinking will get me nowhere. I can feel one of my funks coming on and I must fight it. Maybe I will bake a cake when I get home. Something complicated, which involves skill. It could be my own small celebration for reaching the last lesson of the course?

I certainly deserve a pat on the back for sticking with it. It's fair to say I had a shaky start, mainly because I didn't enjoy the patronizing attitude of the tutor, Alice, an Antipodean who looks about twelve yet always reeks of cigarette smoke. She has a slightly seedy appearance; her small fingers are adorned with chipped, grubby-looking polish and her dark blonde hair has been put into those horrible dreadlocks. Why on earth a white girl would do that with her hair is anyone's guess. They're piled on top of her head every which way giving her the appearance of a young nicotine-stained Medusa. She speaks in a cheerful lilting way that is a little too heavy on the question marks. And she never seems to wear a bra so her small bosom jiggles about like a pair of tennis balls under the vest tops she favours.

She was patient enough when I struggled at the beginning. I'll give her that.

It didn't come to me easily at first. I had a tendency to lift the mouse off the table while trying to master it. When I explained, once, that I was trying to move the cursor 'up', she actually said, 'Aww, bless?' *Bliss.*

I was stunned! You would think I was a child or a little old lady instead of a healthy woman of just 62. I said, 'Young woman, I suggest you show a bit of respect.' That told her. Since then, she still does the annoying laughing thing, but her eyes are always sliding off somewhere other than my face.

No, I'm not sorry this is coming to an end. I only took the course to get myself out of the house, and I am not going to be making friends with any of this lot.

Most of them are much older than me, and the woman nearest my own age – who goes by the name 'Binnie' – isn't really my class of person. She catches my eye now, then looks down again. No doubt she took it personally when I turned down her suggestion to 'go for a cuppa' after the class on the first week. I said, 'I'm afraid I don't really drink tea,' which was a bit of a white lie, because I do in fact drink it a great deal!

But she is one of those women who positively exudes her maternal bounty like an aura. I've heard her going on about 'my daughter' and 'my newest grandson' to anyone who will listen. She even, if you can believe this, has a tote bag with 'World's Best Grandma' and a giant picture of a gurning infant on it. She is one of those women entirely defined by the workings of her womb. I know that, if I had taken her up on her offer, the 'cuppas'

5

would barely be on the table before she would be saying, 'So Hester do you have children?'

Why *do* women ask this question so readily? It's not as though we talk about the intimate workings of our bodies in any other context. It's a very personal question and I have never really found a comfortable way to field it. I want to reply, 'That's none of your business', but I'm aware that would be a little rude.

No, she is not really my sort of person. My mind drifts back to my baking plan and I muse on what sort I could make. A nice lemon drizzle, or a rich fruitcake perhaps. But the gloomy feeling I have been trying to hold off is descending now, falling around my shoulders like a dank shroud.

I know what will happen if I embark on a baking project. I will have a couple of pieces of whatever it will be and then the rest will just sit there, wasted, drying out, until I throw it into the wheelie bin. I can't give any of it to Bertie. It's very bad for dogs to have sweet things. They can get diabetes and heart disease just like we can.

If I was like Binnie over there, I expect the cake would last five minutes before sticky-fingered little ones were cramming pieces into their mouths like hungry birds. It really is so unfair. All of it.

'Are you all right, Hester?' *Hister*.

I look up. Alice is peering directly into my face, for once, with an expression of sugary sympathy. Glancing around I become aware that several of them are looking at me now. Binnie's eyes are wide, and Jackie has paused mid-munch of his sandwich, his bottom lip glistening with grease and hanging slightly open.

So many eyes. All on me.

'Yes, why on earth do you ask?' I bark a short laugh but it sounds entirely unnatural.

Alice hesitates and then actually puts her grubby little paw on my shoulder. I look at it until she takes it away. She clears her throat.

Blushing (rather prettily) she says, 'It's just that you seemed to be, um, muttering something? I wondered who you were talking to?'

My tummy seems to flip over and my breath catches so I have to cover it up by pretending to cough. I can feel the heat creeping up my throat and flooding my cheeks.

Oh dear God. I have finally started talking to myself? What am I doing?

'Hester?' she says again.

I stiffen my spine and meet her gaze full on so that she is then the one who is blushing. I gather my handbag from where it is resting next to the computer monitor and rise to my feet.

'I am quite well, thank you,' I say. 'I think I'm going to go home now.'

'Oh, okay?' she says, in that annoying singsong voice. 'It's just, we're all planning to go the pub? You're very welcome to join us?'

I can't think of anything I'd like to do less. I can just picture it. Alice, all full of fake bonhomie; the oldies getting squiffy and promising loudly (and falsely) to keep in touch.

No. I'd rather stare at my uneaten cake and find out what's on Radio 4.

Yet it stings.

It's the, 'You're very welcome to join us', thing. It wasn't, 'Oh no, Hester, you have to come to the pub! It wouldn't be the same without you!' Ha! It's like I'm an afterthought. And now my silly eyes blur and kaleidoscope Alice's face in front of me.

But I still have my pride. I have achieved what I set out to do. I have learned how to use a computer. I am finished here.

'No thank you,' I say and then the lie just slides out of my mouth. 'My daughter and grandchild are visiting later. I have things to do today.'

'Oh?' Alice seems to chew the word and then the bright smile is plastered over her face once again. 'Well, I hope you have a lovely time with them? It's been great meeting you?'

'Yes, I'm sure,' I say, before walking quickly away towards the exit.

I catch Binnie's eye, and I can see her look of surprise.

I expect Terry is laughing in his grave.

7

MELISSA

As the stylist cocks the mirror to show her the back of her hair, Melissa can't help picturing a shaven-headed teenager in a Moscow bedsit.

'Looking gorgeous, don't you think?' says Susie.

Melissa nods and forces a tight smile. They say the best hair comes from Russia, and this type of blonde is worth every penny of the £400. If only she could get rid of the lurid Gulag imagery.

'Those'll see you right for another six weeks or so,' says Susie, with a kindly squeeze of her shoulders.

'Great, thanks Susie.'

But it's hard to feign the enthusiasm she knows is expected. The whirr and blast of hairdryers and the tinny thud of the background music have anaesthetized her into a kind of stupor. She can't even quite remember what she and Susie had been talking about during the endless hours she has been sitting in this chair. She feels somehow bonded to it.

Her reluctance to get up prompts Susie to speak quietly into her ear.

'Why don't you finish your tea before you go?' she says in her soft Geordie accent. 'Boss likes to get people out the door, if you know what I mean, but you're all right for a bit longer. My eleven o'clock hasn't even arrived yet.'

Melissa murmurs her gratitude as Susie bustles away and reaches for the delicate china teacup cooling next to the jumble of brushes, scissors, and tongs in front of her.

The cloth pyramid of camomile tea has a greasy shine to it and the liquid is tepid and almost slimy as it slips down her throat, which feels scratchy. She coughs experimentally and begins to fret. It would be the worst time to come down with something. She could picture herself croaking miserably at people over the music of the party. There's some zinc and vitamin C at home. She'll dose herself up with them later.

Looking back at her reflection, she runs a hand through her hair, turning her head this way and that. She takes care not to snag the tiny plugs woven into her own thin, expensively dyed tresses, which now hang in glossy waves the colour of butterscotch, wishing yet again that she didn't always *do* this. Wonder about the provenance of the hair, that is.

Surely there's nothing wrong with it? It's no different from the Bio Gel that adorn her fingers in a colour she is told is 'French Nude', although Melissa thinks her fingertips look a bit creepy. Android, almost. She wonders what percentage of her is now artificial.

But the extensions feel different. She pictures some poor pretty girl losing the only asset she has so that a rich woman thousands of miles away can enjoy the weight of it on her shoulders. All too easy to picture the grubby transaction involved in selling your own hair.

It is as she is musing gloomily on this that she feels a strange prickle of unease, like there has been a ripple in the atmosphere, a tiny, fizzing depth charge deep in the primeval part of her brain.

She frowns and looks around.

Someone is watching her. Melissa turns her head sharply to look at the main window. It is slightly steamed up and the displays

9

of flowers – ugly spiky things that she privately detests but which are presumably deemed stylish – obscure the view a little but she can see a swatch of High Street outside.

People drift or march past the window. It's a perfectly ordinary day in North London.

Life bustles on, oblivious to Melissa. No one is looking in at her.

Of course they aren't. What was she expecting? Who was she expecting?

She gets up crisply and walks to the desk to pay, her stomach still roiling queasily from the shock of thinking she was being watched. Her back aches and her bottom is stiff from hours of sitting.

Susie seems to materialize from nowhere and, taking care not to damage her newly faked nails, Melissa rummages for her purse and then opens the small wooden box that has been discreetly placed in front of her, containing the bill.

Melissa knew that this morning wouldn't come cheap, but still, the cost of hair extensions and styling, manicure, pedicure, and eyebrow threading, at almost £600, gives her a thrill of transgressive pleasure.

She hopes Mark will choke on his coffee, as she pushes her credit card across the counter to Susie and looks for a twenty to leave as a tip. If he's going to behave like one of those husbands, then she will be one of those wives.

Outside on the High Street it feels like the contrast button on an old television has been turned up too high. Everything is too bright; nauseatingly colourful. Melissa feels the sharp pinch of a headache beginning in her forehead. She finds her sunglasses and pushes them onto her face a little clumsily, eyes greedy for the shade. A branch of Boots is just over the road and Melissa decides to buy some water and paracetamol before setting off home. Maybe she can head this thing off at the pass so she can enjoy the party later. The caterers will be almost finished now and all that needs to be done is to oversee the Ocado delivery, which is bringing the majority of the booze. It's a bit late, but they let her down yesterday, citing some sort of freezer catastrophe. She hopes the champagne will have enough time to chill for this evening.

It is as she is crossing over to Boots that Melissa feels the crawling sensation again, like fingertips skittering across her skin. She is certain now that it isn't in her head. She read once that it's something to do with peripheral vision.

Someone is definitely watching her.

Melissa's heart begins to thud uncomfortably hard as she whips around in a full circle, eyes narrowed behind her dark lenses. Someone has just been swallowed up by the doors of Superdrug but she didn't see them clearly. The High Street is busy – full of normal people, gazing into phone screens, yanking irritable children along, or, in the case of the few old people dotted about, ambling painstakingly with shoppers or small decrepit dogs. No one is staring at Melissa.

Goosebumps scatter across her arms and she shivers, even though the air is close and heavy. A car alarm shrieks nearby and Melissa flinches. The air feels soupy, with traffic fumes mingling with the cigarette smoke wafting from a doorway, where a young woman's head is bent over her mobile, apparently having a furious conversation at low volume.

At the far end of the High Street, near the library and fire station, Melissa can see a figure who looks familiar. It takes a minute to realize it's her next-door neighbour, Hester. She is a fussy, annoying little woman who was constantly in Melissa's face when she first moved into the street. Hester was far too interested in how Melissa was bringing up Tilly, and although she had occasionally helped with babysitting, she was more trouble than she was worth. Melissa managed to slip free of her attention and the last contact they'd had was earlier this year. Melissa couldn't remember the details because it happened bang in the middle of the Sam thing. Something to do with recycling, or parking.

Melissa is in no mood to see Hester just now. She has enough to worry about. Even though it is only a ten-minute walk home from here, she hurries over to the taxi rank and climbs into the first available car, catching the appreciative look tossed her way by the driver. As she leans forward to give the address, she feels warmed by the attention and thinks about what he sees: a good-looking, well-groomed woman of means. Someone he could only ever admire from a distance. And if he'd known her back then? She doubts he would have allowed her in his taxi.

She is unrecognizable now.

Surely.

Melissa settles back in the seat as the car pulls away and tries to think calming thoughts. No one is watching her. No one is following her.

No one knows.

Her mobile trills, making her jump a little and she inwardly curses herself for her jumpiness.

'Babes, it's me.' Saskia's husky voice pours into her ear like warm oil.

Despite having been educated at an elite girls' boarding school, and growing up riding ponies and skiing, Saskia's diction wouldn't be out of place at a gathering of Pearly Kings and Queens.

Her Mockney affectation sometimes irritates Melissa, but she is also one of the warmest people she has ever met. She laughs like a navvy and can infect Melissa with a dose of humour when she is otherwise unable to feel it. Her loyalty during the Sam episode will never be forgotten by Melissa. Saskia knows all too well what it is like to be cheated on, and the father of her teenage son was sent packing a few years previously.

'What's up?' she says, stifling a yawn. The idea of lying down on the scuffed, smelly seat of the car and taking a nap feels worryingly tempting.

'Not much,' says Saskia. 'Just wondered if you need any last-minute help? I know you have caterers in but I'm about if you need me.'

'That's really sweet, Sass, but I think I'm all sorted.'

There's a brief silence before Saskia speaks again. 'And has there been any change of heart ...?'

Melissa sighs. 'Nope. He claims it's "totally unavoidable". Can you believe him?'

Saskia groans and then Melissa hears the suck and pop of her cigarette.

'Fuck Mark,' says Saskia. 'I'm going to be there to make sure it's the best damned party ever. Nathe is coming along and he can be your barman or something.'

Melissa smiles. 'I can always rely on you.'

'Love ya.' Saskia hangs up.

The car has been stuck in a jam for the last few minutes and Melissa cranes now to see what is going on.

'Some sort of hold-up, is there?' she says to the driver, whose eyes are now framed in the rear-view mirror as he looks back at her.

'There's a lorry that was fannying around unloading something at the back of Asda, but it looks like we're moving now. In a hurry?'

Melissa nods and then turns to the window. She has no interest in chatting through the rest of this journey. As the taxi hums back into movement again, the driver doesn't attempt any further conversation.

They turn down leafy streets where the houses are set back from the road. Several of the houses have original stone sculptures on the gateposts, and when Tilly was little she loved what she called the 'stone piggies' that stand sentry at Hester's gate.

Melissa swears under her breath as she sees the other woman walking just ahead. Hester has managed to get back before her. Not prepared to risk being stuck with her on the doorstep, Melissa switches on a smile for the driver.

'Could I ask you to pull over just here?' she says and she sees his rectangular gaze, harder now.

'Sure,' he says.

She spends some time pretending to look for money, until she is sure Hester is safely inside.

HESTER

I am starting to wonder whether I did the right thing in leaving the library so hastily.

The afternoon has trickled by in a succession of mindless television programmes, which flicker and squawk away in the background. I'm not watching any of them really, but I'm loth to turn them off. They provide a buffer against the silence.

I keep picturing them all in the pub, getting steadily more inebriated. Faces will be flushed now with alcohol, bulbous elderly noses spidered with red veins, mouths open and revealing yellowing dentures as they laugh and laugh and *laugh*. At *me*. I'm sure they will be having a right old time of it. 'Silly, funny old Hester,' they'll say. 'Isn't she the strange one?'

Damn them all.

I know full well what Terry would have made of this.

He was always telling me I was too quick to act, too rash. He'd get that look, the one that seemed to suggest he was a man who required a superhuman level of forbearance.

'Hester, you need to give people a chance,' he'd whine. 'You're so quick to judge.'

What he really meant was, 'Hester, you should let people walk all over you.'

I never anticipated how much he would still haunt me, fifteen years after he died. He seems to be there, yacking away in my head, almost all the time.

My mouth feels stale and I go to pick up my cup of tea but discover that it is quite cold. I must have been sitting here even longer than I had realized. This happens sometimes. I sit down to watch television, and before I know it, it's time to put Bertie out and I don't even remember what I've been watching. I gulp it down anyway, wincing a little at the way it coats my mouth with a milky film.

It is then that I hear the purring of a vehicle stopping outside. I get to my feet and go to the bay window that looks out onto the street. An Ocado van has just pulled up outside, directly below my window. The driver, a balding coloured man of indeterminate middle age, hefts himself out of the front and noisily opens the doors on the side of the van. I part a gap in my nets, noticing the sickly greyness that tells me it's time I washed them again, and stand to the side of the window just so. From this position I can clearly see the contents of the large plastic crates as they are disgorged from the back.

For some reason Melissa has her delivery arrive without carrier bags and it means that I can see exactly what she has ordered from week to week. She has no qualms, it seems, about showing the world all the intimate items, the tampons and deodorants, the panty liners and cotton buds, but I suppose we are all different.

I can tell a lot about the domestic cycles of the house from the shopping. I know when Tilly is home from school because there are slabs of Diet Coca-Cola in the mix, or when Mark is away because the expensive bottled beers he favours are missing. When Melissa is on her own, the shopping contains a lot of organic, low-calorie ready meals. Heaven knows why she needs to diet. Melissa has a wonderful figure and, if anything, could do with a little more meat on her bones.

But this time as I watch the crates emerging from the back of the van it becomes apparent that this is no ordinary delivery.

There's always rather a lot of alcohol but today I see boxes of what looks like champagne. And is that … Pimm's?

More crates are yanked from the van with a scraping sound and now I see forests of French sticks in one. Another is positively crammed with expensive soft fruits such as mangoes and bright strawberries. The colours glow, jewel-like, in this grey afternoon and fill me with a dull ache of longing somewhere around my sternum.

Glancing at my own fruit bowl, I see it contains one banana, stippled and overripe, and a forlorn tangerine that has lost its gloss and looks dry to the touch. I sigh and turn back to the window.

The driver closes the doors of the vehicle with a tinny clang.

And then he turns and looks directly at me, a smirk wrapping around his face.

I pull back from the window so fast I crash painfully into the television. It's an old one and, for a second, the blonde grinning woman on the screen fragments. There is a zigzagging of the image, an angry hiss of static, before the picture rights itself again.

Staggering back into the shadows, rubbing my bruised hip, I reel from the hot scald of humiliation for the second time in a day.

What was he trying to say with that look? That he has seen me before, watching, and finds it odd. I squeeze my hands into fists so tightly my nails bite the soft flesh of my palms.

I walk into the kitchen on trembling legs and slump into a chair, trying to catch my galloping breath.

I have nothing whatsoever to be embarrassed about, yet I seem to ache with shame. Pressing my hand to my cheek I can feel that I am flushed and feverish.

How dare that van driver judge me?

17

How could someone like him possibly understand someone like me?

It's not that I'm *spying* on Melissa. It's just a way of keeping in touch with what's going on in her life.

I sometimes find it hard to make sense of where it all went so wrong.

When that little family first moved in next door, I noticed how she carried Tilly, as though the baby were a grenade. Melissa often looked exhausted but she was still beautiful, still wonderfully turned out. A rush of tender motherly emotion would wash over me as I watched her awkwardly rock the tiny bundle in her arms. I knew I could help her if she would let me.

And she did. For a time. In fact, there was a period when I became quite indispensable to her, if you want the truth.

I was always babysitting at late notice for Tilly. Over time I believe she came to think of me as sort of an aunt, although I couldn't get 'Auntie Hester' to stick as a monica, or whatever that expression is.

There was a time when I fancied I might be invited on holiday with them, even though I was never convinced Mark liked me. Melissa had been complaining about the fact that Tilly would never join the children's holiday clubs when they went to their various resorts. Always classy places, like Mark Warner, or Sandals. Although I imagine these days, with his television career, they go to fancier venues still.

Anyway, all I did was hint that an extra pair of hands could really help but Melissa seemed not to understand. I didn't want to push it.

Now Tilly is away at boarding school and, when she comes home, she smiles politely and answers my questions, but there is a sense that she is keen to get away. I see it in her eyes. How can things have changed so much?

She's certainly not that same girl who liked to make biscuits with me in my kitchen. I think of her small arms moving like pistons inside my big mixing bowl, flour dusting her hair, and it's hard to connect the picture with that near-adult. But there's no point dwelling on it. Time moves on.

But I don't see why Melissa and I can't still be friends, just because Tilly has grown up. She began to drift away as soon as Tilly started primary school, locally.

First, she was never in when I called round to ask her for coffee. At least, I don't think she was there. Once, I thought I saw movement at an upstairs window but I'm sure I must have imagined this.

Why on earth would Melissa hide from *me* of all people?

A few months slipped by, then half a year. We always seemed to be coming in and out at different times. Missing each other.

But I think it was the business with the bins that really caused the rift.

You see there's an alleyway running alongside my house where the bins, for both Melissa's house and my own, are kept. I have always put the bins out on a Monday morning and our little 'system' (as I liked to think of it) was that she would put them back that evening.

When she left them out in the road until Wednesday morning the first couple of times, I thought nothing of it. But then it seemed to become a habit. And that wasn't the only thing. It's very clear that one set of bins is for number 140, mine, and another for 142, hers. But she started to put things in randomly, as though it didn't matter which bin belonged to whom. I'd go to recycle my read copies of the '*Mail* and find it was filled with wine bottles and online shopping packaging. It really was quite irritating. I'm very fond of Melissa, but I suppose this began to really bother me on top of everything else.

At first I'd gently remove the items and put them back into her own bin, hoping that it would get the message across. But it carried on until one day when my entire bin was filled with packaging from Habitat. (It contained a duvet. Duck down. 9.5 tog.) I really felt I should say something. So I went round there. I was perfectly polite and friendly. But I think I may have caught her on a bad day.

She is usually immaculate, as I said, from her shining crown of blonde hair to her prettily painted toenails. That day though, she had on some sort of tracksuit thing and her hair was scraped back into an untidy ponytail. Her eyes looked dull and oddly vacant. It was like no one was there, if that makes sense. Although my heart went out to her (really, I longed to give her a hug and tell her it would be okay) I was determined to say my piece.

But it all seemed to go wrong. She listened without commenting and then simply closed the door in my face. I felt as though I had been slapped. I did something quite out of character at home. I found a dusty old bottle of sherry at the back of my cupboard and had a small glass to calm my nerves. The cloying thickness almost made me sick. God knows how long it had been there. But the whole thing really cut me to the quick.

Such a silly business to fall out over; things have never really been the same since.

I couldn't think of a reason to go round. I would try to make conversation from the front garden (I'd watch for the car and then make sure I was in position) but it has never really been the same.

I so wish that we could be friends again.

Bertie, who always senses when I am distressed, huffs to his feet now. I reach down and scratch the wiry grey hair behind his ears in what I think of as his 'special spot'. He shudders with bliss and his eyes roll back in his head.

My boy.

I've read that King Charles spaniels can live to the age of fifteen. Bertie is only thirteen but I can tell he has lost his lustre a bit lately. He's not the only one.

'Shall Mummy get your dinner?' I say wearily.

His tail jerks and circles like a wonky propeller. I get up. I pour some of his special food into his bowl and place it down on his mat. He starts to eat it with enthusiasm but then loses interest. Sighing again, I open the back door. The kitchen suddenly feels very small.

For one awful moment I think I am going to go quite mad. I'm so very sick of being lonely.

And then, as I stand there, looking out at my overgrown lawn, I have the beginnings of a *wonderful* idea.

Melissa must be having a party, with all that alcohol arriving. There will be such a lot to do. It would take me no time to knock up some scones or a Victoria sponge. She never was much of a baker. She once told me that my lemon drizzle cake was like 'sex on a plate'. I was a bit embarrassed by this, to be honest, but I appreciated that she meant it in a complimentary way. And didn't I have an urge to do some baking earlier? Maybe it was an omen. Perhaps I was meant to leave the library the way I did.

For all I know, Melissa has been waiting for an excuse to patch things up between us. This could be the perfect opportunity to mend bridges.

I'm not even offended that I haven't been invited. I couldn't expect her to, when relations were so strained between us.

'Right, Bertie,' I say, reaching for my apron, which hangs on a hook on the kitchen door. 'Mummy had better get busy.'

I'm the older, more mature, person. It's time to put things right.

MELISSA

The diazepam doesn't seem to be working. She took it more than two hours ago but she's still waiting for the blunting sensation to take effect, for all the hard angles in her mind to soften and blur. The sensation of unease she experienced at the hairdressers has clung to her like a succubus.

She keeps telling herself there's no reason to feel anxious.

Nothing has happened.

All is well.

Melissa stands on the landing and rotates the tips of her fingers into the centre of her forehead. This supposedly wards off headaches, according to Saskia, who picked it up from some alternative therapist. She swears by it, but Melissa remains unconvinced as she gouges hard, rhythmic circles into her skin.

Tilly emerges from her bedroom dressed in pink and green pyjamas that strain across her hips. Her hair is matted on one side and her face is puffy with sleep. She has inherited the distinctive russet brown curls Melissa used to have. It's a lovely colour and Melissa wishes she herself had been able to keep it.

In every other respect Tilly is her father's daughter, from the heavyset shoulders and square, blunt-toed feet, to the almost bovine brown eyes, fringed with enviable lashes. Melissa thinks she carries about a stone more than she should, but she is still a very attractive girl when she makes an effort.

Today she has violet smudges under her eyes. Since the GCSE exams finished, she lives in onesies or pyjamas and thick socks and spends her days padding from fridge to bedroom, where she lies like a large tousled cat, tapping at her iPad and dozing.

But today is a party in her honour and she clearly hasn't been through the shower yet, judging by the cocktail of teenage sweat, stale coffee, and the sickly watermelon-flavoured lip balm she favours rising from her. Her iPad sits lightly on one hand like a prosthesis. Tilly blinks, slowly, as though she has emerged from a subterranean lair.

Mother and daughter eye each other and Tilly attempts an exploratory smile, which morphs into a yawn that smells of sleep. Melissa's face remains impassive. She doesn't want to shout at Tilly and yet it would be so very easy to do right now.

'When are you planning to get ready?' she says crisply. 'This is your party, after all.' Downstairs there is a metallic clatter as the caterers begin to pack away some of their equipment. One of them laughs loudly and says, 'You wish!' A song from Melissa's youth – 'Babooshka' by Kate Bush – wails tinnily from the radio on the windowsill. She has already asked them to turn it down once. Thank God they are almost done.

Tilly's eyes are already being dragged towards the abyss of her iPad, where Walter White is paused, staring out at red, baked earth. She has been on a *Breaking Bad* marathon for the last two days, only pausing to sleep and eat.

'Soon, Mum. I promise.'

Tilly disappears back into her bedroom.

It's the gentleness in her voice that has prompted Melissa's eyes to prickle and ache, unexpectedly. As if Melissa were being humoured. She has made it quite plain that she doesn't really want a party. But she will obviously play along, just to keep her mother happy. In her own time.

23

She'd always imagined, in the days when all her tiny daughter did was cry, shit, and feed, that the compensations would come when she was older; when she was a proper *person*, they would do all the things she never did with her own mother. Melissa pictured her and Tilly cosy on a sofa, bonding over 1980s movies like *The Breakfast Club* and *Pretty in Pink*. Or mother and daughter puffing out their cheeks and complaining good-naturedly about aching feet as they sat down to a good lunch, surrounded by bags from a morning spent shopping.

But none of these fantasies had ever quite come off.

Tilly didn't like what she called 'girly' films, preferring instead to watch violent science fiction thrillers with her father. And the few times Melissa had coaxed her daughter into the West End to shop, they had ended up falling-out and glowering at each other over uneaten salads in Fenwick's café.

Melissa thought it would be nice to celebrate the end of the GCSEs, that was all. It seemed like the kind of thing a family like them – secure, middle class, loving – should be doing.

Secure.

Middle class.

Loving?

That's what she'd thought.

Mark is a doctor, specializing in IVF, who had made a decent living by combining private work with his NHS practice at the Whittington Hospital. But two years ago he had taken part in a BBC documentary set in the private clinic in Bloomsbury where he worked two days a week.

The programme was called *The Baby Business* and it became something of a hit. Every week, thousands of people would discuss the ins and outs of various couples' reproductive failures and successes (more of the former than the latter) over their morning coffees or at bus stops.

There was Janine and Paul, a young man who had almost died

from testicular cancer who longed now to be a father; the Hewlett twins, a pair of sisters who caused a spike in egg donation numbers for a few weeks in late 2013; and a stubbornly un-telegenic, spiky-mannered couple called Trudy and Gary. Every week they bickered with each other on camera and argued with the medical advice given. They were media catnip and Trudy's lugubrious expression even prompted an internet meme in which her face was overlaid by a bleating goat. When their third attempt at IVF failed, the atmosphere shifted and she became Tragic Trudy.

But Mark was the real star of the show. His salt-and-pepper hair, and warm twinkly manner as he delivered both good and bad news, proved to be a ratings winner. Before long he began to receive invitations onto various daytime television sofas.

The BBC commissioned a follow-up series of *TBB*, as they called it. At home Mark privately called it *BBB*, for *Babies Bring Bucks*. All of this had been welcome in terms of money, but for Melissa, having a spotlight shone into her life, a spotlight that could throw every long-abandoned and grubby corner into the sharpest relief, it felt like a particularly cruel cosmic joke.

Mark couldn't understand why Melissa wouldn't accompany him to the various events he was invited to with increasing frequency. She'd always managed to find an excuse. It wasn't her thing. Or she felt like a night in. No one wanted *her* there, after all. They'd only be talking shop.

And it was true that she had no interest in this world. Television people bored her. Their natural privilege was a balm that lubricated their way through life, so they never seemed to snag and falter. They had no idea, the Emmas and the Sachas and the Benedicts, of what the world was like for most of the population, despite the desire to entertain and document them.

But her avoidance of the limelight had blown up in her face in more than one way. Firstly, Mark claimed that her unwillingness to enjoy his success helped push him into the arms of Sam. Mark said that the affair was over, really, before it started.

'It meant nothing. It was a terrible mistake. I'm so sorry. I wouldn't hurt you for the world.'

As though it wasn't far too late to say this.

As a rule, Melissa worked hard to keep her younger self hidden; the small, hard Matryoshka doll that lurked beneath lacquered layers. Mark's grovelling words, which seemed to drip so easily from his lying lips, finally forced her out of hiding.

Melissa was as shocked as he was when she hit him, and the yellowish patina of his bruised cheek was noticed by Make-Up when he next turned up for filming.

But Melissa was being carried on a tide now, one that washed her to Sam's flat in a mansion block in Swiss Cottage. The younger woman's eyes rounded almost comically and she gave a small gasp, like a hiss of gas from a balloon, as Melissa stepped out of the shadows and stood in front of her.

Melissa spoke to her in a measured, calm voice. Afterwards, Sam scurried away on her long, coltish legs, scarlet-cheeked and breathing heavily. She'd left the programme soon after.

They never spoke of it again but the gears of their marriage seemed to turn with more friction now; small irritations Melissa had previously overlooked grated more than ever.

Mark suggested a meal out one evening – 'to talk'. They went to the new restaurant that had opened down the road, which had just appeared in the *Observer* magazine. It was as they stepped towards the white canopy of The Bay, between miniature bay trees in square metal pots, that a photograph was snapped – or stolen – as Melissa thought of it. She hadn't even noticed a flash.

But a week later, a friend of Saskia's had spotted the Society pages piece in *Hello!* magazine. Melissa, smiling, in her black sheath dress and heels, making an *effort*, and 'Handsome Baby Doc Mark', solicitously touching the small of his wife's back as they entered, *'the exciting new eatery that has opened close to the glamorous couple's Dartmouth Park home.'*

Saskia had been surprised by Melissa's muted reaction to the piece, and then sympathetic about the sudden onset of food poisoning that sent Melissa rushing to the downstairs toilet, where she vomited and shook so hard that she could feel her teeth rattling in her skull.

It was just one picture. It meant nothing.

That's what she told herself in the coming weeks, and she almost began to believe it.

But lately Melissa can't seem to shake the feeling that her whole world is simply a snow globe that could tip over and shatter into a million lethal pieces with the slightest push of a fingertip.

Glancing out of the window on the landing now, Melissa sees that the sky seems to be slung low, like a heavy white blanket. The light has a sickly, oppressive edge to it and the house feels full of shadows. Maybe this headache is a warning that a thunderstorm is coming. It feels as though even the weather is out to sabotage the day.

Giving herself a mental shake, Melissa walks into the kitchen and feels marginally better at the industry there. The caterers have been busy all morning and the fridge is heaving with platters and dishes of colourful, tastefully arranged food, but every surface is clean and shining, ready for the guests to arrive a little later.

Ocado have been and gone; the flowers have been delivered – a tall arrangement of lilies that perfectly offsets the newly hung green and gold wallpaper. Really, everything is looking perfect.

Melissa sweeps her hair back from her shoulders, taking care not to ruin its smooth line. Now she only has to slip into the dress and sandals she bought for today and then it won't be long until the first guests arrive.

Finally, she allows herself to feel a ripple of pleasurable anticipation. The house looks great, *she* looks great, and it will be the kind of day that makes all her hard work worthwhile.

Today is about her, Melissa.

And Tilly. Of course.

The doorbell chimes and Melissa walks down the hallway to open the door, wondering if there are any deliveries she has forgotten about.

'Ah,' she sighs. 'Hello.'

Hester – stiff helmet hair, horrible pink blouse, and brown slacks – smiles shyly up at her. She's a small, scurrying sort of a woman who reminds Melissa of a squirrel.

Melissa hates squirrels.

The sight of Hester now causes a claustrophobic sensation of disappointment to crowd in, as if she is literally stealing her air. It takes her brain a second or two to see that the other woman appears to be holding a tray of scones, of all things.

'What can I do for you?' she says, eyeing them suspiciously, her smile tight but bright.

Something shifts in Hester's expression and she lowers the tray a little before her prim lips twitch.

'It's good to see you, Melissa,' she says. 'Well, I can see you're having a function of some kind and I know you must be very busy. I was at a loose end today and I've been doing some baking. I made rather too many scones. I wondered if you might find a use for them?'

Irritation spikes in Melissa's chest.

Function?

It's such a blatant lie that she had accidentally 'made too many scones'. There seem to be a thousand of the bloody things on that tray.

Scones are definitely not going to sit alongside polenta with figs, red onion and goat's cheese, or the balsamic-glazed pecans with rosemary and sea salt.

'It's okay, thank you, Hester,' says Melissa, smiling warmly to stifle the strange urge to scream. 'I'm quite covered for food. I have caterers, you see.'

The polite refusal seems to pierce the other woman. Her face

28

slackens around the jaw and her shoulders sag. She's always been passive-aggressive, Melissa thinks. It's why she has tried to keep her distance in recent times.

Melissa takes a deep, steadying breath. Did people have to be so oversensitive? She knows what she's going to have to say. Mark thinks it's funny to call her the Ice Queen, but she doesn't actually want to go around actively upsetting people. She comforts herself with the thought that Hester will probably be too intimidated to accept the invitation. It isn't really her sort of party, after all; her with her scones and her 1970s 'do'.

'But I'm very grateful for the offer, Hester,' she continues. 'And, um …' The words gather, oversized and chewy, in her mouth. 'Would you like to drop by at some point later? It's nothing fancy,' she adds in a hurry, 'just a small gathering. I'm sure you've got better things to …'

'I'd love to!' Hester's response rings out, a little too shrill, before Melissa has even finished her sentence. Her face and neck flush and blotch with pleasure.

Melissa regards her wearily. 'Marvellous,' she says, forcing her lips into a semblance of a smile. 'Any time from five then. I've still got rather a lot to do, so you'll have to forgive me if I don't chat. See you later.' She closes the door before Hester has time to make any more demands.

Bloody *Hester*.

At least she'd been forced to take her fucking scones back with her.

HESTER

Although Melissa said any time after five, I didn't want to appear too keen so I have waited until almost twenty past to go round. I lift the heavy doorknocker in the shape of a lion's head. With its tarnished gold snout and blank eyes, it seems to assess me unfavourably as I rap once, and then again with more confidence than I am feeling.

My heart is beating a little too fast and my armpits prickle uncomfortably in the flowered dress that was chosen after much painful wardrobe deliberation. It was dispiriting to note that everything I own, although clean and pressed, is a little worn and soft to the touch from wear. This is the best I could do. They will have to take me as they find me.

Strains of music and loud male laughter seep from the house but no one answers. Just for a second, I get the wildest, oddest, sensation that they aren't going to let me in. I will stand here, ignored, until I am forced to take my bottle of Blossom Hill Merlot home. I don't even like wine, and this cost more than five pounds.

But a vague flash of colour through the stippled glass of the door sort of coagulates into a shape and the door opens.

Tilly blinks, then frowns. Finally, she smiles.

'Hester? What are you doing here?'

I swallow and smile brightly, hoping she won't be able to see how much her surprise has stung me. Has she forgotten how close we were, too?

'I'm coming to the party, of course,' I say, tilting my chin. 'Your mother invited me this afternoon.'

Her cheeks flush as she remembers her manners. She's all smiles now, beckoning me inside.

'Go on through and get yourself a drink,' she says. 'Ma's out there holding court, I expect.' She turns to the stairs and her legs scissor away and above me at speed. She is wearing a pair of short dungarees over black tights, which hardly seem like party clothes to me.

I make my way inside. The hallway smells just lovely and I can see that Melissa has new wallpaper since I was last invited round. It's a bit of a funny colour, the sort of dark green you used only to see in institutions, but I expect it cost a bomb. I expect they all favour this overpriced decor round here.

We live in a part of London that I've heard described as 'on the wrong side of the North Circular'. It's always suited me fine, but when the train line was extended into the City, all the yuppies started moving in with their lattes and their big cars and their complicated prams. Now I'd be lucky to afford a garden shed in the area.

But it's just as close and unpleasant in here as in my boring old hallway, that's for sure. The lilies on the hall table are already nodding drowsily and speckling mustard-coloured pollen. It's a devil to get out of clothes, that stuff, so I give the table a wide berth as I make my way towards the kitchen at the back of the house. I pass the sitting room and see a couple of people standing in there smiling and talking animatedly.

I haven't really been that nervous until now but my tummy begins to positively thunder with butterflies as I step down into the packed kitchen.

31

Sensations assail me and I almost stumble. Conversation and laughter billow around me like clouds of smoke. There's a repetitive tsst-tsst musical beat coming from somewhere. And peacock flashes of colour everywhere. Summer frocks cling to bodies in pink, scarlet, turquoise, black. High-heeled, impossible sandals and painted toes. Lipsticked mouths sipping at drinks or parting in wide smiles.

It's so hot in here.

I lift my shoulder and subtly drop my head to check that I don't smell of the perspiration that is prickling my armpits. I have showered and am wearing both deodorant and perfume but I already feel uncomfortable. You wouldn't think it was possible to feel both invisible and horribly self-conscious all at once, but I *do*. I always do at this sort of thing.

'Ah! Hester, isn't it?'

The husky voice makes me turn sharply to my left.

'Oh, hello Saskia,' I say, without enthusiasm.

Melissa's annoying friend is gurning away, revealing a line of healthy pink gum above the white, almost horsey, teeth. A glass of something alcoholic and fizzy is held precariously in one manicured hand.

She laughs, but I don't recall having made a joke. She leans over and I catch a strong scent of the cigarette smoke on her breath along with a pungently spicy perfume.

'Have you just arrived?' she says. 'Can I get you a drinkie?'

I let my gaze sweep over her.

Today she is wearing a bright orange halter-neck dress that is cut very low and the two large brown orbs of her bust are almost popping out. In actual fact, her tan is so deep, she is probably darker-skinned than a good many coloured people. I glance down to see orange toenails with some sort of pattern on them poking out of gold sandals. She has money but absolutely no class, that one.

I force myself to meet her thickly made-up eyes. It always feels

32

like she is secretly mocking me but I force myself to smile and say, 'I can help myself, thank you.'

'No, let me!' she trills. The next thing I know, she has gripped me by the arm and she's almost dragging me through a forest of people to the kitchen island, where we find Melissa, chatting animatedly to a small bespectacled woman.

'Look who I found!' says Saskia.

Melissa gives her a look I can't read.

But then she says, 'So glad you could make it, Hester,' with real warmth. She even touches my wrist lightly and I don't mind that her fingertips feel rather clammy against my skin. Maybe I am not the only person struggling with the muggy heat.

I am quite overcome with relief at her kind welcome. For a second I fear tears may well up. I *did* do the right thing in coming! Oh if only I'd had the courage to make a move sooner. What a waste of time it has been, this silly falling-out business.

'Hello, Melissa!' I say, 'You're looking lovely.'

And she is. She is pretty as a picture in a red and white flow-ered frock that cinches in at the waist. She has more class in her little finger than Saskia. I really don't know what she sees in that woman.

'What can I get you to drink?' she says brightly, her arm sweeping to show the breadth of beverages on offer.

I hesitate. I was going to ask for a sparkling mineral water as usual. I'm not much of a drinker. But maybe it is the happy atmosphere here, or maybe it is the fact that Melissa and I are friends again, which makes me decide to let my hair down for once.

Why not? It can be my little celebration for finishing that computer course. I must tell Melissa about it at some point, but not yet. She is too busy with the party today.

'I'll have some of that lovely Pimm's you've got in, if I may,' I say. A confused frown pinches between her eyebrows and she looks around.

It takes a second for me to realize what I have said. The Pimm's isn't immediately visible. I only know about it, of course, because I happened to see the delivery earlier. It would be terrible if she thought I was spying on her. That isn't at all what I was doing, after all.

Embarrassment congeals like cold fat inside my tummy but at that moment, thank goodness, she is commandeered by a laughing man to her left who seems to have something urgent to impart.

'Pimm's it is,' says Saskia and melts away. I'm just thinking about quietly walking back the other way when I spot the woman Melissa was talking to when I arrived. She's smiling at me in a hopeful sort of way, and I recognize straight away that she is feeling a little out of place, like me. I've always been good at reading people. I have a sort of antenna for it, if you like.

'Hello, I'm Jess,' she says, still smiling.

'Hester,' I say, flinching, as a very tall glass of Pimm's, stuffed with cucumber and a long straw, is thrust at me by a tanned male hand.

'Here you go, get that down your neck!'

Saskia's son, Nathan, is standing next to his mother. The last time I saw him he was about eight years old and crying because he'd fallen off the trampoline, skinning his elbow. I seem to remember an incident involving a wee accident on Melissa's sofa and a loud tantrum too.

Now he must be over six foot tall. He winds a muscular brown forearm around his mother's neck. The boy has an unironed old t-shirt on and his hair hangs over his eyes in mucky blond coils. He grins, showing strong white teeth that look particularly carnivorous, and I notice that his green eyes have little gold flecks in them, as if he is lit by something bright within. I look away from his gaze. It's too much, like looking at the sun. Saskia pulls him in for a loud kiss on the cheek, staring at me the whole time.

'Isn't my boy gorgeous?' she says. 'Go on, isn't he?'

I feel quite sick with confusion. What am I supposed to say? If I say, 'Yes he's very handsome,' she may think I am some kind of pervert who favours teenage boys, and if I say, 'I think he could do with a good bath and a haircut,' they will both be offended. Thankfully I'm saved by Nathan baying, 'Gerroff!' and pulling away from his mother, who bays with laughter.

Jess laughs politely as they move off to bother someone else, Saskia protectively cupping the back of her son's neck.

Jess smiles at me again and I try to smile back, although my cheeks feel stiff and unnatural. I take a too-big sip of my drink and I can feel the alcohol seeping through me instantly.

I regard Jess. She's a small woman, like me, with very short light-brown hair. I'm sure the rectangular glasses perched on her snub nose are very trendy, if you like that sort of thing.

'Do you have any children, Hester?' she says. She looks at me with open curiosity.

I can't stop myself from heaving a sigh of resignation.

I should be inured to it by now.

But, 'No, I do *not*,' I say, perhaps a little sharply. Flustered, I gulp another large mouthful of the Pimm's. It warms me down into my stomach and helps me avoid seeing the inevitable look of pity on Jess's face. So I take another. I had forgotten how nice Pimm's was. It's slipping down so easily.

'Me neither,' she says cheerfully. I look at her with renewed interest.

'I thought you were maybe connected to one of Tilly's friends,' she says conspiratorially. 'It seems most people here are trailing teenagers. Here's to being unencumbered!'

To my surprise, she tips her glass of wine and *chings* it against mine. Her lips quirk and her eyes twinkle. I find that I quite like her.

Emboldened by the alcohol I decide to change the subject.

'So how *do* you know Melissa?' I say.

'Through Zumba classes,' she says with a grin and does a funny little wiggle. 'Have you ever tried it?'

I shake my head vigorously and have another sip. It's only now that I am remembering I didn't have any lunch. Zumba, indeed.

'I've never really been one for foreign cookery,' I say. Jess emits a strange squawk. I think she is laughing at me but all I can see is warmth in her eyes.

'Hester, you are a bit of a hoot,' she says.

'Hmm, am I now.' I've no idea why she has said this. New people should come with an instruction booklet, I think, taking another sip.

I peer at a table laden with food I can't identify. I always find buffet-style eating a bit of a minefield. First there is the business of trying to hold a drink, the food, and a napkin all at the same time. Then there is the worry of having food stuck between your teeth. Terry once very cruelly pointed out that I had spinach in my teeth in front of guests, and I've never really got over it.

I realize Jess is looking at me and it must be time for me to make a comment back to her. I've really quite forgotten how to behave in public. Since I stopped working, I probably do spend a little bit too much time alone.

I suppose it's a little like tennis: conversation. For some reason this makes me want to laugh and, to compensate, I take another sip of the drink. To my complete surprise, I realize I have finished it. I really am starting to feel quite relaxed.

'Wow, that barely touched the sides!' says Jess and before I know it, I'm grinning back. I don't know why. It isn't very funny. I really should have something to eat before too long.

'I've finished mine too,' says Jess. 'Let's get a top-up.'

'Allow me, ladies!'

That annoying boy pops up next to us. I hand him my empty glass and he disappears off with it.

I smile at Jess. She really does seem terribly nice.

MELISSA

Melissa winces at the sudden starburst of pain behind her eyes. She slicks on more lipstick and then sighs, closing her eyes and leaning her forehead against the blissfully cool glass of the bathroom mirror.

The diazepam has done nothing but give her a dry mouth and her headache hasn't responded to double painkillers. She has been sipping champagne all afternoon, yet remains completely sober. It seems her body is depressingly resistant to chemical help today, when she needs it the most.

She washes her hands and comes out of the en-suite. Mark has left a balled-up pair of socks in the middle of the floor. Melissa picks them up and then throws them savagely against the far wall. They drop to the carpet with a disappointing lack of bounce.

'Fuck you Mark,' she murmurs.

Mark was meant to return from a medical conference in Durham this afternoon, in time for the party. Then two days ago he'd announced that the BBC wanted to fit in some studio filming, to be slotted around the location scenes for the next series. The studio is in Manchester.

He had argued strongly that he had no choice, but when he'd

added, 'It's not like Tilly wants this party, is it?' it had been obvious how he really felt.

A few days ago she'd watched him throw his suit bag onto the bed, whistling like a man who has no real cares. Like a man who thinks everything is fixed now. He'd been wearing only a turquoise towel around his middle and she could see a new softness there. The bedroom was filled with steam and the scent of the Czech & Speake aftershave she'd bought him for Christmas.

He hadn't even bothered with aftershave before his television career had taken off. Mark used to get his suits from John Lewis and he'd wear whatever ties and shirts Melissa put into his wardrobe. Now, despite putting on weight, he fusses about haircuts and Melissa has caught him patting under his chin and examining the line of his jaw in the mirror.

Always an attractive man, with his dark brown eyes and the smattering of salt-and-pepper in his hair, as he approaches 44, he looks more comfortable in his skin than ever before.

And look where that led us, she thinks.

A wave of torpid, sapping exhaustion washes over Melissa now. For a second she longs to crawl under the sheets, close her aching eyes and allow darkness to press her into oblivion.

Apart from Saskia, there are very few people downstairs who she actually wants to talk to. They are mostly parents she has met over the years or neighbours. The conversations with parents always felt like jousting matches, each jabbing the other with pointed boasts about their children. She doesn't know any of Tilly's boarding school friends, so these guests were mainly from primary school days. They had little in common anymore anyway.

Sometimes she imagined what would happen if any of them found out about the things she had done. A cold chill creeps over her arms and she rubs them briskly. The chances of anyone from *Before* recognizing her in that picture must be infinitesimal. She has been told that her light green eyes are distinctive. But lots of people have light green eyes.

Giving herself a mental shake, she arranges her face into one of friendly hospitality. She can do this. It's really no different from putting on her make-up.

As Melissa comes to the bottom of the stairs she hears a piercing, high-pitched laugh she doesn't recognize.

The party feels *thinner* somehow – like it has lost fat and heft, rather than individuals – and she wonders whether some guests have left without saying goodbye. Maybe she was upstairs for longer than she thought? Or maybe it is just that all the young people have decamped to the summerhouse at the bottom of the garden. She can hear the thump of music coming from there and hopes Tilly is finally enjoying herself.

There's that baying laugh again. Emerging onto the patio she spies Hester, talking animatedly to a couple from the tennis club, who regard her with blank expressions. The scene is so unexpected it takes a moment to make sense of it. Hester's hair is sticking damply to her forehead and her eyes have a bright, unfocused glaze. Is she … drunk?

The woman who once said, 'Mind my French', after using the word 'bloody' and who Mark once joked wears a chastity belt under her old-lady skirts? Hester, drunk?

'Here she is!' Hester trills as Melissa cautiously approaches.

Gary and Sue meet her puzzled gaze and Sue raises an eyebrow, quizzically, at Melissa, barely stifling a smile.

Melissa gives her a stricken look back.

'I was just telling your friends Gary and … um … Thing, that I used to look after Tilly all the time when she was little. I was like an aunty to her, wasn't I, Melissa? We're all terribly proud of her now, aren't we?'

Melissa grimaces and tries to convey an apology with her eyes to Gary and Sue.

'Well, you certainly helped me out once or twice,' she says. 'And yes, we are very proud of her.'

Hester hiccups and then turns to look around the garden, her eyes narrowed.

'Where did that Jess one go? I liked her. Although I'm not completely sure she isn't one of those. Not that I care! Live and let live, I say. As long as they are not rubbing our noses in it.'

Sue tuts.

'Oh dear God,' says Melissa under her breath.

'Gosh, look at the time!' says Gary, pretending to look at his watch, not very convincingly.

'It's Pimm's o'clock!' trills Hester and collapses into giggles, staggering slightly against Melissa, who takes hold of her arm.

Hester leans into her. For a small woman, she feels surprisingly solid. Melissa is momentarily reminded of holding Tilly as a toddler; the dense heat of her compact body.

'You seem to be having a good time, Hester,' says Melissa tightly. 'Have you had any water?'

Hester hiccups and belatedly puts a hand over her mouth.

'I've only had two drinks but I do feel a little squiffy. Perhaps I should have some of your lovely nibbles! I was just telling, um, Thing …', Sue smiles primly but doesn't help her out, 'that I offered some of my scones but it seems you have done a wonderful job of catering. It's all lovely! Darned if I can identify any of it, though!'

At this she breaks into peals of laughter. Melissa realizes that she has never really heard Hester laugh properly before. The high-pitched seal bark hurts her head a little bit more.

'Okay, maybe you should have a drink of water and something to eat, hmm?' Melissa begins to steer her back into the kitchen, mouthing 'sorry' at Gary and Sue, who are already turning to each other and leaning in with conspiratorial grins.

Nathan watches her with a small smile as she comes into the kitchen. Melissa privately thinks that Saskia panders to him far too much. He and Tilly seem to have some sort of awkwardness between them and Tilly has called him, 'a bit of an airhead'.

He'd even half come-on to Melissa at Christmas and she'd had to pretend it was all a joke. He certainly seems very amused by something as he studies Hester stumbling towards the table of food, which is now a wreck of weary salad leaves, smeared plates, and crumbs.

She wishes they would all go home. She only had this party as a sort of 'fuck you'; to prove to herself that Mark's betrayal hasn't destroyed her. She is a survivor. Not that any of them even knew about it, apart from Saskia. But it all feels so much more trouble than it is worth.

Hester is now folding a mini pavlova into her mouth in one piece so cream dribbles from the corner of her lips. Melissa sighs and says, 'Wait there,' and goes to the sink. A woman she knows from the tennis club, Jennie, is nearby. She does a comical staggering motion and murmurs, 'Gosh, she's a bit worse for wear! Who on earth *is* that?'

'My next-door neighbour,' says Melissa in a low voice as water from the filter tap splashes noisily into the tall green glass. Normally she would add ice and some fresh mint but there's no point wasting that on Hester. 'She's totally off her face, isn't she? I didn't even want her here but she sort of invited herself.'

The other woman laughs. 'She banged on to me earlier about being one of the family or something,' she says. 'I thought it was a bit strange when you've never mentioned her!'

'Oh God,' says Melissa with feeling, turning off the tap.

'Well she's certainly making up for lost time with the food now!' says Jennie stifling another laugh.

Melissa turns to see Hester cramming crisps into her mouth with a robotic regularity. She takes the water over and places it on the table next to where she stands.

'Here,' she says, no longer bothering to hide her irritation, 'you'd better drink this and then maybe it's time to go home for a lie-down. I think you're going to need it, don't you?'

Hester gazes up with unfocused eyes. Her skin looks clammy and blotchy now. She sways gently on the spot.

The doorbell trills. The sound, like a hard flick on a lighter wheel, ignites hope in Melissa's chest. The pure joy of it comes as a surprise.

Could Mark have come home after all? But no, that's ridiculous. He would use his key, wouldn't he? She hurries to the door and can see straight away that it is a smallish man who stands there. She can't think of any single men who were invited to the party.

As quickly as it came, the euphoria melts away and ice seems to form in the pit of her belly. Melissa has the strangest feeling that she can't move. That she *shouldn't* move. It would be a foolish act to take those few steps towards the front door.

She doesn't believe in premonitions. But she does believe in following her instincts and something is telling her that she must not open that door.

She tries to breathe slowly. *Be rational*, she thinks.

Hasn't she been feeling strange and paranoid all day? Thinking people are looking at her on the High Street? Peering in at her through the hairdresser's windows?

It's absurd.

She turns and looks at herself in the gilt-edged mirror she and Mark bought in an antique shop in Camden Passage when they first got together. He called it 'shabby chic' and the expression pleased her greatly. It was new to her and she liked very much that she was now a woman for whom shabby no longer necessarily meant poor, inferior, or dirty.

Melissa tries to breathe slowly as she gazes at her reflection. She sees someone poised and elegant who lives a safe, comfortable, middle-class life. Someone with no reason to be frightened.

The doorbell trills again, insistent as an angry fly banging against glass.

Licking her dry lips, Melissa moves towards the door.

HESTER

I've had such a wonderful time but I think perhaps I should have stayed away from all that rich food.

My tummy is churning and when I look around Melissa's kitchen, it's like all the edges of things have run in the wash. Everything is a bit blurry.

I'm not feeling too clever.

That's one of Terry's expressions. 'Not feeling too clever, old girl?' he'd say and it annoyed the heck out of me because he was eleven years my elder.

'Bugger off, Terry,' I say out loud and it surprises me so much that I *belch*, to my horror, really quite loudly. I mumble an 'excuse me' and realize a strange woman is standing very close to me. I think we spoke earlier but darned if I know what about.

I don't know where she came from now.

She's there with her big wobbly face, saying, 'Are you all right? Are you okay?' I can smell her perfume and it makes me think of the inside of old handbags that we would get in Scope, which contained all sorts of disgusting things. Old tissues. Sanitary ware. Sweeties stuck to the lining like tumours. This image is so horrible it brings bile into my mouth and the ground does a strange shift sideways. I clutch the table. The woman says, 'Do you need to sit down?'

It's the second time today someone has spoken to me like this.

I look her squarely in the eye. Hers are large and very dark. I think she is probably foreign. With all the dignity I can muster I say, 'I am absolutely tickety-boo', and then wonder why, because this is another irritating Terry expression. But the words skid and skate into each other like cars on an icy road. 'Going to the bathroom,' I say and this time it comes out a bit more clearly.

I am on the landing upstairs now. I remember, too late, that there is a downstairs toilet that would have been closer.

My head is swimming and my insides feel wrong. Maybe it was the pâté on those tiny blinis. It smelled so very *meaty*. Sometimes I am eating a chop, or a piece of pork, and I remember that it is a dead thing on my plate. It puts me right off. Then all I can think about are tumours and carcasses, which makes my stomach squeeze and relax like a big fist.

Oh dear.

I can't quite remember which room is the bathroom.

I'm not sure I've ever been upstairs here in all these years of living next door. It's certainly very different to mine. It really is twice the size. But how silly that I don't know where to go! A small laugh turns into another belch. 'Whoops, pardon me,' I say to no one.

I can hear Melissa's voice, pitched low, at the front door. Melissa! I'm so very happy and relieved that we are friends again. I think I will offer to help tidy up later. There will be such a lot to do. But I may need a small rest first.

If only I could find the bathroom.

I lean over the stairs, intending to ask her where I might find it, but there's something strange about the way she is standing. Despite my fuzziness I can tell she is somehow *braced*. Her feet are apart and her shoulders seem to be high. She's clutching the side of the door like a lifeline. How very odd.

Maybe it's one of those Chuggers. Chugger buggers! I must say this to Melissa later when we're clearing up, maybe over a well-earned cup of tea. It will really tickle her.

I lean over the banister a little further and somehow knock my ribs, quite hard. The pain makes me even more queasy. And now something strange is happening to the walls and landing, which tip and pulse around me.

I really must find …

I shove open the nearest door.

Sweat breaks out all over me, greasy and cold. My stomach turns inside out.

I'm staring into Tilly's face. She's saying something but I can't hear because the sour sickness rises up, engulfing me and then spurting out onto the soft pale carpet.

I stare down at the small pool, pink with Pimm's.

Things have gone terribly wrong.

MELISSA

'Hello, Mel. Well don't just stand there, gawping. You going to invite me in, or what?'

Melissa clutches the doorframe. Viscous shock floods her spine. She can't think of a single word to say.

He can't be *here*? On her doorstep?

He's laughing; enjoying the moment. Immersing himself gleefully in her distress like a dog cavorting in a filthy puddle.

When she manages to find words, they tumble out messily.

'What are you …? Why …?' It feels imperative that she doesn't say his name aloud. If she does, it will make this all the more real.

Jamie? At her *house*?

'Come on, aren't you even a little bit pleased to see me after all these years?'

Blind instinct makes Melissa try to close the door, but he is too quick for her and pushes his white trainered foot into the gap. She immediately feels foolish.

'Really? Come on!' he says, head cocked to one side, not smiling now.

Of course, she can't just slam the door in his face. Can she?

'This is a bit of a surprise.' Her voice sounds very far away to her own ears.

'I bet.'

Jamie holds out his arms, as if to say, 'this is me!', and she looks at him properly now, registering that he is both unchanged and yet completely different.

The dark brown eyes are feathered by lines but the features that once crowded his teenage face, gawky and out of proportion, now suit him. His face is thicker, more square-jawed, but it is his body that is quite transformed. Although still on the short side, the skinny, concave-chested boy now looks like someone who works out with dedication. A broad chest and arms rounded with muscle are showcased in a tight t-shirt. His hair is cropped short.

The last time Melissa had seen him, his face was covered with snot and tears. He'd looked like the little boy he still was inside: sixteen to her seventeen.

He has a large holdall slung across one shoulder and an expectant tilt to his eyebrows. Surely he can't think …

'What the *fuck* are you doing here, Jamie?' she says in little more than a whisper. Saying his name makes it all feel worse, just as she'd anticipated. 'How did you …', she swallows, 'find me?'

Jamie shifts position, moving the bag onto the other shoulder, and his expression slackens. He's always done that puppy dog thing to guilt trip her, but then his eyes and mouth thin and harden and she feels a flash of something else. The back of her neck prickles. This is new.

'That's not very welcoming, is it?' he says, shifting the holdall in a way designed to emphasize how very heavy it is. 'After all we've been through together? Can't a girl make an effort for her own brother?'

She's about to speak when she feels a hot, clammy hand on her bare arm.

'Mum!'

Tilly has materialized at the front door. Her eyes are wide, shining, and she bristles with appalled excitement.

'You won't believe what's happened! Hester has been *sick*! All over my …'

She stops speaking abruptly, staring openly at Jamie. 'Did you just say, *brother*?' Her mouth drops open and she seems to shed years. She's once more the tiny girl who has just discovered Father Christmas has 'been'.

Jamie chuckles easily. His gaze drifts up and down Tilly's entire length.

Tilly flushes. Melissa wants to lean over and rake her newly done nails across Jamie's face. Instead she steps in front of her daughter, creating a physical barrier. She wants to erase this moment from history. She wants to make it all un-happen.

'He's not my *brother*.' She tries to laugh dismissively but her face is too rigid. It's all she can do to spit words out through tight lips.

'Well, *foster* brother, so close enough,' says Jamie with a twinkle, holding out his arms. 'I'm Jamie. And who are you? No, hang on … I reckon you should be called something like Aphrodite, or Kate Moss, or something.'

Tilly emits a shrill giggle, still blushing furiously. Melissa's head feels like it's going to explode. How could her privately educated, clever daughter lap up such bullshit?

Why is he here? What does he *want*? She has to clamp her lips together to stop a soft moan from seeping out.

'What is it, Tilly?' she snaps. She's distantly aware of some other issue she must absorb. 'What did you say about someone being sick?'

Tilly starts at her mother's tone. 'Oh … Hester's puked on my carpet.'

'*What*?'

Melissa opens her mouth and closes it again. Her head throbs.

The light is almost sepia now. Bruise-coloured clouds have gathered over the low sky and seem to roil and move too fast.

Everything has a sickly, unreal feel. The sticky air presses in all around her and sweat breaks out along her hairline.

'What on earth do you mean?' She has to grasp this information, she knows this, yet cannot.

Tilly mimes throwing up, expressively. Jamie hoots with laughter and Tilly beams at the appreciation. 'She's totally rat-arsed,' she says cheerfully. 'Now she's flat out in the guest room, snoring her head off.'

'Wow, it sounds like some party you've got going on here, Mel!' says Jamie.

Tilly, still glowing in the heat of his attention, shoots him an arch smile. It looks all wrong, like a toddler wearing its mother's shoes. 'You'd think, wouldn't you?' she says.

No. This has to stop right *now*.

Melissa opens her mouth to tell Jamie he has to go when a clap of thunder as loud as a gunshot cracks the still air. All three flinch in surprise. Fat raindrops plop onto Jamie's head and confetti the step around him. He cartoon cowers, arms up to fend off the rain. A hot concrete smell wafts upwards.

'Mum! Let him come in! What's wrong with you?'

And then somehow Jamie is crossing the threshold and here he is, inside.

He's in her house and she has lost control of the situation.

'Jesus,' says Melissa. 'All right! Just go and ... wait in there.' She gestures to the sitting room. 'I'll be as quick as I can dealing with this. Just don't ... move.' What she wants to say is, 'Don't touch anything. Don't steal anything. *Piss off.*'

Jamie walks quickly past her and flumps down onto the plush sofa. He strokes its arm luxuriously, stretching out his legs, before turning to flash a grin that seems to say, 'I should have all this too.'

The band of pain tightens around Melissa's head.

***

49

As hot water thunders into the bucket in the bathroom upstairs, she sits on the edge of the bath and holds her head in her hands. She squeezes her eyes shut and moans softly, a long sibilant hiss. '*Shit-shit-shit-shit.*'

She and Jamie had been separated before her days in Asquith Mansions but it's too close for comfort. Was that why he was here? And how did he find her? Holding her breath and scrubbing at the foul pink mess, she thinks about doing this before, many times over, back when she was Melanie Ronson. But then it was cheap scratchy carpets pocked with fag burns that rubbed your knees raw, or lino that was cracked and sticky. Not this oatmeal-coloured pure wool, which Tilly's bare toes scrunch into every day and which is proving to be astonishingly absorbent to vomit.

However hard she scrubs, she can't stop the pictures that start flicker-booking through her mind:

– Her mother slumped, weeping, at the yellow Formica table, smelling bad. Melissa, then Melanie, hiding behind the sofa and *pick-pick-picking* at the swirly green and black wallpaper. She'd seen a programme about Narnia on telly. They don't have any big wardrobes but she is obsessed with hiding places just in case;

– The purplish grey swelling of her mother's eyes one morning that made her think of lizards and dinosaurs;

– Lying in bed, pulling the sour-smelling Barbie duvet up to her face when her mother flings open the bedroom door. She is silhouetted against the yellowish landing light. Flecks of spit fly from her mouth as she screams that she could have 'made something' of herself and that she should have 'just dealt with it' when she had the opportunity.

And finally.

– Coming into the dark living room, a little unsteady after too many Bacardi and Cokes and a little sore from pounding against the bonnet of Gary Mottram's Vauxhall Viva in the Camelot car park, to find her mother dead in the stripy brown and orange chair that always smelled musty.

She had been fifteen then.

No one would believe that she had been looking after herself for years. That she had found money around the house and bought the chips for dinner, spreading margarine on slices of bread and, once, putting some dandelions in a jar in the centre of the table because she had seen something like it on telly. Mum had taken one look and then burst into tears, so Melanie never did it again.

Melissa sits back on her heels now, staring down at the damp carpet. She hopes she won't have to replace it.

Rain patters against the sash window where Tilly has hung a blue feathery dreamcatcher that Melissa has never seen before. Getting up with a sigh, she lifts the bucket of dirty water.

She will get rid of him.

It's going to be okay.

HESTER

I'm looking up at an unfamiliar ceiling.

The inside of my head thrums and pulses in sickening waves. Have I had an accident? Maybe I was hit by a car and I'm in hospital.

I run my tongue over my dry lips, grimacing at the terrible taste in my mouth.

As I turn my head and look to the right, I can see a pale blue wooden bedside table. It looks far too pretty and upmarket to be in a hospital. That's not all. The wallpaper is textured with roses and looks like raw silk. Gauzy curtains shimmer and flutter at a window where a light breeze drifts in. The light is the pale bluish milk of very early morning.

My brain scrambles to assemble a jigsaw puzzle of jagged information.

Computer club. A party.

Laughing and then feeling peculiar.

Oh no, oh no, oh no …

Memories crash into my mind with the violence of bumper cars. I'm talking too loud to the couple whose faces are frozen with embarrassment. I'm on the landing, feeling queer. And then I'm in Tilly's room and …

Oh my goodness. I start to cry a little, but am so dehydrated I don't seem to make any tears. All I can do is a strange sort of mewling, like a cat in distress. That's when I remember poor Bertie. My darling boy has been alone all night long. My guilt and horror increase tenfold.

I groan and turn onto my other side. I wish I could hide in this room forever but I can't leave my boy any longer. I have to get up. I have to face what I have done. Peering at my watch with eyeballs that don't seem to fit the sockets anymore, I see that it is only 5 a.m. in the morning. I must leave, but I will somehow have to make amends later.

It's then I notice the glass of water next to the bed and a packet of paracetamol. The kindness of this simple act twists my insides with more guilt. I don't deserve it. I start to cry again. But my head hurts too much for that so I stop.

Almost without realizing I'm doing it, I reach for the soft skin of my inner arm and pinch myself viciously. The thin, tender skin burns and the pain makes me gasp but I deserve the pain after what I have done. I won't take the medicine or the water. I will take my punishment, at least while I am still at the scene of my crime.

Clambering out of the big soft bed, my balance wobbles and I almost fall back down again. Nausea rolls over me, coating me in a clammy layer of sweat, and I try to breathe steadily for a moment. I mustn't be sick again!

Finally steady, I walk to the middle of the floor. There's a full-length mirror on a stand in one corner but I can't bear to look. I try to rake my fingers through my hair, knowing it to be a futile gesture. My hair feels dirty and matted with sweat and I can taste something horrible. Sweetish and rotten.

Slowly, with shaking hands, I make the bed and try to rearrange the beautifully soft cushions on the floor, presumably tossed carelessly there by me last night. But I don't really know what to do with them. They are imprinted with a river scene like something from a Chinese painting, with tall herons standing proudly in water. But they look all wrong however I arrange them. I don't have a flair for that sort of thing, like Melissa does. Frustrated, I give up and just lay them in a neat row.

A throw made from heavy cotton in a deep turquoise colour lies half on the floor and it is so lovely I can't help but hold it to my throbbing forehead for a moment. I hope to catch some kind of comforting scent from it. But it is curiously without any odour at all. I place it neatly along the bottom of the bed. This, at least, I can do because I have seen it on decor programmes on television. The bed is so perfect, even with the cushions out of place, that it fills me with a strange sense of longing, and then, another hot blast of shame.

Poor Tilly. And poor, poor Melissa. She must hate me for this. I can't understand how it happened. I don't even remember the last time I was under the influence. It must be *years* ago. Any tolerance I once had must have completely disappeared.

Miserably, I slip my feet into my court shoes and that's when I notice a globule of something pink and lumpy on the toe of my right one. Disgust ripples through me as I reach for a tissue from the neat metal container at the side of the bed and rub at the crustiness, trying to quell the heaving sensation in my stomach as I do so.

There's no way I can put the tissue in the bin for poor Melissa to deal with, so, shuddering a little, I fold it over as much as possible to obscure the shameful contents and push it inside the cuff of my blouse.

When I open the door, I listen for a moment, willing with every fibre of my being that no one will be around. I will come back later, with flowers, to apologize. I simply can't face seeing anyone yet.

It's as I creep towards the stairs that I hear a door opening behind me. Oh please no …

But it isn't Melissa, or Mark, or Tilly. It's a man.

I have no idea who he is. He is perhaps in his thirties and he is dressed only in his underwear. He's not very tall but all muscled chest and arms. Then my eyes are drawn downwards and I gasp in shock; I can clearly see the tented distortion of his boxer shorts.

He gives a deep, throaty laugh. 'Oops, sorry, Grandma,' he says. 'Morning glory and all that.'

My cheeks flame. I scurry down the stairs as fast as I can. I am sure I can hear mocking laughter behind me.

Thankfully the front door isn't locked. Wrenching it open, I almost throw myself down the front steps, twisting my knee a little in the process.

Home! Please let me just get home.

I run up my own steps. It's as I get inside, relief flooding my veins, that I realize the tissue containing the vomit must have fallen out of my sleeve. Panicking, I quickly retrace my steps but it isn't on Melissa's steps either. It is obviously lying somewhere inside.

'I'm so sorry. I'm so sorry,' I whisper.

Bertie runs from the kitchen, yapping wildly. Telling me off, no doubt. I pick him up and hug him to my chest, kissing his rough little head and murmuring my apologies, but he scrambles to be put down. When I open the back door, he darts outside and squats straight away. The poor thing; what a clever boy he is for not having an accident on the floor. He must be hungry too.

I think then of someone else washing up *my* 'accident' on the floor, and I have to close my eyes at the poisonous sensation of shame. I go straight to bed.

When I awake, I am shocked to see it is the afternoon already. Forcing down tea and toast, I run a bath, and ease my aching body into the water.

It is almost hotter than I can stand, and when I lift my leg the skin is bright and mottled. I'm not at all comfortable but I feel

I am being purged. If only the shame could be leached from my skin along with the traces of alcohol.

Images from last night keep racing through my mind: talking to that woman at the start who kept laughing like I was the funniest woman ever. Saying 'Pimm's o'clock!' to someone and finding it almost unbearably funny. Someone (Tilly?) speaking to me gently and telling me a 'nice lie-down' would 'sort me out'.

My mind drifts to that man on the landing this morning. Who on earth was that? He didn't look at all like one of Mark's friends. Come to think of it, where was Mark?

He had *tattoos*. I keep picturing the coarse black hair on his chest and arms. Some men are like monkeys under their clothes. And the sight of … *that*. Mocking me with his lack of modesty.

I close my eyes in disgust.

My head still aches, despite the aspirin I forced down with my cup of tea when I got back. So much for taking my punishment. But it did hurt so very much.

It really is odd that I should have had quite such a strong reaction to the alcohol. I've never been a drinker but I'm sure I didn't have *that* much Pimm's. Maybe it is just more potent than I ever realized? The memory of its cloying taste makes my stomach churn again, and I close my eyes then sink under the surface of the water, allowing it to close over my head like a baptism.

When I emerge I am crying in great gulps. I keep picturing Terry laughing at me being in this state. Oh yes, he would have found this very amusing, I'm sure. He was always trying to encourage me to 'have a drink and let go a little'.

I was always the butt of his jokes. Always the 'funny old thing' who took things too seriously and didn't seem to know how to enjoy herself. Funny old, silly old Hester.

This is another reason to avoid alcohol. It causes all sorts of unwanted memories to surface. The dirty silt at the bottom of my mind has been stirred up.

'Leave me alone, Terry,' I gulp into the steamy air.

He once suggested we take a bath in here together, in the early days. I was quite unable to think of an excuse. My parents were gone by then and the house was all mine, but it still felt wrong.

But I agreed. It was the early days, as I said.

We met at Bentley's, the engineering works that has long been closed down. I was an Office Manager, having started as an assistant straight from secretarial college and working my way up. He worked on the shop floor.

It took a year of him asking before I gave in and went out with him for a drink. At 35, I was seeing colleague after colleague leave to have babies and time was beginning to pinch.

I went for the drink, then we had some country walks together. He told me he was 'really falling for me', after a couple of months. He'd been married before, but she died quite young. As for me, well, I'd never really met the right person.

He had all sorts of ideas and he was quite unlike anyone else I'd ever met. He liked to invent things in his spare time and was always saying he would come up with a gadget that would make our fortune.

It all turned out to be rubbish, of course, from the remote control that was also a holder for a cup of tea (for goodness' sake) to the teddy bear that contained a 'nappy pouch'. Rubbish, all of it. No one wanted to invest in any of his ideas, and in the end he had to set up a painting and decorating business. He couldn't get a job anywhere else after Bentley's closed down. I didn't know about how weak and useless he was in the early days. He behaved like a gentleman and seemed to have something about him, so I suppose I was fooled.

When he proposed, after a rather lovely evening in an Italian restaurant, he went down on one knee, and I think I was genuinely happy in that moment. The future seemed so rich and full of possibility.

In those early days, I still thought that the 'other' side of things would start to be more enjoyable with a little practice.

When he made the bath suggestion, I'd tried to laugh it off, saying it was far too small. Then he'd caught me up in his arms and whispered into my hair that it would only be nice and snug. So we tried it and it was every bit as uncomfortable and unpleasant as I'd imagined. He insisted that I lay between his legs, facing away from him, and I could feel bits digging into my lower back straight away.

I closed my eyes and pictured the wonderful prize that was waiting for me after all this: a smiling, pink-cheeked baby.

I had so much love to pour into a child. I would have been the very best mother. It had always been my goal, ever since I was small. I had a baby doll called Susie-Sue that I loved until she was merely a torso with staring eyes and a grubby grey patina to her once-pink flesh.

I even thought I might call my own daughter Susie, although I also loved the name Rachel. For a boy, I had William and Daniel picked out long before there was any chance of a conception.

I waited so long. So very long.

'Damn you, Terry,' I say loudly, shocking myself when the words bounce back at me. I realize I have been digging my fingers into my arm again, the old habit resurfacing today. It is almost as though I have been outside myself, and I blink, a little shocked to see I am still in the bath and that the water is now quite cool.

I'm only aware now of an insistent sharp ringing and realize with a start that it is the front doorbell. I can't possibly answer. Whoever it is has to go away.

But what if it's Melissa? I don't want her to think I wasn't going to apologize.

I quickly climb out of the bath and pull on my robe, which clings unpleasantly to my damp, mottled skin. Stuffing my feet into slippers, I hurry out of the bathroom, calling out, 'Hang on!' in a voice that sounds shrill even to my own ears.

There are two shapes lurking behind the frosted glass and I

hesitate as I get to the bottom of the stairs. It could be Jehovah's Witnesses or something. Whoever it is, they are very insistent. The doorbell rings sharply again.

'All right, I'm coming!' I say to shut them up and fling open the door.

'Oh,' I say.

Jehovah's Witnesses suddenly seem like very much the better alternative.

'Hello Hester. I'm sorry if we got you out of bed.'

Saskia is wearing highly age-inappropriate shorts, a tight t-shirt, and oversized sunglasses that obscure most of her face.

Nathan looms just behind her. He's looking down at the toe of his grimy white plimsoll as if it's the most fascinating thing he's ever seen. Most bizarrely, he's holding two bunches of flowers wrapped in brown paper that I recognize from Petal and Vine, the overpriced flower shop down the road. One must be for Melissa, to say thank you for the party. But why the heck are they here, on my doorstep?

Have they come to tell me off? I am incensed by this thought and find myself blurting words out before Saskia can speak again.

'If you've come round here to make me feel guilty,' I say, 'then I can assure you there is no need. I plan to apologize later. You can't possibly make me feel any worse than I already do.'

Saskia reaches out her hand to touch my wrist, but I take a step back. She's always touching people; it's like she can't speak without making physical contact with the person opposite her. Well, I'm in no mood for her nonsense today.

'No, no, you've got it all wrong,' she says in a voice that is even more gravelly than usual. 'We've come to apologize to you. At least, Nathan has. Haven't you?' She says his name sternly and he steps forward.

The boy – and he really looks like a boy today – turns his strangely coloured eyes on me and his cheeks flush a deep pink under his light tan.

'Yeah,' he says and clears his throat before continuing. 'The thing is, I did something really stupid. So it's sort of my fault you puked up everywhere.'

I flinch at his coarseness. As if I need reminding!

'Fuck's sake, Nathe!'

I tut, loudly. She's almost as bad as he is! No wonder he speaks like that. The boy shoots a panicked look at her.

'Sorry! Um, what I mean is, I did a really moronic thing for a laugh. I didn't think it would be such a big deal.'

'What did you do?' I want nothing more than for these ghastly people to disappear.

'I spiked your drink,' he says in a rush, glancing at his mother. The thin, tight line of her lips reveals the true age of her face.

'What?' I can't seem to make sense of any of this.

'You asked for a Pimm's and I added a massive slug of vodka to it,' he says, blushing harder.

My stomach seems to drop. 'Why?' I manage to breathe. 'Why would you do something like that?'

He shrugs with one shoulder. I want to slap him hard around the face for being such a childish, pathetic specimen of a boy at sixteen.

'I dunno, I only did it for a joke,' he says. 'I thought it would be funny to see you a bit pissed because you're always so …'

'Nathan!' barks Saskia.

'Sorry,' he shoots another panicked look at his mother, then turns back to me. I can't help feeling this entire apology is only really aimed at her.

'I mean, I just didn't … think,' he says.

'No,' I say.

I can imagine so very clearly what it would feel like to strike that cheek. The smoothness, despite the speckle of juvenile beard. It's so vivid in my mind, the satisfying slapping ring, the warm tautness of his young skin against my palm, that for a second I think I have actually hit him.

They are both staring at me, a little curiously now.

'I really am sorry, Hester,' he says, a bit more boldly. 'I bought you these to apologize.'

I eye the flowers and then reach for them. They are beautiful and totally out of my budget. But I can't bring myself to say thank you.

'He bought them with his own money,' says Saskia, a wheedling note to her voice. As if I should be impressed!

I want to tell them to go away but force myself to be polite. I will not stoop to the level of these appalling people.

'I have things to attend to,' I say. 'Good afternoon.' And I close the door in their faces.

I do still have some vestige of dignity.

MELISSA

Melissa takes the last bag of bottles out to the recycling bins in the alley at the side of the house. She has been working on the aftermath of the party all day. Furious, almost frenzied, cleaning that has made her old lower back injury throb and her arms ache. But the activity has done nothing to quash the thoughts that still swirl in her mind like dirty, buzzing flies.

Tilly, thank God, wanted to sleepover at a friend's house tonight. Melissa had jumped to the task of driving her to Chloe's in a way that made Tilly look at her askance.

As she was climbing into the car, she'd wondered about leaving Jamie alone in the house and hastily hid her laptop and jewellery in the safe upstairs. When she got back, he was still sleeping in the second guest bedroom. He has been there all day. No doubt luxuriating in her good sheets, like a pig in mud. Maybe he realizes that she's getting rid of him the minute he pops his head out of that door.

She lifts a weary hand now to wipe away a strand of hair that has fallen from the band of her ponytail. Coming into the kitchen she tries to take pleasure in the way surfaces gleam, taps and sink sparkle. Nothing is cluttering the surfaces, which hold only a large pewter bowl, crowded with bright green limes, and the heavy stone pestle and mortar set that she had found in a village in Tuscany last year. It was so heavy they'd had to pay a fortune to get it shipped home. It is bluish-grey and speckled with little chips of gold and silver; a thing of such beauty that she has never actually used it to crush spices.

The rain has passed and the sun streams buttery light over the floor. Usually this room can calm her like no other place. This is *her home*. Everything in it is beautiful or useful. A great deal of money, time, and care have gone into making it like this.

It's her sanctuary.

No one can take it away. But the gravitational pull of the past seems to suck at her.

The kitchen feels as insubstantial as if it were projected on one of those green screens they use for special effects in the movie business. Like it would be a second's work to make it vanish.

She looks down at her hands and presses them to the table in an attempt to stop the trembling. Acid sloshes in her stomach. She has only had a piece of toast and honey all day but can't face eating anything else. Sliding onto one of the kitchen chairs, Melissa puts her head in her hands, resting her elbows on the table.

Oh God, what have I done? she thinks. If someone had handed her a script for what not to do last night, she couldn't have handled it worse.

The first mistake was letting Jamie cross the threshold. She should have quietly pulled the door behind her and told him that she didn't want him here; that he wasn't welcome. He would have complained, of course, put up an argument. But she could handle Jamie. Or, she could, once.

If Tilly hadn't arrived at that precise moment, bursting with good intentions like the nice, well-brought-up girl she is; all wide-eyed with curiosity about this blast from her mother's past, it would have been so much easier to get rid of him.

Blast was right. Jamie's presence felt incendiary.

When she had emerged from cleaning up Hester's sick, and got the bleary-eyed, apologetic woman into the main guest bedroom, Jamie was still in the sitting room as instructed, but he was now holding a beer and chatting to Tom and Lucy from down the road, who were among the last straggling guests.

Her one piece of luck had been that Saskia had taken a very drunk Nathan home early and had somehow missed Jamie entirely.

Tilly wasn't there; perhaps, thought Melissa, she had trotted off to get him a fresh drink, an extra cushion, or a three course bloody meal.

He was telling a story; something about an old lady with a well-spoken voice berating a group of teenagers with a barrage of foul language on the bus. Melissa winced at the words, 'And don't you forget that, you little cunts!'

Tom in particular was laughing so hard he'd gone quite purple in the face.

'The gob on her!' said Jamie, basking in the attention.

This was new too. This raconteur who was comfortable taking centre stage in a house like this one.

Melissa had been swept up in conversations with other guests who were leaving then, but a little later, she'd come back to find Tilly ensconced on the sofa, long legs curled to the side, feet bare.

She'd let her hair down from the habitual bird's-nesty bun and even brushed it, so it lay in soft waves around her face. Melissa peered at her daughter. Was that mascara? She barely ever wore make-up. Melissa felt a sick lurch.

But she was more concerned about what they may have been discussing. Flickers of real fear licked at her.

Her daughter knew her mother had had a difficult childhood with a short period (so she thought) with foster parents. But she hadn't given her many details, just said that her mother had been ill and died young. Tilly had a phase, when she was seven or eight, of being quite obsessed with the subject. 'Did your mummy have freckles on her nose like me?' she'd ask. Or, 'Were you really, really sad when your mummy died?'

Melissa thinks Mark eventually took Tilly to one side and explained that Mummy didn't like to talk about her past. He had long since stopped asking and so had she.

Tilly's voice now, still so high and young, despite her belief in her own sophistication, was filling the room. She was telling Jamie about her Duke of Edinburgh Gold, which had involved a night rough camping in the Lakes. And exaggerating wildly. She made it sound as though a bunch of wealthy teenagers, North Faced to the eyeballs, were polar explorers.

Jamie was all smiles and open body language, listening to Tilly speak, and Melissa had the strongest urge to grab this dirty magpie by the shoulders and forcibly eject him. He was sprawled with his legs apart, arms stretched proprietarily along the back of the sofa. Owning the space. Showing that he too might belong here, given the right circumstances, just like she did.

No.

But she knew she'd have to play this just right, remembering a hard seam of stubbornness in Jamie.

'Mum, I've been trying to find out what you were like from Jamie but he's a man of mystery,' said Tilly, smiling up at her as she entered the room. 'Keeps telling me to ask *you* about when you two were brother and sister.'

She'd met his eyes. He gazed coolly back at her, a slight smile playing on his lips.

'We just lived with the same foster parents for a while, as I said.' Melissa kept her voice light. 'We're not related in any way.'

Jamie flashed her a sly grin and leaned over to pick up the voluminous glass of red wine he'd acquired since she had last seen him.

Melissa bought those wine glasses for Mark on his last birthday; they were almost eighty pounds each. Mark always said they made red wine taste even better because they were so pleasing to hold. Melissa had to fight an impulse to lean over and remove the glass from Jamie's hand.

He took a deep sip, as though he was swigging lager, and placed the glass back on the coffee table with a satisfied little sigh before speaking again.

'It's much more interesting to hear about your lives, than all that crappy old stuff from the past,' he said. 'It was a hundred years ago! It probably seems that long to someone as young as you, anyway. Who wants to go back to the past, eh, Mel? We were different people then, weren't we?'

Tilly giggled lightly. Melissa met his eyes again and they were cold. She had to keep reminding herself it was the old Jamie she knew. This muscular man sprawled over her furniture was essentially a stranger. But if he called her Mel one more time she was going to punch him.

Out. She needed him out of her house. Out of her life.

'Tills,' she said in a calm, clear tone. 'I'd like a private chat with Jamie, so can you please go do something else?'

Tilly's mouth rounded in outrage.

'But my bedroom smells of puke!' she'd squawked; Jamie over-laughed in response.

Smiling, somehow, Melissa had said patiently, 'It's been completely cleaned and aired in there. And anyway, you can go to the den and watch telly or something. It's been a long day and Jamie is going to need to go home soon, I'm sure.'

'But you can't make him go now! It's still pouring!'

They all went quiet as if on cue. Rain was hitting the sitting room windows like handfuls of flung gravel.

'We've got another guest bedroom,' said Tilly. 'Unless,' she dipped another sly look at Jamie, 'you want to bunk up with Hester …'

Jamie started to laugh. It was surprisingly high-pitched. 'I think she sounds a bit too much of a party girl for me!' he said. 'Not sure I'm man enough to handle her!'

Melissa felt something boil over inside.

'I mean it, Tilly. Off you go.'

Grumbling and rolling her eyes, Tilly finally uncoiled herself from the sofa.

'All right, I'm going!' she said. 'But you have to let him stay over, Mum. It's a really horrible night.'

'Close the door behind you, please.'

Sighing but moving a little faster now, Tilly got up and pulled the heavy oak door until it clicked behind her.

Melissa regarded Jamie steadily.

The laughter had gone, snapped off with light-switch speed. He stared back at her, blank-faced and expectant.

Melissa sat down on the chair opposite the sofa. She leaned forward, her arms dangling from her knees like a boxer during rounds.

'What the fuck are you doing here, Jamie?' She kept her voice quiet and managed a tight smile. Had to keep this light. Stay in control.

He reached for the wine glass and took another long swig, with a satisfied 'ah', as though a bottle of £20 Merlot were designed to quench thirst. It was all for effect. She knew this. She just had to play along and then get him the hell out of her house.

'I need to kip here for tonight, Mel,' he'd said. 'Maybe two. And then I'll get right out of your hair, I promise.'

Melissa forced herself to breathe slowly through her nose.

'So ... how did you find me after all these years?'

Jamie laughed and made a questioning sort of face, as though she had said something ridiculous.

'You're a bit of a celebrity, aren't you, these days?' he said. 'You and the handsome doctor? Once I realized it was you, it wasn't very difficult. I just used my initiative.'

He grinned and gave a little sigh, entirely comfortable in his skin.

Melissa swallowed the urge to scream that felt like a hard, bitter lump in her throat. She nodded slowly, gathering herself, literally putting her arms around her body and tucking her legs up alongside her.

'So,' she said carefully, 'my husband is the jealous type. What do you think he's going to say when he comes back in a while and sees a strange man sprawled all over his sofa, drinking his wine?'

Jamie laughed, easily, just as though they really were old friends, catching up.

'I saw him going off with his little wheelie case earlier, didn't I?' he said. 'I'm not an idiot. You always did underestimate me.' His eyes flashed hard then and she felt another real twist of unease.

Jamie rubbed his face as though this conversation was beginning to bore him now.

'Like I say, I'm not here to cause trouble. I just want a bed for a night or two.'

He sounded weary; all his fight seemed to drain away then.

Melissa felt it too, like a change in air pressure. Her shoulders seemed to drop and she suddenly felt exhausted. Was it really such a big deal? She could get rid of him first thing tomorrow, couldn't she?

She'd let him drink her wine and stay the night. This would be over soon.

'Okay,' she said, allowing herself to smile warily. 'Let me get a glass of wine and you can fill me in on what you've been up to for the past twenty years.'

They'd talked until late. Or at least, he had and she had been the perfect listener. He told her about how he'd made a series of 'fuck-ups' that had landed him in prison, the most recent stint ending only a couple of weeks previously. But he was 'turning over a new leaf' now. 'It's all going to change, Mel,' he'd said. 'I'm tired of it. I've had enough of behaving like a kid.'

As Melissa listened, she began to relax. It was obvious that he knew nothing about what had happened later; the pivot on which the rest of her life had turned. The relief was like slipping into a perfectly warm bath; she snuggled further into the sofa, drank more wine and found herself laughing at all his jokes.

It had been fun. But it had still been a mistake, because it had led to a much bigger one.

Melissa runs her finger along her jaw, squeezing her eyes closed. She'd had to apply her foundation carefully to hide the slight stubble rash that had erupted on her chin. The evidence of last night was there too in the residual ache between her legs.

There was no point in pretending to herself that it had been a surprise. The squeak on the landing. The bedroom door opening; the slice of moonlight on the floor crossed by a dark shape.

By her third glass of Merlot it had started to feel inevitable. She told herself it was a little 'fuck you' to Mark that he would never need to know about.

She hadn't been sleeping when he'd climbed into her bed.

They didn't speak.

His body was so different to Mark's and not just because he was younger. Mark was soft and familiar. Jamie was ripples of velvet skin over taut muscle. Everything silken smooth and hard at the same time. While Mark smelled of aftershave and soap, Jamie had a hint of clean sweat about him that made Melissa bite and scratch, hating him at the same time as wanting him to burrow into every part of her.

It was good to feel that desirable again.

When it was over they lay for a while in the dark, listening to the sounds of the sleeping house and their own gasped breaths, bodies bathed in soapy sweat. And then Jamie had rolled over, ready for her again. This was a novelty too. She and Mark hadn't been like this since the earliest days. No one was, surely, when there were kids, late-night conversations about putting the bins out, or the box set they'd just watched?

She'd kicked him out at five a.m. and it was the only time they'd spoken since he came into the room. All the words had been used up earlier in the evening.

She didn't want specifics of why he was here. She couldn't have cared less. Her main priority was waiting until Tilly was out of the house today before she could get him to leave. The half-light in the bedroom last night had made everything seem sexy and illicit. Now it all just felt squalid and cheap and she wanted to wash all evidence of him away.

Melissa runs the filtered water tap and pours herself a long glass before taking a desultory sip.

She wonders how Hester is feeling. She hopes Hester won't try to be friends again. The thought of her cringing all over the place and apologizing makes Melissa feel even more weary.

In the end, Tilly had been remarkably sensible about the whole thing. She hadn't gone so far as to help mop it all up, but she had been the one who insisted Hester be covered by a duvet and she laid out water and painkillers for her. When Nathan had confessed to what he'd done, Tilly had let rip at him in a way that had surprised and impressed her mother. She said that Hester could have been on medication for all he knew, and that alcohol could have killed her. This thought hadn't really occurred to Melissa, who had then fretted her neighbour was dying all over her spare room.

She'd forced herself to check on her at one point, just in case she choked on her own vomit, but the older woman appeared to be sleeping quite peacefully, gentle snores puffing from her lips.

It was funny, but sometimes Tilly could be very mature for her age. Other times, well …

Melissa pictures herself at fifteen. Mature, yes, but in all the ways she shouldn't have been.

When she'd first met Jamie, back when she was Mel for short and Melanie for long, he'd been living with their foster parents, Greg and Kathie, for six months.

She remembered that first evening in Technicolour clarity. They were sitting round a table to have their tea, which had seemed way over the top. She'd sat back in her chair and rhythmically lifted dollops of the mashed potato (which tasted weird and not at all like Smash) before letting it slop back onto her plate.

Jamie had watched her with wide brown eyes, his mouth hanging open a bit to reveal a mess of masticated chop and liquid potato. Eventually, Kathie had lightly reprimanded him in her soft Glaswegian accent.

'You just concentrate on your own dinner, Jamie,' she'd said. And then, 'Are you no' enjoying that, hen?'

Melissa had shrugged, exaggeratedly. She wanted them to kick off at her. Angry lava was bubbling up inside her and she was aching for a way to let it out. '*Come on,*' she'd thought, '*just give me a reason.*'

There was no point in getting comfortable, like that weird boy. Didn't he understand anything? She wouldn't be allowed to stay for long and neither would he, in the long run.

'Maybe she isn't used to good cooking,' said Jamie smugly.

It was almost a relief.

Smiling broadly, she'd given him the finger, then lifted a forkful of potato. She'd then flipped it neatly across the table, splattering hot stickiness across his cheek. Jamie let out a howl of pain and outrage.

And so she sat back and waited for the explosion of anger. But it didn't come. Jamie had started to cry and rock, very softly. Greg went to the boy, wrapping his burly arms around him tightly and muttering, 'Shoosh, it's okay, it's all right.' Soft, meaningless words that seemed to comfort Jamie quickly, and then Greg was wiping away the remains of the globby potato with a paper napkin.

Kathie told Mel sharply that she was to help tidy and wash up. And that later on she would apologize to Jamie.

Mel had obeyed the first command at least, surprised into meek submission by the lack of violence.

She'd then avoided talking to Jamie at all for the first week, but felt his eyes roaming over her constantly. It was obvious that he fancied her, but at thirteen had no idea what to do with the seismic feelings she invoked.

Melissa kneads a fist between her eyebrows now and makes a small sound of repressed frustration. Why is he here, bringing all these unwanted memories in his wake? He carries the past about him, like body odour, and she can't stand it.

The sound of footsteps above fills her with resolve. He's up. Time to get him to leave, however badly he takes it. This can't go on for another night.

HESTER

I don't know why Saskia would think these flowers were an appropriate gift.

I hadn't looked at them properly outside. Now I am staring down at them on my kitchen table and I can see they aren't at all the sort of thing I would buy.

Everything is ugly and alien-looking. There are ornamental cabbages, which I hate, plus white pom-pom things, and orchids with thick purple petals and long red tongues that seem to leer. The worst ones though are almost black; with their spiky tendrils, they look like those fascination hats women wear to the races.

Black flowers! What an idiotic idea.

The entire bouquet makes me think about death. I rush to my bin and thrust the whole thing in there, head first. What on earth would have been wrong with some nice gerbera or some tulips?

I remember now that Saskia had another bouquet, which must surely have been meant for Melissa.

I had also been intending to go round with flowers, albeit from Tesco, rather than Petal and Vine. So those ghastly people have effectively scuppered my own apology.

Damn them.

A tear slides down my cheek again and I angrily swipe it away.

None of it was my fault. But I can't imagine what Melissa must think of me. Getting drunk like some kind of teenager and being sick like that. Another hot burst of shame washes over me now.

I've never been someone who drinks very much. Growing up, we only had sherry in the house for occasional guests, so when I met Terry it didn't occur to me that he would expect to go to pubs all the time and have wine with dinner. I hated when his face would get all red. He'd start talking too loudly and drape a heavy arm around my shoulders when we were out, as though I belonged to him. I never much liked his friends either. They were all a bit loud for my taste. Plus they all liked pubs just a little *too* much. In the end, I told him to go out on his own.

So I am the last person in the world who would ever drink too much and behave like that. It makes the cruel joke that was played on me even more savage.

I wipe another tear that slips down my face and look across at Bertie, who is fast asleep in his bed. Such a carefree existence. I envy him sometimes.

It's then, out of the blue, that I have an idea. Instead of flowers, I'll make my lemon drizzle cake. It was her favourite, after all. Who can resist a warm slice of lemon drizzle? She may not have needed my help with the catering yesterday, but this is different; a peace offering.

As I'm pulling on my pinny, my still-tender stomach gives a little ripple of protest. But I ignore it and set to work.

Before too long the kitchen is filled with comforting smells, but today the meditative nature of baking doesn't work its usual magic. I still feel unsettled, ill-fitting in my own skin, and it's as though my mind is filled with shadows.

When I am done, I look doubtfully at the cake cooling on the counter. Nothing went quite right. The cake feels heavier than it should, sagging in the centre. The colour is all wrong. Still, it is kindly meant. I'm sure Melissa will accept it in the good grace with which it is intended.

I tidy myself up in the hall mirror, breathing slowly, in and out, in an attempt to calm my jumpy heart. I sigh at my appearance; eyes baggy and skin the colour of porridge. But then I suppose I look like a woman who feels truly penitent, and that is as it should be. I'd dress in sackcloth and ashes if I could.

I walk around to the front door, holding the cake carefully, and knock sharply.

No one comes. But Melissa's Range Rover is parked outside so she must be in. I ring the bell.

Still nothing. Looking up, I see that windows are open at the front. I'm sure someone is there. Maybe it's just Tilly, but at least I can leave the cake and perhaps apologize to her at the same time.

When our friendship was at its zenith, I would sometimes bypass the front door and go through the garden gate and down to the kitchen at the back of the house. Then I noticed that it started to be locked, which I had to admit was a sensible security move when you live in a city.

Hesitating, I walk to the gate and gently push on the handle. It opens easily.

I'll just pop the cake inside if the patio doors are open. I'll find a piece of paper and write a note.

Coming into the back garden I spy some cigarette ends that haven't been cleared up. I will deal with those when I come back out. There must have been an awful lot to do, cleaning up after the party. Another little puff of shame and humiliation spreads in my chest.

I go to the French windows and peer inside.

The light is shining on them so I can't really see anything, but one of them is slightly open. Tentatively, I push it wider and step into the cool kitchen.

It is lovely in here. Melissa has such good taste. I hope she will forgive me. I was so looking forward to sitting here and drinking coffee with her again, like we used to.

I will leave the cake for her on the table. I simply cannot let things slide back to the way they were. Not when it seemed as though our bridges may be mended.

'Coo-ee?' I say, not too loudly. The air feels thick and unnatural, only punctuated by the ticking of the large railway clock on the far wall. It feels as though there is no living soul here. Melissa is not one for plants, or pets, though I've never felt the lack until now.

But there is a strangeness in the air I can't identify.

I'm just about to place the cake on one of her beautiful granite counters when there is an indistinct but recognizably human noise from the other side of the kitchen, from just out of sight beyond the table. I swivel round so fast in shock I almost drop the lemon drizzle onto the floor.

Then I realize I can see the gold of Melissa's pretty hair, tied in a ponytail, just beyond. She is kneeling down on the other side of the table.

'Oh my goodness!' I say. My heart is galloping uncomfortably fast. 'What are you doing down there, Melissa?'

I come closer and see that she is crouching on her haunches, like toddlers do with such ease. Her hands are over her mouth. She is looking down at something just out of sight on the floor. Oh no, I do hope it's not a spider or a mouse. I would go a long way to help Melissa, but I'm not sure I'm up to that.

'What is it?' I say gently, moving closer. 'Are you …?'

The rest of my sentence is whisked away in an out-breath that seems to go on and on. I am aware of the thud and whoosh of my own blood.

'Oh …', I say, but it comes out as a strangled whisper.

There is a man lying on the floor in front of her.

It's the one I saw this morning, dressed now, thankfully, his head turned away from Melissa. A heavy-looking stone implement lies at her feet on the floor and it takes a moment or two for me to understand that it's the pestle from that ugly pestle and mortar set she went on about so much.

My brain is slow to make sense of this strange scene. I look at the sticky redness on the side of the man's head for several minutes before I connect it with the pestle and with Melissa.

She rocks back and forth a little, seemingly unaware of me, until I come and kneel beside her, taking her hands and forcing her to look into my eyes. Hers are cloudy with shock so I speak slowly, while gently chafing her hands to comfort her.

'Melissa, look at me,' I say, forcing authority into my voice. 'Tell me what happened'.

'He's dead.'

The words are whisper soft and I feel her breath on my face.

'I killed him. I didn't mean it. I just …' She breathes in a big suck of air. Her lips tremble. They are deathly white.

I understand then, with a rush of bright clarity.

'Did he … did that man try to hurt you?'

She doesn't answer me so I gently press on.

'Did he … force himself on you?'

She doesn't reply, just stares into my face as though there are answers there. I've never seen her look so young. Oh my poor, dear girl. My heart twists with sympathy and affection.

'You poor baby!'

I pull her into an embrace. She falls willingly into my arms, limp as a rag doll. I breathe in the sweet smell of her hair before she struggles slightly and pulls back.

'Are you hurt?' I say.

Finally, she finds her voice, which comes out flat and toneless.

'I … I just lashed out.' She stares down at the pestle, which has a patch of jammy wetness and a few black hairs stuck to it. 'I didn't, I didn't mean to.'

I shudder in distaste then force a briskness into my voice.

'Go and wash your face in the bathroom. Take a few moments

77

to calm yourself down and then I'll make tea and we can talk.'

Almost meekly, she rises to her feet and almost stumbles out of the kitchen.

I think I may be experiencing a delayed reaction. It is only now that my own legs begin to shake so hard I almost collapse. I lean back against the table, breathing hard.

I wish someone would tell me what to do. I'm aware that we should call the police, and when I have watched dramas on television I have always been very dismissive of characters who fail to do this obvious thing.

But let me tell you, the aftermath of violence feels very different to television programmes. It's as though the normal rules of life have been crumpled up and tossed aside. Surely it is an impossible thing to lift a telephone and alert the outside world to the intimacy of the scene in this kitchen? How would they ever understand?

I saw him this morning, strutting about like Cock of the North.

I glance at the body and feel disgust rising in my throat. I don't want to be near it. I walk over to the sink, taking deep breaths. And as my breathing starts to settle, I make a decision.

I will help her. I will do whatever it takes. A feeling of euphoria dares to trickle into my tummy. We have a bond now that she can't share with another living person.

PART TWO

MELISSA

Melissa grips the sink and focuses on trying to breathe. It seems incredible that her body once sucked air in and out again by its own volition. If she stops willing it to happen, her lungs will simply stop working.

Toxic oil seems to pump around her body and the insistent mosquito-whine of her panic is threatening to engulf her. Hurrying to bend over the toilet, she vomits repeatedly until she is only bringing up bitter yellow bile. Afterwards she reaches for mouthwash with a hand that shakes so much she almost drops the bottle. She finally manages to get the minty liquid into her mouth to swill but it makes her feel sick again.

I didn't mean to.

That's what she said to Hester.

Those words. She could feel herself saying them before, over and over again, at the side of a road, while rain lashed her bruised face and the world tipped and expanded like it was made from stretchy rubber. No one had cared that she hadn't 'meant to' then.

No one would care now.

It wasn't entirely true that she hadn't meant this either. In that moment, after Jamie said what he said, she wanted to *stop him*.

Not to kill him, not that, but to stop him from saying those terrible words and doing what he was threatening to do.

She was stupid to think there was any other reason for him turning up at her door.

Melissa brushes her teeth now in hard circles until her gums throb and she has to spit pink froth into the sink.

She tries to picture what is happening downstairs. Hester is probably calling the police. Melissa sees herself down at the station on a hard plastic seat, vending machine coffee cups multiplying on the desk as the strata of lies she has cocooned herself in all these years begins to unravel.

Tilly.

Saliva floods her mouth. She cannot think about her daughter just now.

She has to get herself together. Get through this – one moment at a time. If she can only concentrate on the *very next few minutes*, she might be able to find some kind of road map through this nightmare.

After splashing water on her face she fumbles in the cupboard for her make-up bag. It is only as she has the lipstick in her shaking hand, poised at her lips, that she realizes something; this is the tipping point between putting on a game face and behaving like a crazy person.

When Melissa gets to the kitchen she is suddenly certain that all will be normal again. There will be no Jamie. Or he'll be sitting at the table with a coffee and a cocky smile. The back of his skull won't be smashed in. His heart will be working. Blood will be pumping around his body, rather than pooling on the floor.

But he's still lying there, head to the side, eyes closed. One arm is stretched out, his hand palm up. She pictures him flailing and grabbing only air as he fell so shockingly fast and hard. The *crump* as his body hit the cool, smooth tiles.

She tears her eyes away from him and it hits her forcefully that she can't hear the wail of sirens.

Hester isn't on the phone, but standing by the table, slightly smiling at her. Her expression seems as inappropriate as whistling a tune but, then, she has no clue what is normal anymore. The world has spun out of shape and is rearranging itself into a pattern she doesn't understand any longer.

For one fleeting moment Melissa has the sensation that there is something wrong about all this. Or at least, that there is another layer of wrongness. Is Hester behaving like someone who has stumbled upon a murder?

But perhaps Hester is acting strangely because she is frightened of Melissa. This thought causes a vertiginous dip in her stomach because funny old annoying Hester is all she has right now. She seems like the grown-up who can make it right again.

'Are you all right?' says Hester with such gentleness that Melissa's eyes fill with tears.

'I don't know,' she says in a small, cracked voice. 'I don't know what I'm going to do, Hester. I'm so frightened.' She's aware of the dry click of her tongue against the roof of her mouth.

Hester makes a small sound that's somewhere between a word and a sigh. But Melissa can't be sure it isn't just the sea pounding in her own ears.

Hester's bright chocolate-button eyes shine, the pupils large and black. When she speaks her voice is thick with emotion.

'You can rely on me,' she says. 'We'll sort this out, somehow. We just need to think things through clearly.'

She makes her way to the counter and climbs onto a stool. Her legs are only just long enough to reach the lower bar of the stool, something Tilly had been able to do since she was eleven.

Melissa walks to the sink and finds two tumblers then moves to the freezer where she retrieves the half-empty bottle of Stolichnaya. She sloshes some into the first glass, and Hester's voice seems to slice through her clogged thoughts.

'It's a little early for that, don't you think? I'll just have some water.'

'It's … what?'

Melissa's hand, holding the ice-cold bottle, wavers in mid-air. She carefully puts it on the sink as laughter spasms through her; it hurts, like contractions. There's a dead man on her floor. *Jamie is dead.* She killed Jamie. But Hester thinks a drink would be inappropriate. Melissa bends double, laughing in brittle waves that scare her. But it's impossible to stop and now she's crying and gasping, grasping for air.

And then Hester is right next to her, firmly taking her hand with her own small dry one. She leads her to the table, where she almost forces Melissa into a chair.

'Put your head between your legs,' she says, pushing Melissa's head downwards.

The irritation at this – all this *touching* – finally forces Melissa back into control of herself.

She is going to be fine. *Fine.*

She gently bats Hester's hand away and goes to pick up her glass of vodka, which she almost downs in one go, enjoying the sharp coldness slithering into her belly.

The alcohol instantly calms her. Her hands have stopped shaking at last. Melissa now regards her neighbour, who is staring at her intently. What is she thinking? What is she going to *do?*

She gets a funny mental image of a couple of gunslingers in an old Western. But it's not funny really. Nothing will ever be funny again.

The fridge hums noisily into life, breaking the bubble of silence that seems to surround them and Hester speaks.

'Melissa,' she says, 'who is that man?'

Melissa reaches for the glass and almost throws the last inch of vodka into her mouth. 'He's …' she croaks. 'He's someone I knew a thousand years ago. I let him stay last night because he had nowhere to go, but I never expected …'

Jamie's body seems to be obscenely large and present in the room.

He is dead.

Dead, dead, dead, dead, dead …

'Hester, what am I going to do?' she whispers.

'Everything depends on whether someone is likely to come looking for him,' says Hester, surprising Melissa so much that she looks up sharply. 'Are they? Did anyone know he was here?'

The implications of Hester's words sink in. Melissa puts a knuckle to her lips and bites on it until it hurts and she has to stop.

Surely she doesn't mean …?

But maybe this is the right question. She has no idea anymore.

Melissa swallows. 'I don't think so,' she says. 'He's just come out of prison. He said he had nowhere to go and wanted somewhere to stay for a while.'

Just for old times' sake. C'mon Mel.

She stands abruptly and goes to pour another, smaller, draught of vodka, before returning to the table and sipping it, slowly.

'Well I can't see that there would be any benefit in going to the police,' says Hester. 'Much better that we just deal with it ourselves.'

Melissa nods, waiting for her to expand on this thought, which she can't seem to understand.

'I mean,' says Hester patiently, 'we need to think about getting rid of it.'

Melissa stares at the other woman.

The idea is so seductive and so terrible she feels her eyes prick with tears again, which she blinks away.

'You seem very calm about all this!' she barks finally with a hysterical lilt to the end of her sentence. She snatches up the glass to take another sip of the vodka. But it has all gone. It's probably for the best. The alcohol was starting to dull the edges a bit too much and she needs to stay sharp. 'Are you really suggesting we don't tell anyone?'

Hester gives a small sniff. 'I read a lot of books,' she says. 'Plus, I watch television. We have done nothing wrong, Melissa, but it could look bad for us. I have nothing much to lose, but you … well. Think of everything you have. Think of Tilly!'

Bad for us? This all feels discordant; a bum note in a musical score, but Melissa is too befuddled and shocked to question it.

Hester continues, 'You could lose everything you have. Your beautiful home, your family. Everything you've worked for, all gone, because of one moment of self-defence.'

Melissa nods eagerly, her vision fracturing with the tears brimming in her eyes. Hester's voice is soft and mellifluous. She is right about how much Melissa has to lose.

But, self-defence?

It may have felt like it in that brief, sickening moment, but Melissa knows enough about the law to know the definition doesn't encompass what really happened.

How could anyone ever understand? She eyes Hester, desperately. She needs her. The thought of Hester backing away is more than she can stand right now.

The sound of the front door opening blasts terror through her now and her hands fly to her mouth, blocking the small shriek that rises from her throat. She and Hester stare at each other with wild, wide eyes.

'Only me!' trills Tilly from the hallway. 'Forgot my phone!'

Melissa's frozen muscles somehow unlock themselves and she flings herself towards the kitchen door and out into the hall.

Tilly is reaching for the bright pink iPhone on the hall table. Her cheeks are pink and her eyes shine. She looks like a visitor from a clean, healthy place. Everything about her is wrong and unwelcome.

'Oh hey!' she says, glancing up in a too-loud voice. 'Not stopping. God, Mum, you look like shit. Are you all right?'

'Just a bit … hung-over.'

Melissa is astonished to find that her lips and mouth and lungs can work together to make normal words. If they sound strange then Tilly is too distracted to notice. She is already gazing into the long-cracked screen of her phone with a look of concentration.

'Aw, well, have a bacon sandwich. That usually sorts you out,' she says vaguely. 'See you tomorrow.'

The door is open and then it is closed again. She is gone. The outside world is once more sealed away.

Melissa goes back into the kitchen on leaden limbs and looks at Hester, who hasn't moved from the spot. Her eyes are round and her small mouth is slightly open.

She feels an overwhelming urge to laugh and wraps her arms around herself, trying to control new shakes that have begun to rip through her. She's so *cold*.

'My word,' says Hester, holding a hand to her chest. 'That was a bit close.'

She slides into one of the chairs at the kitchen island.

'Look, I've had a thought.' Hester is businesslike again. 'About what we can do about … this.' She pauses and they both look at Jamie's body. 'The important thing is to get it out of your kitchen so you can get on with your life. What's done is done and there is no use whatsoever in making this situation worse than it needs to be. Agreed?'

Melissa nods uncertainly and hugs herself, chafing her goose-pimpled arms.

'There's a place in Dorset, where Terry used to go fishing,' says Hester. 'It was by a stately home. I forget the name, but anyway, there was an old well there. A really deep one, apparently. It was near where they used to park their van. Terry once remarked that you could hide anything down there and no one would know.'

She taps at her bottom lip with two fingers, scrunching her brow. 'We could take this … it … to the well, couldn't we? Oh, what was its *name*?'

Melissa can only stare in amazement at this extraordinary woman; she's taking this in her stride, with no apparent qualms about disposing of Jamie's body. Melissa knows she should be on her knees with gratitude but instead she feels an unreasonable rush of anger towards her neighbour.

'How do you suppose we'd find this place?' she says. 'And who's to say there isn't a gigantic housing estate there now?'

'Well, can't you look it up on the web or something?' Hester is clearly stung.

'Look what up, exactly?' says Melissa, aware that she is raising her voice. '*Convenient wells in Dorset where you can hide a body?*'

'There's no need to be facetious, Melissa. I'm only trying to be helpful.'

Hester's eyes film over with tears. Shit. She has to keep her on board. She needs her.

Melissa rubs her own face, hard, with both hands. 'Sorry! Sorry,' she says. 'It's just … I can't think with … him … there.'

Both women regard the body that somehow seems more dominating of her attention every time Melissa looks at it. It's almost as though it's growing. Soon it will have expanded to fill the entire room. *Stop it. That's crazy thinking. Keep it together.*

'Terry's van,' says Hester decisively. 'I've never driven it but I'm sure it still works. He used to take great care of that thing. We can put … it, there, while we think of somewhere to dispose of it.'

'Right, okay, yes,' says Melissa, getting up, hugely grateful to be acting at last. There is always the possibility that Tilly might come back early, or Mark's filming could have been curtailed. The thought of this sets off a silent scream in her mind. This is better than no plan. And maybe they could locate the place Hester mentioned. Maybe they could really do this. Maybe it will all be okay again.

Then her eye snags on the pestle, lying on the floor, its grim smearings hidden.

'What should I do with … that, Hester?' she says, pointing at it and swallowing deeply.

Hester peers at the pestle and gestures at Melissa. 'Get me a bin bag. I'll get rid of it.'

Melissa meekly retrieves a black sack from the drawer and passes it to Hester, before going through the inner door to the double garage. Here she finds two dust sheets that had been bought in anticipation of work on the bathroom. In the end the decorators had brought their own and they hadn't been needed. They are still in their plastic covers, which slide and crinkle in Melissa's arms. Goose pimples scatter across her chest. She feels as though there are people watching all of this. The police are just waiting for the best moment to swoop in and arrest her. Several police cars will come screeching to a stop outside. Black-clad men will descend from the ceiling on ropes.

She wants to laugh again. Melissa clamps her jaw shut to stop her teeth from slamming together and goes back into the kitchen.

'I found these, I think they'll—' But she stops speaking abruptly.

Hester has gone.

Dropping the bulky contents of her arms with a ragged gasp, she runs to the hallway. Melissa pictures her on a witness stand, giving evidence against her. 'Oh yes, she was quite ready to dispose of the body. I went along with it because I was frightened she might hurt me too.' She can even see the suit Hester would wear, with some sort of Thatcher blouse underneath.

Melissa lets out a deep animal moan. Hester has lost her nerve.

The doorbell shrieks into her consciousness and her whole body jerks at the shock. The police, then?

Walking on shaky, newborn-Bambi legs to the front door, she can make out one shape. A smallish female shape with helmet hair.

She flings the door open.

'Oh Hester, thank Christ. Where did you go?'

Hester glances up at her as she steps inside, carrying what looks like a Marks and Spencer cool bag. It *is* a Marks and Spencer cool bag.

Melissa can feel the slender threads fixing her to a state of control begin to twist and buckle again.

Hester walks into the kitchen with a new boldness. As though she owns the space.

'What have you got there?' cries Melissa. 'We're not going on a fucking picnic, are we?'

The other woman's mouth primps into a tight squiggle of disapproval.

'Of course we're not,' says Hester, eyebrows raised. 'I'm merely using this to transport all the cool packs I could find in my freezer. We don't want things to start getting unpleasant in the van, do we? I don't know how soon there may be a smell.'

Melissa breathes slowly, in through her nose and out through her mouth, just like she had been taught to do at her yoga classes. They are going to pack Jamie in ice packs like some kind of cooked ham. Then they're going to throw him away.

Practical help like this is what she needs. But it feels all wrong. Grotesque.

'What about the pestle?' she manages to say. She almost said, 'weapon' instead.

Hester gestures at the bag.

'In there, wrapped, but washed. I used some of Terry's special cleaning fluids on it, but really, I think we have to get rid of it, to be on the safe side. The other bit too. The bowl. But you can do that later. The priority now is … well …', she trails off.

Both women look down at the body cooling on the floor.

HESTER

I think I'm doing a very good job of keeping this terrible situation under control, given the circumstances.

Melissa looks rather wild. I've never seen her like this before. She keeps speaking really fast and then staring into space. She doesn't seem to be able to focus on anything.

Luckily I am feeling sharper than I have for a long time.

I don't think it is too fanciful to say that this was maybe meant to be. All those years that we have known each other, perhaps they were all building up to this strange day when Melissa really needed me? After all, what would she do if I wasn't here right now?

Together we work to lay out the large dust sheets that she has found in my absence. We work in silence and all I can hear is her rather heavy breathing. I keep flicking glances at her to make sure she isn't going to become hysterical again, but she seems quieter now, as though the reality of this situation is finally sinking in. It's a relief.

But once the sheets are neatly laid out, we both stare down at the body. Neither of us wants to touch the thing really.

Then, to my relief, she hands me a pair of disposable gloves. They feel slippery and unpleasant in my hands. She is already

91

wearing some, I notice with surprise. A little late for that, I think, but I say nothing.

'Right,' she says, with only the slightest quiver in her voice, 'let's move him onto the plastic sheets.'

That's my girl.

She lifts the arms, with only a small moue of distaste, and I take hold of the feet.

We both haul with all our might, but goodness, it is heavy. He was quite a short man, but strongly built. It seems death has now added its own burden – do bodies become heavier post-mortem? I have no idea – but he is almost impossible to move.

Melissa's face is quite pink and I can feel sweat breaking out all over my body. She releases the arms to the ground with a strange gentleness. I feel like pointing out that he is hardly going to bother about being manhandled now, but sense this wouldn't be well received.

We exchange dispirited looks. All we have managed to do is cause the dust sheet to bunch up unhelpfully.

'We'll have to roll him,' I say, getting down on my knees, despite the discomfort from my arthritic joints. 'Come on, Melissa, I can't do this alone!'

Melissa hurriedly gets down to the floor at the other end of the man. We straighten the limbs in an attempt to get the body into the right shape to be rolled. His shoulders seem to be in the way now.

Sweat pools unpleasantly at my armpits as we push and pull, push and pull, both grunting with exertion. We make progress inch by inch.

It feels like forever but somehow, eventually, we have managed to get the body onto the dust sheet. But just as one problem is solved, another presents itself.

How are we, two women, going to transport it to the van, let alone to Dorset and down a well?

It's funny, but despite all this, there is still no question of abandoning her. I am in this for the duration now, as they say.

'Wait!' she says suddenly. 'What are we meant to do with these ice packs?'

I regard her with a sense of satisfaction. *Now* she sees the wisdom of my plan, despite being quite rude about it when it was suggested.

I believe there is no point pretending that certain realities don't exist. At some point, that body is going to go 'off'. But I'm never one to crow so I simply ask her to pass the cool packs. I place the smaller ones underneath the small of the back and knees; the larger, I lay on top of the body. Without speaking, Melissa goes to her own freezer and finds some more, which we arrange in a similar fashion. This is going to add considerable weight but I think this is unavoidable.

We manage to roll the sheeting around the bulky shape until we have something rather like a large plastic mummy lying before us.

It reminds me too of a chrysalis. But there will be no rebirth here.

Then it strikes me that maybe there will. Maybe it is the dawning of a new level of friendship between Melissa and myself. I like this thought.

But we still need to find a way to move this huge *thing*.

My mind's eye roams around the garage, where Terry kept all sorts of things from his decorating business. And then, bingo, I have an idea. There's a sort of metal trolley there, under some boxes, I think. He used it to move heavy paint cans and whatnot. I'm sure it's just about big enough to fit this onto.

I'm about to tell Melissa when the doorbell shrieks, unnaturally loud.

We stare at each other, mouths fish-like, gaping. Who is it now?

It rings again and again, insistent and bossy. The letterbox rattles. Why can't the world leave us *alone?*

'Lissa? Honey, please talk to me,' says a familiar husky voice. 'I know you're in because all your windows are open.'

Saskia. That damned woman, again.

We have to get rid of her. I start to rise and Melissa's hand shoots out, grabbing my arm in a painful grasp. Her eyes are wide as she mimes a shushing motion.

'Look, I'm not going away,' says the nightmare creature on the doorstep. 'It's just me. And I'm staying here until you talk to me.'

I don't know where the image comes from but for a moment I picture her wrapped in plastic too. Silent for once. Compliant. The image brings a thrill of satisfaction. But no, there are too many people who would miss her, not least that alarming man-child she drags around the place.

Melissa gets decisively to her feet, ripping off the gloves and throwing them onto the table. For a second, I think she's gone quite mad, because she suddenly ruffles her hair with both hands and rubs her eyes fiercely. She stalks out of the room without giving me a second glance. I confess my heart is in my mouth as I hear her open the front door. What is she doing?

'Honey!' The voice seems to fill the hallway. 'Did I wake you?'

'Yeah,' says Melissa in a very weak voice that I can only just make out. 'I'm sick, Tams. I ate some prawns late last night that had been out in the heat all day. I'm not ignoring you. I'm just ... not well.'

'Let me come in and look after you,' says Saskia.

Melissa's acting performance slips slightly for a second as she squeaks, 'No! I mean there's really no need!' Then, more calmly. 'I just want to sleep, honey. We can catch up later, yeah? And don't worry about Nathan and the Hester thing. I'm sure she'll see the funny side. Eventually.'

This hurts me, I don't mind saying. I know she is only acting but it still rankles.

'Okay darling,' says Saskia at last, reluctantly. 'You go back to bed. I'm so sorry about Nathan's idea of a joke. I've told him he's in the fucking doghouse for a year.' She gives one of her trademark deep laughs and I hear Melissa laughing too. She really is a very good actress. It's not half an hour ago that she was virtually hysterical.

I think it's only now that I understand this could all work out okay. Between my common sense and her ability to put on a front, well, we really are quite a team.

There's a flurry of '*love you, babe*'s' and other nonsense, before the door closes and Melissa comes back into the room.

She straightens her hair and regards me coolly.

'Right, so you need to get your van into my garage. I'm going to move my car out the front. We'll get … him', she nods at the plastic chrysalis on the floor and I see her swallow deeply before continuing, 'into the van. Then we'll look up that place you talked about.'

An hour later we've made real progress.

The trolley proved to be a godsend in terms of transporting it from the kitchen. But getting the body and then the trolley into the van itself was a lot more difficult, and with all the pushing and shoving I think I may have pulled a muscle in my back. Between us, though, we managed it.

Thankfully, most of the decorating stuff in the van had been cleared out and there is a decent space. Terry mainly used it for his fishing gear after he retired, but once he was gone from my life, I did a proper tidy.

When the doors are nicely closed up again, a sort of euphoric relief takes hold of both of us. I think it's because we don't have that horrible sight in front of us anymore. Truly, anything seems possible now.

We go to work in silence with a bleach-based detergent and cloths, scrubbing the floor tiles, arms pumping back and forth in unison. I really do feel a sense of camaraderie as we scrub and scrub. From television I know all about Luminol and how the police can find the tiniest splash of blood; but they would need a reason to look in the first place, wouldn't they? People may have seen Jamie here, but he clearly had no settled lifestyle and there would be no reason to suspect Melissa's part in any perceived disappearance. Who would suspect a woman like her of murder?

After we've finished, Melissa gets on the phone to Tilly and tells her she is going away for a night to visit an old friend whose mother has just died of cancer.

Unfortunately, I can hear from this one-sided conversation that Melissa is having problems convincing her daughter of this story.

'Why would you have heard of her before now?' she says and, after a pause, 'You don't necessarily know all my old friends, do you?' and, 'Of course I have old friends, don't be cheeky.'

When she finally comes off the phone she looks pale. I persuade her to eat the sandwiches I have been making during her conversation. She gives me a very strange look as I offer the plate, and it's only when I say, 'If you go fainting on us, it really could draw the wrong sort of attention,' that she eventually reaches for one and takes a couple of small bites, chewing as though her mouth is filled with sand.

I have quite an appetite. I eat three sandwiches and feel much the better for it.

And I think it's because my blood sugar has risen again that I suddenly have a jolt of real brainpower.

'Scarrow Hall!' I say.

'What?' says Melissa blankly.

'That's the name of the place where Terry used to go fishing! Let's look it up! Do you have a computer?'

She gives me another of her rather impenetrable looks and goes to one of the cupboards, from which she removes an impossibly thin silver laptop computer. Flipping the lid open, she taps away for a moment until a screen with Google on it appears.

'Scarrow Hall,' I say again, slowly but she is already typing.

A page opens and we both bend a little closer to read. 'Forgotten Dorset' says the banner across the top. We read on:

A few miles from the thundering A303 lies a pocket of England in which time has stood still. Scarrow Hall was, in its day, the home of the Parkstone family, who were major landowners in the North Dorset area.

But in the latter half of the twentieth century the house fell into a state of disrepair and when the final member of the Parkstone family, Emily, died in 2009 at the age of 91, a complicated probate situation has meant the old house is now derelict and unloved.

Take a pictorial trip with us as we explore this once *grande dame* of local architecture.

She deftly clicks and enlarges picture after picture of the house, including one of the well.

'Well I think it looks as though it's much the same,' I say triumphantly but Melissa is doing something complicated on a map page and doesn't appear to be listening to me.

'Hmm,' she murmurs after a while. 'There's no Street View in that area at all so there can't be any major housing developments there.'

I don't really know what she's talking about but it doesn't matter, because she slaps down the lid of the laptop and half smiles at me for the first time in ... well, I don't know how long.

Then her shoulders slump again. 'But how would we find the well? There's no guarantee that it's still there, is there?'

I muse on this, wanting so much to bring that hopefulness back into her face, and a wonderful thought comes to me. I can see it very clearly in my mind's eye.

That photograph: Terry beaming into the camera, holding aloft some manner of fish or other as though it were the crown jewels.

And then bringing it home and expecting *me* to gut, clean, and cook it. I refused, of course. But he insisted on having that picture up until he died. I'm sure it's in a drawer somewhere, and I could swear the well can be seen in the background.

'Hester!'

Melissa has slapped her hand on the table and the sound shocks me deeply, as though I, myself, have been struck.

'Can you fucking concentrate! What are we going to do?'

I'm conscious of my spine stiffening and my cheeks glow with an unwelcome warmth. When my words come out, they are clipped but I keep my cool and speak quietly.

'I am very happy to help you in any way I can, Melissa,' I say. 'But I will not be sworn at. Are we clear on this?'

Her bottom lip gapes a little before she closes her mouth and runs her hand across her face. Her eyes look dull and tired.

'I'm so sorry, Hester,' she says quietly. 'But I am very, very upset and frightened. I have …' she gulps, visibly, 'killed a man in my kitchen and I don't know what I'm going to do.'

Her voice skids away into a choked sort of sob and I feel compassion flood my heart. I would like to hold her again and let her cry it all out but I sense too much contact might not be welcome. Instead I stretch my hand across the table and pat hers.

'Please don't worry,' I say in a soothing voice. 'I was just remembering that I have something which will help us. I'll go get it right now and then we can plan our route.'

She's watching me, blinking hard to dispel the threatening tears, and she nods. I know how much she wants to believe me.

And how much she needs me right now.

MELISSA

Melissa roots desperately through the kitchen drawer, pushing aside packs of cards, string, broken bits of toy from when Tilly was small, and assorted other rubbish she can't believe she hasn't thrown away. Stabbing her thumb painfully on a mini screwdriver that came in a Christmas cracker a couple of years ago, she swears expressively, then sucks the thumb. The coppery taste of her own blood causes another swell of panic.

Don't do this, a small voice says in her head. *Stop this now. It's not too late. Tell the police he attacked you.*

But the sensible little voice doesn't suggest how she would explain that Jamie's wound is on the back of his head and not the front.

She turns back to the drawer and roots inside it, more cautiously now. She hasn't smoked properly in years, but had bought a packet during the Sam episode and was happy to find she was able to stop again at will.

The action of placing the cigarette between her lips is rooted deep in her muscle memory. The papery toasted taste floods her mouth with anticipation of the hit to come.

Finding the cook's matches in another drawer, she sparks up and lights the cigarette. The nicotine burn hits her in a dizzying wave and she sucks greedily, instantly feeling a pleasurable rough-ness in her throat. Christ, she's missed this.

Her hand shakes as she takes another deep drag and her head spins a little. She pictures Hester's disapproval and the strange reprimand about swearing.

'Well *fucking fuck* it all,' she whispers to the empty kitchen.

She is acutely aware that her strange little neighbour has crossed the threshold into a dark place for her. She can't imagine a single other person who would have done what Hester has done for her already. Mark would have called the police straight away. Saskia would have been no use to anyone. But Hester is almost calm. There is no reason for her to help like this and Melissa is grateful for her cool, practical sense.

She's suddenly aware of the nipple that Jamie sucked chafing against her bra and she closes her eyes in distress. How can these physical sensations have outlived him? Damp misery slaps at her and she feels sure that she will never feel pleasure or happiness in anything again. Melissa finishes the cigarette in a few deep puffs then stabs it out viciously in the sink before running the tap and putting the wet, squashed remains in the bin.

Catching sight of the notepad she leaves on the side, she reads the words, 'Flowers 10 a.m.' and 'Pay Zofia.'

The ordinariness of this other life, which existed just yesterday, seems sweeter and more remote now than she can believe. Cleaners, day-to-day quibbles with Tilly over homework, laziness, and laundry seem like precious jewels that have slipped out of her fingers and been lost forever. Even her relationship with Mark has taken on a rosy hue, as though her life before today were more perfect than she had ever appreciated. Who cares if Mark fucked another woman? What does that really matter?

She glances at the clock. Time seems to move strangely in this new reality, like a liquid that turns without warning from fast-flowing water to something muddy and listless. Last night seems like another lifetime. Yet four o'clock this afternoon seems to have only just passed but now it is almost eight. In just a few hours, everything has changed.

He's dead. She really did kill him.

Jamie had waited until late into the following afternoon to make his move, when they were alone. Long enough for her to think that maybe she had got him all wrong and her only problem was how to get rid of him. She had resolved to tell him that enough was enough. They'd had some fun and bonded over old times.

But now he needed to get out of her life again and never come back.

He must have guessed what was coming because, as if continuing an earlier conversation, he'd suddenly said, 'So I used to hear about what you were up to, on the grapevine.' He'd paused and given her an almost lazy smile. 'Back when you were ordinary old Mel Ronson. Before all *this*.' He'd made an expansive gesture to indicate everything she now had.

Melissa's heart had begun to thud with dread. Jamie wagged his finger in front of his face as though scolding her.

'Dear, dear, you really were a naughty girl, weren't you?' he'd said and then, coldly, 'So the sixty-four million dollar question is, does he know? Your Mark?'

Her expression told him all he wanted to know. Jamie smiled again. 'Or should I say, the ten grand question? Because that's what it will take. Really, Melanie, what do you think the red tops would make of it all, eh? Wife of the handsome telly doc, a little jailbird? Someone with blood on her hands?'

Everything she had, everything she'd worked so *damned hard* for, was suddenly quicksand-soft under her feet. All of it could be taken away.

'Fuck off, Jamie,' she'd bluffed. 'I don't care what the papers say. And Mark knows already.' This was a lie.

But Jamie hadn't finished yet.

'Yeah,' he'd said, 'but what about that girl of yours? What would young Tilly, with her jolly fucking hockey sticks school and her Duke of Fucking Edinburgh *whatever*, make of knowing what her mother had done? How would she feel about carrying those genes around in that fuckable little body of hers, eh?'

And he'd turned away, actually chuckling to himself, like it was all so very funny.

Her response had felt primeval and completely out of her control. Her fingers were around the pestle and, before the rational part of her mind could take over, stone was crunching into skin and bone. It had felt exactly like self-defence at the time. She'd had to stop him. To protect herself.

The doorbell pulls her out of her reverie and she cautiously goes to check that it is Hester, returning with whatever it was she went to get next door.

The little woman bustles in and her nasty little dog comes trotting behind. It smells and makes odd grunting sounds. Melissa wrinkles her nose as the dog wags its tail at her and pants expectantly.

'Found it!' says Hester brightly, as though she'd gone to get a borrowed casserole dish.

The dog has darted off ahead of them and, when they come into the room, they see that it is sniffing enthusiastically at the floor where Jamie had lain. Melissa feels a wave of horror that the dog can smell blood, despite all that cleaning. Her stomach roils and Hester shoos the animal away, clearly having the same thought.

Hester is holding a wooden picture frame towards her now and beaming triumphantly. Melissa cautiously takes it and begins to study the picture.

It shows a bald man with a moustache and a safari-style short-sleeved shirt. He's holding some kind of fish in the air with a proud expression. This, presumably, is Terry, who was long gone by the time Melissa moved in. Hester has never really talked about him but, from the odd comment made here and there, Melissa got the impression the marriage wasn't a happy one.

Melissa focuses now on the background to the picture. Behind him is a river. She can just see distinctive spiky reeds fringing the bank. The well is to his right and the house itself in the background. There is an unusual red-brick tower that is almost equidistant to the well. If it is still there (and this in itself is a long shot) it should be possible to locate it.

Hester is beaming at her in that way that causes an unpleasant ripple of emotion. There's still something 'off' about her energy. It's as though she has more colour in her cheeks than Melissa has ever seen in her before.

It's all wrong. None of this should be happening. In a moment, the rational person she really is will take charge of things. Call the police and try to make it right.

Instead, she finds herself saying, 'Thank you, Hester, this is really helpful. But I think we should get going soon.'

Hester pulls a doubtful face. 'Well,' she says, 'as much as I am loth to try and find this place in the dark, I really think we should wait until much later. There is far less risk of us being seen that way.'

Panic rises up inside her again. 'I can't just *sit here*,' says Melissa, her voice wobbling. 'We could at least be doing something. And we could make sure we're there for first light.'

Hester regards her, her expression patient. 'It will take a few hours to get there but dawn doesn't come until around 5 a.m. at the moment. I know because the light always comes around the edges of my curtains and wakes me. We should ideally leave at about 2 a.m.'

Her tone is decisive and bossy. Melissa wants to lash out at her, even though Hester is helping her with this terrible mess.

'No,' she says with forced calm. 'I can't wait until then. I just can't.'

Melissa and Hester stare at each other and then Hester makes a small sound of frustration.

'Look,' her tone is unctuous now, 'let's just be sensible and wait a *little* while longer, then? If we have to sit at the side of the road until dawn comes, so be it, but we should at least give it another hour or two.'

'Fine,' says Melissa, wearily. 'Why don't you go and get whatever you're going to need for the journey now and take your dog back, while I get a few things together.'

Hester actually gasps.

'I can't leave Bertie all night!' she says. 'He must come with us!'

'But won't it …?' Melissa starts to ask the question but her vocabulary can't accommodate the monstrous images her mind is creating; the dog sniffing and snuffling at Jamie's plastic-wrapped corpse, desperate to get at the juiciness inside. That's all he is now … rotting meat. Her stomach heaves.

Luckily, Hester seems to understand what she cannot say.

'No, no,' she says hurriedly, 'of course he won't because he will have to sit up in the front with us. He'll be fine. Won't you, Bertie?' She reaches down and strokes the dog's ears. It gazes up at its owner.

Melissa looks away. It is clear that Hester has drawn a line that Melissa will not be allowed to cross. One way or another, that mutt is coming with them to Dorset.

Melissa sighs. She needs to be alone.

Upstairs she showers and changes her clothes. For some time, she sits numbly on the edge of her bed, wrapped in the towel, until her skin begins to chill and she forces herself to get dressed.

She stares into the wardrobe for a good five minutes because she can't seem to work out what she should do next. Finally, still shivering, she goes to the chest of drawers to find underwear, then jeans, and a long-sleeved t-shirt, which she puts on with the slowness of a much older woman. Her body aches strangely and she feels mildly feverish as she pulls on her fleece hoodie and scrapes her hair back into a ponytail. Glancing at the mirror, she sees a haunted woman staring balefully back at her.

The dress she wore at the party is pooled on the pale blue armchair by the window and she has the strange sensation that if she put it on she could climb back into Before.

Yesterday she was a different person. How naive she had been to think there would be only one Before and After in her life. Yet here was another chasm between her old life and this new one.

Jamie is dead. She *murdered* him. The words roll around like marbles inside her skull.

A thought jolts through her mind then, making her gasp audibly.

The bag Jamie had with him last night. Where did he put it?

She hurries into the guest room and stops when she sees the evidence of his presence straight away. The bed is made and she pictures his body warming the sheets last night before he came into her room. The bed probably still smells of him.

She turns away hurriedly to the chest of drawers, where he'd lain out a Lynx deodorant, a small soap bag, a handful of change, and a mobile phone. There's something neat about the way he has put them there. Then she realizes. It is a habit from prison: keeping your small amount of belongings neat and tidy. She wishes she didn't know this and, at the same time, feels a belly punch of sorrow.

Melissa scoops the mobile into her pocket. They'll have to dump it somewhere on the way to Dorset. She glances around the bedroom, searching for the holdall he'd arrived with. It isn't lying anywhere obvious and so, grumbling under her breath, Melissa pulls out drawers and looks in the wardrobe. Then she spots that one of the big drawers under the bed, where she keeps spare bed linen, isn't flush. It's jutting out a little on one side. Dropping the items on the bed, she gets to her knees and pulls the large drawer towards her. It rolls smoothly on its runners until it is entirely free of the bed.

Crouching low, Melissa leans forward and feels around with her fingertips until they meet the roughness of an unfamiliar material. It's an ugly, cheap bag that looks as though it came from some army surplus shop about thirty years ago. It's slightly greasy to the touch and Melissa grimaces as she yanks at the zip and peels the sides back to look inside.

Pants, socks, a t-shirt or two, and another pair of jeans, which are folded neatly.

It's as she is about to zip up the bag again that she notices a Hamleys' carrier bag with its familiar black and red logo at the bottom. Hesitating, Melissa pulls it out and reaches inside.

It contains a teddy bear with a wide smile and a little gold bell on a red ribbon around its neck. The fur is soft and cool under her fingers and Melissa knows the bear was expensive; she once bought something similar for a friend who'd had a baby. The bear's lifeless eyes shine up at her.

Angrily stuffing the bear back into the bag, she zips the whole thing up again. Getting to her feet, she hefts the holdall over her shoulder before going downstairs to Hester and whatever comes next.

HESTER

Melissa takes a very long time upstairs.

When an hour has passed, I think about going to find her. To check she is all right, of course, but also …

Well …

She's in such a state that my imagination is playing all sorts of tricks on me. I'm picturing her opening a window, shinning down a drainpipe and leaving me with all this. But then I hear her moving around and am surprised by the sensation of relief I experience.

While I wait for her to come down, I walk around her kitchen, letting my fingers trail over the surfaces. I wonder what it would be like to live here? I used to spend a fair bit of time in this kitchen, holding Tilly for her while she bustled about doing whatever it was that she had to do.

An unwanted memory forces its way into my mind. I wish I could bat it away, like an insect, but it lodges itself there.

Tilly had been teething and fractious all night. Melissa was pale and tired and I offered to sit and look after the baby while she had a nap.

I had a knack for calming Tilly. Babies always responded well to me, which was one of the reasons I was so good at my job at the nursery.

I'd heard one of the parents there talking about a new shop that had opened up, which sold baby clothes. The bonnet I'd picked out, in the palest primrose yellow with tiny sprigs of cherries, was one of the prettiest things I'd ever seen.

I couldn't wait to see what it looked like on Tilly's little curly head. So when Melissa was upstairs, I got it out of the bag and slipped it onto her. Melissa had some strange ideas about how to dress her and I sometimes wished she would favour more classic baby clothes.

Tilly looked up at me with her beautiful round eyes, her thumb embedded in her rosebud mouth, sucking noisily. The bonnet framed her face perfectly and she seemed to like it. Or at least, she certainly didn't complain.

I bent down and kissed her downy forehead and breathed in her sweet, biscuit smell. And then I looked up to find Melissa standing in the doorway.

A guilty feeling flooded through me, even though I had done nothing wrong. Melissa's expression was stony.

'What have you put on her head?' she asked in a cold tone of voice.

'It's just a bonnet I thought would suit her!' I said, smiling and trying to keep the tone light.

But Melissa had taken the baby from my arms and snatched it off her head.

'I don't like hats on babies,' she'd said, bafflingly. She'd been strange with me for the rest of that afternoon, even though I'd offered to stay and cook dinner for all three of them. Melissa does have her funny ways.

I find myself lifting the glass she drank from almost unconsciously now. I can see an intimate smudge where her lips touched the rim. Flustered, I hurriedly place the glass in the sink.

Nerves begin to flutter inside me again.

I am having to gear myself up psychologically to the idea of driving. I'm not even confident that the vehicle will start after being shut up in the garage for several years. Terry always said it was 'a great little runner', but it would be just like my luck for it to refuse to start.

We will simply have to hope for the best. Melissa's Land Rover would be no good for this task, huge though that vehicle is. I am not prepared to let her drive the van, either. I don't think she is in a fit state. She's been drinking. Plus, her mood is all over the place, veering between zombie-like calm and sudden bursts of temper.

I am insured for the van, of course. I once had to transport something when Terry had inconveniently broken a wrist, and even though I never use it, I find myself renewing both the tax and the insurance when I get the reminders. I am aware this may seem like an extravagance but you never know when you might need a vehicle, as today has demonstrated.

When Melissa finally emerges, I am as calm as I will ever be at the prospect of a motorway drive. At least it will be quiet at this time of the night.

I notice straight away that she is carrying some sort of bag.

'What's that?'

'It's nothing. Just his bag. Jamie's,' she says. She seems even more nervy than before she went up there. Her eyes keep bobbing around the room as though looking for somewhere to rest.

'Melissa?' I say hesitantly. 'Are you okay?' I force myself to say something that almost makes me feel sick. 'If you're having second thoughts, it's still not too late to—'

'NO!' she says. Almost shouts, in fact.

I give her a weak smile of relief.

What on earth would I have done if she'd said yes? She would like to call the police now?

She sits down at the opposite end of the kitchen table and

begins to fiddle with her phone, barely looking at me. It's clear she is in no mood to communicate.

So we just sit there, in silence, waiting for the evening to move on. It's actually quite pleasant in a strange way.

We stay like this for half an hour or more and then she seems to erupt from the table like an explosion, announcing, 'That's it, we're going. I can't do this any longer.'

'Fine,' I say with a sigh. 'Let's go.'

Of course then we have a tedious row about which of us is going to drive.

'You don't know this van,' I say. As if I drive it all the time.

'How bloody hard can it be?!' she snaps, but I will not be budged. We go back and forth for a few minutes until she gives in.

It is a lovely evening, quite balmy, after yesterday's rain. No other neighbours are about as we get into the van, which is a relief. Now all I have to do is drive.

I glance at Melissa in the passenger seat. She has a mutinous look plastered on her face that quite spoils her looks. I think she is still sulking.

When the engine turns over first time I give a silent prayer of thanks. But the journey gets off to a bad start nonetheless. Backing out of the drive, there is a thump as I accidentally reverse into the gatepost. There's a nasty grinding sound of metal against metal and the wheels spin in an alarming way for a moment. Melissa cries out and Bertie begins to bark in earnest from the footwell.

'Be quiet, Bertie!' I snap.

With a whine, he turns in a circle and snuggles down next to Melissa's feet. I don't think she likes dogs very much because she keeps moving her legs to the side. She made rather a fuss about him lying there, in fact, but when I pointed out that the alternative was to have him on her lap, she backed down. However, I have noticed her shifting her legs whenever the poor dog looks for comfort by trying to lie close. Honestly. How can she object to Bertie when he is lying there so sweetly? Some people are very strange.

Neither of us speaks as I pull out onto the road, accidentally crunching the gears from one through to three until I get the hang of things. *Come on, Hester. You can do this*, I tell myself.

I hope I haven't caused any damage to the gatepost. I don't much care about the van, as long as it can get us from A to B. But it will be inconvenient to have to mend the fence between our houses.

We have agreed the route in advance and so head out through the quiet streets of North London towards the M25. The quicker way is via the North Circular, but that feels so much more conspicuous.

I'm still having trouble with the gears and there are a few unpleasant noises before I get the hang of things again. Melissa melodramatically winces every time this happens, which is really rather unnecessary, not to mention off-putting.

I glance at her. Her face looks gaunt in the wash of the street lights, her eyes hollowed out, as though she has aged in just twenty-four hours. It's strange, but I feel quite the opposite.

The air heater seems to be fixed so warm air blasts into our faces. Melissa fiddles with the controls for some time to no avail before sighing and turning her face to the window. There is a residual smell of paint in the van and the atmosphere could become quite unpleasant in time. Still, we have bigger concerns on that front. Let's just hope those ice packs do the business.

We're coming through the quiet country roads of Hadley Wood when she finally speaks in a tightly wound tone.

'Hester,' she says, 'I sincerely hope you aren't going to drive at 30 miles per hour the whole way. We won't get to Dorset until tomorrow afternoon at this rate.'

It's only then that I realize I'm gripping the steering wheel so hard my knuckles bleach white. The nervous driving is something Terry used to like to tease me about and it was very unfair, not to mention unfunny. He would say things like 'Oh look, a hearse is about to overtake us', or 'Here comes a toddler on a tricycle' when we were on the motorway.

I didn't rise to the bait but what he didn't know was that I would picture his face, quite clearly, slamming against the dashboard. I could see his nose splintering like plywood and the plum-coloured black eyes. It all helped stop me from shouting at him and losing control of myself. Yes, that's a little extreme perhaps, but there was no need for unkind teasing.

I breathe slowly in through my nose and out through my mouth now before I reply.

'There are speed cameras around here, actually. I think the very last thing we want is to be noticed, don't you? Under the circumstances?'

She huffs a bit and then says, 'Yeah, but if you drive like this you'll attract just as much attention anyway.'

'I assure you,' I say, through gritted teeth, 'that I will drive at the acceptable speed on the motorway.'

We lapse into silence then.

It's extraordinary, how easy it is to forget about the cargo we are carrying back there. I could almost convince myself we are going on a girls-only camping trip somewhere, if it weren't for the fact that it was night-time. Maybe when all this is over we really can do something of that nature?

Tilly could come along too. We could spend the evening talking and toasting marshmallows over a campfire. I've always wanted to do that. It would be such a lot of fun.

'*Hester.*'

'Yes?' It's hard to keep the smile out of my voice; the fantasy was so delicious.

'You're making a weird noise!'

Am I? I'm horrified by this. Terry picked up on that too. I think I make a sort of humming sound sometimes when I'm lost in my thoughts. I must try very hard not to do that. 'I do apologize,' I say stiffly.

There's a very loaded pause before she speaks again.

'Really, if you're feeling very tired and not up to this, I am completely okay to drive.'

I'm slapping my hand onto the steering wheel before I even know I'm going to do it. It stings and the sound rings out, disproportionately loud. I think we are both a little shocked by the sudden violence of this.

'Please stop undermining me, Melissa. I am fine. Everything is *fine*.' I try to catch my breath, which has become shallow, as though I have been running. 'Why don't you try and have a little sleep?' I say a little more gently.

She lets out a strange sound that is somewhere between a gasp and a laugh then but doesn't say anything else. To calm myself, I glance down at Bertie, who is now fast asleep by Melissa's feet. I'm glad because the poor dog must have been wondering what on earth is going on.

He's not the only one.

Before too long I'm indicating for the westbound M25. I push myself back in the seat and grip the steering wheel as we come down the slip road and it seems to help my nerves a little.

It's quite busy, despite the late hour, but this is a good thing because before long we have run out of overhead lighting. I am nervous about driving in the dark as it is, particularly at these speeds. But I find that I can stay close to other cars and follow their lights.

We drive in silence for some time then and, to my surprise, I begin to relax and a rather comforting feeling settles over me. Here we are, hurtling through the darkness in this metal container, linked by what we have been through together in a way that, hopefully, cannot now be undone. It's just me and Melissa against the world.

Nothing can change what happened earlier. There are only two people, well, three, I suppose, who were party to the events in Melissa's kitchen. Saskia, Tilly, and Mark may as well all be on another planet now. I am the one helping Melissa.

Only *me*.

It's hard to stop the smile in my heart from spreading to my face.

Every now and then I glance to my left to check Melissa is all right. It's hard to tell though, because she just looks straight ahead, her face as impassive as a sphinx. Her hands are tightly wound together and resting between her knees. She doesn't even seem to mind the fact that Bertie is lying on her feet in their Ugg boots. I privately call them Uggly boots and can't understand why so many women wear them. Still, perhaps Bertie feels they are comforting, as Melissa presumably does. And heaven knows we all need a little comfort today.

To be perfectly honest, as unpleasant as this all is, I'm enjoying having something *to do* at last. Life used to be so busy, but the days do drag now.

I had planned a life that would follow certain lines, you see. Bringing up children would fill my days. I would be just like those women you see in the advertisements. You know, the ones who look so happy and busy, settling down to a dinner table with the family, while everyone competes good-naturedly to share details of their days. I'd be dishing out mashed potato to one child while gently chiding another to eat their broccoli. It's all so clear in my mind that I could almost write the script.

And then, when it became clear this life was not the one meant for me, I threw myself into my work.

I try not to dwell on it but, on some days, I still miss my job so much it gives me actual pains.

It wasn't as though I needed the money, even with Terry's poor career choices. Mum and Dad had left me the house and a tidy nest egg. Terry was always on at me to spend it and 'splash out' on this and that, but what point was there in the two of us going away on cruises or staying in hotels? I couldn't think of anything worse. It wasn't about the income. It was all I ever wanted, to have a family of my own. Working in the office at Butterflies Nursery was a poor substitute but the next best thing, I suppose.

They'd had fifteen years of my life at that nursery. Fifteen years of caring for those children and being the most organized Office Manager they could have wished for. I ran that office like the CEO of a successful business.

But then the company was bought by a successful chain and the regime changed entirely. The officious, ferret-faced Manager, a young woman called Irena, told me that there was no longer any need for an Office Manager under the 'new model'.

I put up a fight, of course I did.

But as Irena continued to speak her Judas words, it transpired that there had been *complaints* about me. Parents who didn't approve of their toddler coming home from school with a fuzzy lolly stick in their pocket, or were disgruntled when I told them their child could do with a scarf on a cold day.

And yes, I did reprimand the odd child and make them sit on a naughty chair if they were rude or unkind at playtime. You don't need a degree in Education to know how to do that. No one had ever complained under the old regime, as far as I was aware. The previous owners had never minded and, apart from the occasional snippy comment from some of the younger guard of nursery nurses, I had never felt that I was anything other than an integral part of that place.

I couldn't count the number of scraped knees I'd swabbed and bandaged, the number of toddler squabbles that were solved simply by lending a sympathetic, fair ear. And yes, there were cuddles and sometimes the odd illicit lollypop, too; but what kind of world are we living in where comforting an unhappy child is seen as aberrant behaviour? For some of those children, it was the only affection they ever got. But it turned out I had no choice in the matter. I was being asked to retire. So, come the end of the year, I was forced out to pasture.

I tried to fill my time with work in the local charity shop after that, but it wasn't for me. The other women there weren't my sort of people.

But I must try not to think about this now. I have to be here for Melissa. And for Tilly. I have a job to do and I must not let them down. I am the strong one in this whole equation.

A gentle rain begins to dot the windscreen. I switch on the wipers, which drag and sweep across the glass with a thumping beat that could become hypnotic. I sit up straighter in the seat, the cushion under my bottom sliding uncomfortably.

My eyes are starting to feel grainy and, despite all my protestations, I'm wondering if I am going to be able to drive the whole way after all. The dashboard clock tells me it is close to eleven o'clock. It is hours until dawn breaks and I am still very concerned about finding this place in the dark. We should stop at a service station and kill some time. I don't think Melissa is thinking straight. It's up to me to be the mature, sensible one.

I'm just gathering the courage to broach this suggestion to Melissa when the van starts to judder and shake and smoke begins to pour from the bonnet.

MELISSA

Until the moment they joined the motorway (travelling, Melissa noted, at 55 miles per hour), she told herself there was still time to stop this. None of it was set in stone yet and she could change her mind at any moment. They could still go back. Confess.

She pictured them reversing their earlier work, like a film played backwards at speed. But how would they explain the delay? The fact that the pestle had been cleaned and the floor bleached?

Now they are on the M25, she is suffused with an almost pleasurable feeling of helplessness. After all, they can't easily turn round here. For now, at least, she must go with the flow.

Bundling her sweatshirt against the window, she lays her head against it and closes her eyes. There's no possibility that she will sleep – possibly ever again. But her eyes ache and she needs to rest them for a short while.

Soon, the swish and thump of the wipers, the gentle snoring from the dog, and the throb of the engine begin to lull her into an almost hypnotic state. The physical effects of shock combined with last night's lack of sleep start to drag at her and before long, as she is pitching into a light doze, her mind roams like a fisheye lens around the house at Fernley Close, where her world had collided with Jamie's for the first time.

A small cluttered house on a respectable estate, the hallway was an obstacle course of bags of footballs and plastic cones; Greg was manager of a junior football team. Kathie always grumbled about tripping over it all but there was never any real heat in her words.

They didn't drink or smoke and they never argued.

Melissa would watch their casual affection and stolen kisses in the kitchen with a mixture of fascination and revulsion. Sometimes she would amuse herself by imagining David Attenborough narrating them. '*And now the male of the species smacks the huge arse of the female, who laughs and tells him he is a "one".*'

They were good, kind people. But Melissa, or Melanie as she was then, was too tightly wound, her heart too sealed away, to let them come near.

Jamie had a long-term foster arrangement at Kathie and Greg's and he'd believed they would one day adopt him. He confessed that to her one night when they'd crammed into Greg's shed with a bottle of sweet, sticky sherry Mel had nicked from the back of the drinks cabinet. She'd laughed at him then. Told him he was a deluded fuckwit if he thought Kathie and Greg really *wanted* him.

Jamie did the puppy dog eyes thing but he no longer threw tantrums.

He understood that Mel wouldn't spend time with him if he did and was learning to control himself. Really, she was helping him more than anyone in social services ever had.

She had no idea, really, whether they wanted to adopt Jamie. They went overboard in the whole 'treating you both the same' thing. They treated her no differently, not in any real sense.

But she felt as though they were able to see the treacly rotten-ness that lay deep inside her, to see whatever it was that made her difficult to love. You heard about mothers giving their lives for their kids all the time. And yet her own mother wasn't even able to get out of bed for her. What other conclusion could she draw than that she wasn't worth the effort?

Kathie and Greg tried to compensate by showing that extra bit of tolerance with Melanie. With Jamie, they acted more like real parents, becoming exasperated, irritated, and finding him comical sometimes. With Melanie it all felt as though it was coming from the 'Book of Dealing with Difficult Teens'.

This was Jamie's first and only stint in foster care. His parents had died within a few months of each other; wiped out in a house fire. He had no other family. At least he'd had one before, she thought. He seemed to inspire a soppiness in people. Poor little Jamie. Diddums.

Who cared about her, Melanie Ronson? Exactly no one. And so she'd begun to look for small ways to undermine Jamie in Kathie and Greg's eyes. She was quite impressed with her own creativity, especially when she took one of his trainers and used it to track dog shit onto the hallway carpet. And because he was naturally forgetful, it was easy to make sure he lost his bus pass twice in one fortnight, or couldn't find a chemistry textbook the night before a test. All too easy.

So after a while, she upped her game by luring Jamie with the odd grope here and there to carry out various dares. One of them had been to tell Greg to fuck off when he told Jamie to go up to bed.

When he'd done it, there had been a shocked silence in the room for a few moments in which Jamie's face had seemed to crumple with shame. He'd been sharply reprimanded by Kathie and, later, she found him in his room, face down on the duvet, tearful and red-cheeked. Jamie was upset, okay, but it all worked out well for him. She'd turned him over, unzipped his flies and taken him in her mouth for the first time. It hadn't been any fun and she'd only done it for a few moments before finishing him off with her hand.

Before long, he'd do anything for her.

None of it brought her any pleasure and she didn't really know why she was doing it. Maybe it was just envy because Kathie and Greg favoured him. Or maybe it was just the fact that, despite everything that had happened to him, he seemed to have a kernel of hope inside him, when she knew there was none really.

And then they had been caught, one rainy afternoon when the theme tune from *Bullseye* played on the telly downstairs, and the smell of Kathie's roast beef and overcooked carrots permeated the air. Naked in Jamie's bed where they had accidentally fallen asleep, entwined together.

Melissa's thoughts are beginning to dissolve into sleepy scraps when she feels the van slowing down. At first, she thinks they must have reached their destination, and, alert now, she sits up, wiping a little drool from the side of her mouth.

But for some reason they appear to be on the hard shoulder of the motorway. Melissa looks to Hester, whose shoulders are high and rigidly set, her hands gripping the steering wheel. She stares straight ahead, her mouth open a little, giving her an odd, idiotic look.

'What's going on?' says Melissa groggily.

As she gropes for the bottle of water by her side, something hot and wet brushes against her hand. She gives a little shriek. That dog is staring up at her expectantly with its horrible leaky eyes. She pushes it away surreptitiously.

'What's happened, Hester?' She is suddenly wide awake.

There's a pause. Hester clears her throat. 'We seem to have broken down,' she says in a tight little voice.

Melissa almost levitates off her seat. 'What the *fuck*?' she yelps. 'Broken *down*?' She looks around wildly. 'We can't have broken down! What are we going to do?'

Hester is taking deep, noisy breaths, in and out. She turns to

Melissa. 'We're going to have to call the AA,' she says in a stran-gled voice.

'What? *What*?' Melissa drags her hands across her scalp and lets out a hysterical, high-pitched laugh. 'Call the AA? Call the *AA*? Has it escaped your knowledge that we have a *fucking dead man in the back of this van*?'

Hester closes her eyes for a second in the patronizing manner of a parent who is being pushed to the limit. When she speaks, her voice is low and measured.

'Of course I hadn't forgotten. But unless you have taken an advanced mechanics course – and I know that *I* haven't – then we have no choice about this. And there is no reason for the AA to look in the back of the van, is there? Even with my limited car knowledge I am aware that the engine is at the front of the —'

But the end of her sentence is cut off because Melissa has wrenched open the car door and is clambering out. Bertie gets up excitedly, tail wagging, and Hester cries out and only just manages to grab his collar in time to stop him from exiting with her.

Melissa marches to the front of the van and kicks viciously at the bonnet. Her Ugg boot offers little protection; pain shoots through her foot. She screams 'Fuck!' at the top of her voice and then starts to slap ferociously at the bonnet. A car goes past, impossibly close and fast, and she forces herself to try and stop this loss of control. Anyone could go by and see them. The police even.

Hester, now out of the van, runs around to where Melissa stands and fans at her face, gasping. 'Oh my goodness!' she says, 'you really have no idea how fast and how *close* it all is when you are driving, do you?'

Melissa starts to shiver. It has stopped raining but the air is chill. She yanks her hood up and over her head. 'What should we do?' she murmurs. The fight has drained from her as quickly as it arrived. She needs Hester to make a decision. She is incapable.

'Are you in the AA or the RAC?' says Hester in her practical, clipped voice.

Melissa wants to laugh again. And again, it isn't funny at all. 'I'm in the AA. But what if—?' That hysterical whine is back now inside her head; the feeling that she is a hair's breadth away from screaming.

Hester cuts her off. 'There is no reason for the mechanic to look inside the van. None at all. It will be fine. You'll see. Get your membership card for me.'

Obediently, Melissa goes to the car and finds her purse.

The AA assure Hester that two women stranded on a motorway in the middle of the night qualify as the very highest customer priority and a mechanic will be with them in no more than forty minutes. This feels like a very mixed sort of blessing.

Despite Hester's plaintive pleas that they must sit 'on the bank, away from the vehicle', Melissa clambers back into the van and wraps an old tartan blanket she finds between the seats around her shoulders. It smells of the dog but she doesn't much care.

Neither does she care about any supposed danger in staying in the van. There is nothing that could induce her to sit out there, where the roaring hornet drone of passing traffic feels like the cruellest of jokes that could be played right now.

Maybe it is justice, she thinks, pulling the blanket even tighter around her shoulders. The circle was closing.

The past is hurtling towards her like the cars that now rip past them.

***

After she and Jamie had been separated, Melissa spent the remaining year of her care in a children's home about twenty miles from the house in Fernley Close. As soon as she was eighteen, she moved to London and, working as a waitress in a greasy spoon in Archway, she had moved into a squat in Arnos Grove.

This, she'd thought, was the real start of her life. Everything that came before had been practice for living.

When she thought of that house, it was a cocktail of smells that she remembered most: fishy rot from the damp patch on the ceiling. Burnt-sugar woodiness of the ever-present weed. Stale armpits, feet, and breath from the bodies that covered every scrap of floor space after a party. And always, the carbon smell of burnt toast. They all ate so much toast then, slice after slice turning black in the broken toaster, late at night when the munchies made them limp and liquid from giggling, or on those grey mornings after, when no one wanted to speak too loudly and coming down felt like drowning.

Melissa squeezes her eyes shut and wipes fresh tears from her cheeks now.

'I'm sorry,' she whispers to no one. 'I'm so sorry.'

For a few moments she is broken. Lost in the guilt again. She pictures a car slamming into the van and thinks it would be a good thing. A few seconds of terror and pain and it would all be wiped out. The slate would be clean again.

But then she thinks about her daughter and panic thrums across her skin. *Oh God, Tilly. Baby.*

She pictures Tilly's eyes widening in shock as some spotty copper breaks the news that will change her life for ever; her hands, habitually covered by her sleeves like they're in mittens, snaking around her middle, and her whole body collapsing in on itself in misery.

And what about Mark? Whatever he has done, he doesn't deserve this.

Melissa rummages in her bag for a tissue and blows her nose. She looks at Hester sitting high on the bank, anxiously peering at the traffic and tries to force herself to be calm again.

She has to get through this with the only resources she has.

Decisively, Melissa reaches into her handbag for the emergency make-up she keeps there. Holding her phone awkwardly on her knees as lighting, she attempts to repair her face. Taking a few minutes to apply liner, more mascara, and a slick of lipstick, she snaps the overhead mirror back into place. Hester is now watching her from the bank.

What a strange woman she is, thinks Melissa. So buttoned-up and repressed, but totally and utterly calm about the scene she witnessed in Melissa's kitchen. It's almost as though she is slightly enjoying it all. Melissa feels a ripple of distaste, even as she tells herself she mustn't be unfair. Something is bothering her about the helpfulness though. It feels disproportionate. But she doesn't have the space in her head to allow these thoughts to expand and fester.

She remembers how Hester was before. Too keen, too ready to be involved with her business and to offer her opinions. She had a way of taking over, of ingratiating herself into every corner of Melissa's life that had been uncomfortable. And now what?

Now they were bound. Melissa has no one else.

Melissa tries to force her thoughts back on track, to the here and now. She wonders whether they should somehow get Jamie's body onto the road.

Images of his body being pulped by passing cars bombard her. She can almost hear the sickening thumps of metal hitting flesh and she swallows bile. It could cause an accident. Yet more deaths.

No. There's no other way. For now, they just have to push forward with the plan.

This reminds her of the phone and she quickly looks for it in her handbag, glancing up to check there are no slowing lights of the AA. Clambering out of the van again, she climbs up the bank and looks at the thick bushes growing there.

Jamie's iPhone is an old model whose curvy shape feels strange and bulky in her hand. She had believed it to be turned off but she accidentally touches the home button and the screen saver blooms into life.

A baby beams out at her, all blonde hair and cheeks flushed rosy from teething. The merry blue eyes have the distinctive folded lids of Down's syndrome.

Melissa scrabbles about in her brain for any mention of a child in their conversation but can find none. Then a casually tossed remark floats into her mind.

'It's time to grow up.' She hadn't asked him what he meant at the time.

Would knowing he was a father have made any difference to what she'd done? Would it have been different, if her fingers had found only the scrubbed kitchen surface behind her? Or if she had been a few inches shorter, or taller?

It was the work of a couple of seconds. And it couldn't be undone now. It was too late.

There's a sour, dirty taste in Melissa's mouth and a terrible heaviness in her heart. There will never be a time when she feels any better. She believes this absolutely.

Glancing down at the phone again, a realization slams into her and she scrabbles to turn it off. Can't they track people by where they've used mobiles? *Shit*. The smiling cherub's face disappears.

Melissa brings back her arm and throws the phone into the bushes with all her strength. She doesn't hear it land.

HESTER

I have managed to think up a reason for why we're driving in the middle of the night. I'll say that we are sisters (I find this notion rather pleasing) and that we are on a mercy mission to visit our dying mother. Melissa has had to borrow her husband's van because he's away at the moment with the car. Or something like that.

We had to leave so late because Mother might not make it to morning …

Yes, this seems plausible. I told Melissa there is no way the mechanic would need to go into the back of the van, but I can't say that I really know for sure. There could be any number of technical reasons why he might suggest it. All I can do is hope and pray.

Bertie has fallen asleep on my lap and I stroke his soft ears and feel thankful for his trust and warmth.

Cars pass with aggressive speed, their sound like giant sheets of paper being angrily ripped apart. The vibrations rumble through the bank and into my sore hips. I'm sitting on my spare cagoule but the chill from the ground still seeps through and into my bones. It doesn't feel like June. It could be October right now.

I glance at the van. I can see Melissa's face in the glow of the mirror light and it looks as though she is applying make-up. We're not likely to be appearing in *Vogue* as far as I am aware but I suppose I mustn't judge. Younger women care about these things inordinately these days.

But I do wish she would join me here on the bank, as one is supposed to in these circumstances. Anything could happen.

I sigh, knowing that is a hopeless wish. If there is one thing I have learned in the last few, strange hours, it's that this girl won't do anything she doesn't want to. I haven't had time to run my story past her either. I can only hope she will employ that acting ability she demonstrated earlier.

The strobing light of the breakdown truck would be a comforting sight on any other occasion. Tonight though, it makes my stomach jolt with nerves, as it gradually gets larger and closer. It's a little too similar to another sort of light in these present circumstances. The driver spends a minute reading something before making his leisurely way out of the truck. He's a portly man, bald, in his forties, and looks tired and fed up.

'Evening ladies,' he says and then I notice the little spark of interest when he sees Melissa close up. I wonder if she is even aware of this any more?

'Bit past your bedtimes, is it?'

Melissa gives a little giggle, and I think, *Oh yes, she's aware, all right.*

I open my mouth to speak, ready with our story, but realize quickly that it is just one of those things people say. He doesn't really care why we are driving in the middle of the night and moves straight onto a question about what has happened before we can answer.

It never ceases to amaze me, how little people are interested in each other anymore. It never occurred to me until tonight that this could ever be a *good* thing.

I quickly tell him what happened with the smoke and so on,

and he nods knowingly before asking me to unlatch the bonnet. Naturally, I have no idea how to do this and my expression must betray this because, wordlessly, he's already opening the driver's door and fumbling below the steering wheel. The bonnet makes a clunking sound and he goes round to lift it up. He peers inside for a while. I can hardly breathe. I glance at Melissa, whose eyes look large and luminous in the light. She still has the tartan blanket around her although she has let it hang open a little at the front, I notice.

The AA man rummages about inside the bonnet for a while.

I am suddenly so acutely aware of the dead body crumpled just a few feet from him that I have a very inappropriate urge to start laughing. How would I explain that? It's such a terrible but almost comical thought that I can't seem to control my face and I feel the corners of my mouth hitch up of their own accord. I think I must have made a small sound too because Melissa is staring at me now, an expression of such terror and fury on her pretty face that I almost take a step backwards.

My heartbeat pounds in my ears. I have to appear like a woman who just wants to get on her way. *Just be normal, Hester,* I tell myself. Just be normal. But I can't entirely remember how.

A few minutes later the AA man holds aloft a rectangular sort of grid that is covered in dust and dirt.

'There you go,' he says. 'Your air filter is all chocked up.'

'Oh dear, is that a big problem?' says Melissa. The slight tremor in her voice betrays her nerves, which she has done a good job of hiding until now.

The AA man emerges from the bonnet and bends backwards, rotating his shoulders and groaning a little.

'Bloody back,' he says, then, 'Nah, just need to give it a clean and you'll be on your way again. Won't take five minutes.'

Oh thank God. My knees almost give way as I meet Melissa's eyes. Neither of us can help exchanging a small smile. The relief is so intense it feels like a drug flooding through my system. Not that I've ever taken drugs, but I imagine it must be a similar sensation.

True to his word, he doesn't take long and soon he's putting the filter back where it belongs. Melissa's nervous energy is almost crackling around her now like static, and I sense she is desperate to get this over with and be on our way. I'm expecting the AA man to get some paperwork from his vehicle for her to sign, but he doesn't do that.

Instead, he walks past us to the back of the van, without glancing at either of us.

I stare at Melissa, my mouth circling in horror. Her face is a mask of shock as she follows him. I hurry after her.

'What's up?' she says in a strange squeaky voice.

The AA man gestures at the lower end of the back of the van and then taps it with the toe of his boot. The proximity of his large frame – so near the body on the other side of those doors – makes my throat close over.

'See that?' he says in a relaxed tone. 'One of your taillights is gone. Noticed it was smashed as I pulled over.'

Looking down I can see that, sure enough, there is broken glass or plastic or whatever it is on one of the lights. I realize with a plummeting sensation that this probably happened when I was reversing out of Melissa's driveway. She shoots me a look that makes my skin shrivel, then clears her throat.

'Really, it's okay,' she says then, and I wonder if it's only me who can hear the tightness in her voice. 'We'll get that sorted when we get, um, home. You must have another job you should be getting to!'

The false brightness in her voice makes me think of the sound made when you run a finger around a wine glass. It's too high, too sharp, not *normal*.

'Nope, this is my last job,' says the AA man, rolling his fist over a small belch. 'Pop open the back of the van for me and I'll sort it for you now.'

Melissa doesn't move, and neither do I.

The man seems to turn slowly, taking us both in.

Everything seems to go very quiet. I am no longer aware of the passing vehicles.

I have the strangest notion that we will be stuck in this odd tableau forever: Melissa, the AA man, and me. Time is unable to move forward.

My mind fills with vivid images. I see the van being opened and the AA man peering in. Asking what's in the back. Maybe reaching out in our silence and unrolling some of the plastic to see the cool, stiff flesh beneath. I picture the look of slight confusion and then horror on his face as he reaches into his pocket for his mobile phone. I see him stumbling back a little as he rings 999.

I think I'm actually going to vomit.

And then another picture comes to me. This time I see myself finding a rock from the side of the road. I see it smashing against his bald, shiny head and splitting it like an egg. Or maybe I could find some sort of heavy spanner from his own breakdown truck. I quickly try to calculate the chances of this working. He's quite a big man. It would also be enormously problematic if we found ourselves with two bodies to dispose of.

What's more, all his movements tonight will have been logged …

Melissa is speaking and I'm too flustered and caught up in my own panic to make sense of what she is saying.

'No really, my husband has planned to sort that himself … we'd better leave it, but honestly, *thanks a million*. You're a total gem.'

The AA man looks understandably confused. 'Well, it won't take a moment, love. And I really shouldn't send you on your way with a defective light. Did you know the police can pull you over for that?'

I gaze at Melissa. I am shaking, hard, from my legs up to my chattering teeth.

The notion of finding some kind of heavy implement in his truck is starting to feel like our only option.

Melissa casts her eyes down and seems to hunch her shoulders, visibly shrinking.

'The thing is,' she says in a small voice, 'I wasn't really supposed to borrow the van at all. My old man is away on a golf weekend and my, er, cousin and I have been to a friend's party. I was hoping he'd never know about this breakdown. I deal with AA stuff so there's no reason for him to know. But if you mend the light ...'

Despite how shaken I am, I notice that her normally well-spoken voice is morphing into an Estuary twang.

She looks up, slyly. But maybe he can't see that. Men are so stupid sometimes. No woman would ever believe that story about a party when neither of us is remotely dressed for one.

But she hasn't finished. 'He has a bit of a temper, you see.' This last bit is almost a whisper and she gazes at the AA man with wide eyes.

He seems to grow taller as she shrinks. This appeal to his testosterone has quite done the trick.

'Okay love,' he says in a gruff voice. 'I get it. I'll leave it for now but make sure he does get it fixed, won't you?'

'I will,' she says, rewarding him with a sweet, melancholy smile.

'And ... love?'

'Yes?'

'Take care of yourself, won't you?'

A few minutes later she waves him away. I haven't been able to find my voice yet and wasn't even able to thank him before he left, which is very unlike me. I put my hand to my chest, feeling my heart beat like a trapped bird against a window. Melissa turns shining eyes to me.

'Christ! That was a bit close, wasn't it?'

I get the sense that she is close to tears. Her chin trembles a little and she gives a slightly hysterical laugh.

131

'It certainly was,' I say quietly. Then, 'Come on, we'd better go.' The thought of driving again is monstrous right now but I lower my eyes and trudge back to the driver's side.

'Hester?' says Melissa, as we settle back into our seats. 'Do you mind if we stop for a bit at the next services? I need to pee and get some coffee. That whole thing almost finished me off. And we've got hours still, haven't we?'

I look over at her as the occasional car streaks past outside and stripes our interior with yellow light. She is smiling at me, hopefully, and she looks young and tired. There is a softness in her eyes that feels like something new between us.

I feel a surge of affection and do believe that this is the closest we have ever been. Five minutes ago, I felt as though I were experiencing one of the worst moments of my life, but this one I would like to bathe in for a little longer.

'Of course we can, dear girl,' I say. 'Of course we can.'

Before long we see the sign for Fleet Services and I pull into the car park, which isn't as empty as you might imagine at 2.30 a.m. in the morning.

I have to leave Bertie in the van once he has relieved himself but, he is such a good little dog, I know I can trust him not to make a lot of noise. He looks at me trustingly as I whisper to him that Mummy will be back in a little while.

These are such strange places, I think, as we go through the main doors. People come and go, all night long. There are lots of places to eat and drink now, not like my day when we would sit at the side of the road on a picnic blanket with our boiled eggs and thermos tea. Now it's all cappuccinos and paninis, or burgers and Coke, depending on where you are on the social spectrum.

I get myself a cup of insipid tea from the least offensive-looking of the options and sit in the main seating area, where Melissa will be able to find me once she has gone to the toilet. I try to concentrate on the timing of our night ahead.

If we stay here for an hour or so, it should mean that we get to our destination as daylight arrives.

I'm terribly tired now and the tea isn't helping all that much. What a night!

I keep trying to picture the practicalities of moving the body and getting it down the well, but it sounds like an almost impossible task.

It's a terrible thing to say, and, of course, I could never have countenanced such a barbaric act, but it does rather make one understand why bodies are sometimes … well, separated into more manageable pieces to make disposal easier. I'm not sure whether we would have had the necessary tools, however. Dexter has all sorts of complicated saws and things, not to mention all that plastic sheeting he uses. It's not exactly what you'd find in the average kitchen.

We're just going to have to work with what we've got but I am concerned about the rigor mortis issue. What if the thing is now as stiff as an ironing board? However will we get it in the well?

I'm half wishing I hadn't suggested this plan, although I have no idea what the alternative would be. We couldn't exactly put the body out with the bins.

Cradling my cooling cup of tea, I realize now Melissa has been in the Ladies for rather a long time. I wonder whether I should check on her.

The silly thought occurs to me that she has somehow left me here.

Alone.

Maybe she walked back outside and is hitch-hiking home, hip cocked cheekily and her thumb out. This thought makes me squeeze my hands into fists so tightly that my nails dig into my palms in quite a painful way. It would be a terrible thing to do to me. Evil, almost. Surely she couldn't do that?

I really am starting to fret about this when I see her coming towards me across the concourse, holding a large Starbucks' cup, even though this is a separate café and I believe you're only supposed to consume items bought here. But I suppose it's a very small misdemeanour, given our current circumstances.

She slides into the seat in front of me. Her eyes are puffy and I can see that she has been crying. This thought really rips at my heart and gives me new resolve.

I have to help this poor, lost girl. I really don't think that, despite the riches she has (both literally and metaphorically), she is a very happy person. Mark is nice enough, I suppose but, like Saskia, I always felt that he resented my place in Melissa's life. Sometimes I even believed he was secretly mocking me, when we had one of our rare conversations.

One thing I know for sure. There is no way we will be returning to how things used to be. Not now we have been through this together. Saskia and Mark and anyone else with an opinion will just have to get used to my new place in her life. We are a team now.

Melissa takes a sip of her drink and closes her eyes. I would like to let her rest awhile, but we have matters that must be discussed and they can't wait.

'So, I've been thinking about the rigor mortis issue,' I say.

Her eyes snap open and her cheeks flood with blotchy colour. 'Keep your voice down!' she hisses, looking around the café area. 'Why don't you just take over the Tannoy and tell the entire place for Christ's sake?'

This stings.

There aren't that many people in here. There are a few men who look like truck drivers dotted about at this hour but none of them has paid us any attention. A young coloured teenager runs a huge mop around in a desultory fashion at the far end of the café area. I think she is really making an unnecessary fuss, but I do nonetheless drop my voice when I speak again.

'I'm sorry! But I know from watching dramas that rigor mortis isn't a permanent state, so I'm hoping we will be beyond that bit when the time comes. But even so, it's going to be difficult to manoeuvre it, isn't it?'

She leans forward, placing her hand on the table in front of her. Her face is so thunderous it almost frightens me.

'*Him*, Hester,' she hisses. 'Him. That's a person in the back of that van. Not an "it".' Her words seem to skid off into tearfulness then. She jabs angry looks around the café. 'I think it's about time you remembered that.'

Well! I can feel the tears rising up and I can't stop them. After everything I've done for that girl and am still prepared to do, she speaks to me like that. The ingratitude …

My tea is only half-drunk and I am so exhausted now that my eyes seem to be filled with sand but I can't stay here a moment longer.

I push back my chair and lift my chin, mustering my dignity.

'I will be in the van, resting. You should stay here for a while. I think you need time alone.' I pause. 'And quite frankly, so do I!'

With that, I march away from the table and across the concourse, back to my Bertie.

MELISSA

Melissa gulps the coffee and winces as she burns her tongue. She watches Hester bustle out of sight and wonders if she should follow her and apologize. She hadn't meant to snap. It was the matter-of-fact nature of the words that had offended her, not their volume.

Ice packs, talk of rigor mortis … it makes it all so *real*. The way Hester refers to Jamie's body as 'it'.

But isn't that all that's left? Jamie has gone. It's too late to help him now.

These thoughts seem to set off a silent scream inside her and she reaches for the coffee, slopping it a little through the drinking hole. She sucks the brown foam from her hand and lifts her eyes. A few sleepy-looking men – lorry drivers she presumes – are dotted about, and a member of staff dragging a mop in desultory circles across the floor.

And then, looking towards the entrance again, she sees something that makes her entire body thrill with horror.

Two police officers – a man and a woman – are walking towards her.

He is bald and portly. Older. She is delicate-boned and dark-skinned.

The man is scanning the café area and, after a brief exchange of words, the woman peels off from his side and moves out of sight.

Melissa's heart pounds so hard she can hear its throbbing beat in her head. She can't breathe. Sweat slimes her back.

Wildly she looks around to see if there is any prospect of running away but there is only one entrance. The policeman is almost with her now. She is a second away from standing up and holding out her wrists for the handcuffs when he gives her a small nod and walks past. Melissa begins to tremble, hard, all over.

She can't stop herself from glancing behind her. He has taken a seat further back and is picking up a newspaper that has been left on the table.

He clears his throat loudly and rubs his nose, his head down. Oblivious to her.

After a few minutes, in which Melissa barely breathes, the policewoman comes over with a tray laden with red and yellow McDonald's' packages. Melissa drops her eyes to her coffee until the policewoman passes her.

She should wait a few moments and then leave.

She knows that's what she should do.

But as the seconds tick by, a powerfully seductive feeling creeps over her.

Maybe this is a sign?

What are the chances of a couple of coppers being right *here*, right *now*?

This is her opportunity to make it all right. She never really meant for it to get this far. Kill someone? Dispose of the body? It was all ridiculous. It was all a terrible, terrible misunderstanding and, if she can only explain, things will start to get better again.

If she got up right now, walked over to them, and said, 'I want to report a murder', what would they do? Would there be a moment of incredulity, maybe even laughter, at the improbability of these words being true? Maybe their training and profession-alism would kick in straight away. Maybe Melissa would be over the table, hands and feet spread, while they roughly patted her down before she had time to blink.

For a moment she wants this. She downs the last of the coffee in a decisive swig. It would be so easy.

I'm sorry. I'm so very sorry. Take me away now.

The cocoon of shock that has encased her until this moment is finally cracking, and the plan she and Hester had hatched in her kitchen seems ridiculous. Almost laughable.

Melissa is on her feet before the next thought seeps into her brain.

What about Hester?

She has to give the other woman the opportunity to get away first. It's only right.

An airy joy fills her up inside as she snatches her handbag from the table and hurries out of the service station towards the car park.

At first, she can't remember where the van is parked. She sees the police car and she clearly pictures sitting in the back of it all the way back to London. She hesitates, suddenly incapable of deciding what to do next, and she sees the van, at last, parked at a slightly skewed angle. As she gets closer Melissa can't see any sign of Hester, then she appears suddenly from the back of the van, clutching her dog to her stout bosom.

She gives a little start when she sees Melissa. Her lips tighten and thin in disapproval.

'I was just attending to Bertie,' she says in a clipped voice. 'Have you had enough of a rest? We should probably get on our way soon.'

Melissa reaches out and gently places a hand on Hester's arm. Hester gazes down at it before looking up, blinking owlishly.

'I'm so sorry if I offended you,' says Melissa. 'I truly am grateful for everything you've done for me, Hester. But look ...', she hesitates, stuck for a moment, and then something is uncorked in her. 'We can't really do this. It's insane! Can't you see that? I wanted to tell you just to leave, to go home. I'm going to hand myself in.' She speaks too fast but can't stop the words from flooding out.

Hester's face is a pale oval in the floodlit car park. Her eyes seem to be all pupil now and Melissa can't see any expression in them at all.

'Melissa,' she says, at last, very quietly. It is as though she forgets to continue for a moment. Then she says, 'You're still in shock and you're not thinking clearly. You have to get a grip on yourself. This is quite ridiculous. Have you forgotten that you are a *mother*?'

Melissa flinches at the hissed word and blinks fast, twice. She can feel her euphoria begin to seep away like a puncture into the still night air.

Hester speaks again.

'You have a life, Melissa. A good life. You can go back to it but we have to deal with this unfortunate situation first.' She pauses and then gives a small, high-pitched laugh that is entirely without mirth. 'And my number plate will have been registered the second we drove into this service station. Do you seriously think I would be able to just go home and stay out of this?' Her voice becomes feather-soft again. 'Darling girl, none of us meant for this to happen. But we simply have to follow through with it now we've started.'

Melissa's chin wobbles and her eyes gloss over with tears. She shakes her head vehemently and takes a wobbly, loud in-breath. Hester gives a small, stoical laugh.

'It's quite all right, darling Melissa,' she says gently. 'You've been through a terrible ordeal. But don't worry about anything because you can count on me.'

Melissa nods. She is cold and her knees knock together, her teeth chattering.

'Come on, let's get going,' Hester says gently.

With that she climbs into the driver's seat again, hauling the dog onto the passenger side. Melissa slides into her own seat. Four moist adoring eyes greet her inside the van.

Hester starts the engine and pulls out of the parking space and towards the exit signs. There are no other cars around. She carefully checks her wing mirror and indicates anyway.

HESTER

Before too long we are filtering onto the A303, the main route down to the West Country. I know this journey quite well from childhood holidays in Cornwall and when Terry and I used to take the caravan this way.

I must say, I am relieved to be off the motorway.

But while the good hot tea and the rest have settled me inside, it's a mixed blessing. The jangling of nerves was keeping me alert and now I feel more sluggish.

I glance across at Melissa and see the shine of her open eyes. I cannot believe she was seriously considering handing herself in. What a silly girl she is sometimes. Her hands are twisted together in her lap, pale in the reflected dashboard lights. She looks so hunched and lost in thought, so, well ... *sad*, I don't like to disturb her. I think she has always been sad. I don't know why but I sense she is a troubled girl underneath her glamorous exterior.

My eyes are becoming gritty and I think a little conversation will help me to concentrate. I clear my throat.

'So,' I say. My voice seems especially loud in the stillness of the car. 'How is Mark?' It was the first thing that came into my mind. I don't really care about Mark. Melissa turns to stare at me. I can feel the graze of her eyes on the side of my face.

'Why do you ask?' she says tightly.

I can't help but glance away from the road to look at her. Maybe I have touched a nerve in some way. I suddenly feel overcome with how difficult life can be. Why are people so hard to read?

'I don't really know,' I say wearily. 'It seems like the sort of thing people ask in these circumstances.' I didn't quite intend to be so honest but, to my surprise, I hear the ripple of low laughter from my left.

'These circumstances?' says Melissa. 'Do you think people do this a lot then? What we're doing?' There is a slight edge to her voice. I don't want to say the wrong thing again.

'I suppose it must be unusual,' I say, and then, 'Although it's a lovely part of the country. Have you been to Dorset before?'

The silence that follows my words feels bloated and uncomfortable. When I hear a noise next to me, I think she has started to cry again. She has her hands cupped over her face and she is shaking uncontrollably. It's only then that I realize she is actually *laughing*.

I glance at her in astonishment as she splutters and squeals, quite helpless now. And it's the strangest thing; like a chain reaction, I can feel rumbles of laughter start to shake my ribcage and, before I know it, I am hooting too. Terry used to say I had a rotten sense of humour. Sometimes we would watch comedy programmes on television and he would be quite insensible with mirth. I never understood it. But now ticklish waves are breaking over me and I feel myself give into it. I don't know what's funny and I don't care either. It feels wonderful: healing and cleansing me.

'Oh Hester,' she manages to say at last. 'What are you like?' And she starts to laugh again.

I'm giggling so hard, I fear for my bladder control. I'm not sure I have ever really laughed like this before. I feel as though I am quite lost.

Gusts of our mirth break over us again and again, as the rain begins to dot the windscreen.

Wiping my eyes, I manage to speak at last.

'Goodness,' I say, 'I'm not sure where that came from! But it has certainly helped keep me awake. Not that I'm having problems,' I add hurriedly. I want to keep the new, lighter atmosphere going so quickly think of more conversation. 'So, did you ever come this way on holiday as a child?' I ask.

She is quiet again and I curse myself inwardly. Have I done it again? Said the wrong thing. She gives a long sigh.

'No,' she says. 'I didn't really have that sort of childhood, to be honest. Holidays weren't really on the agenda.' She doesn't elaborate but then speaks again. 'What about you? Do you know Dorset?'

'Not so much, but my parents used to take me to Carbis Bay every year,' I say and I can feel the smile warming my voice at the memory. 'We had such wonderful times there. Donkey rides on the beach, crabbing in the rock pools. We always stayed in the same guest house. It was run by a formidable woman called Mrs Hoskins and my dad joked she was older than Methuselah!'

Melissa laughs kindly. 'Carbis Bay's lovely,' she says. 'Mark and I stayed in a gorgeous boutique hotel down there for our wedding anniversary.'

'Well this place wasn't exactly in that league,' I murmur.

You can keep your 'boutique hotels'. I wouldn't have changed a thing about those holidays.

I can still picture it all so clearly. The memories are like Polaroids tinted in sunshine colours; the yellow Formica-topped tables in the dining room; the stack of tourist brochures in reception that seemed to hold the promise of so many wonderful attractions. Golden sunlight dancing on the water like fireflies. The salty thrill of the waves and the rough feeling of my red spotted costume as Mum and Dad waved from the beach.

I was blessed. For a short time at least, I was truly blessed. It's what I'd always hoped to share with a child of my own.

'Are your parents still around?' asks Melissa gently, bringing me back to the present.

Ribbons of pale road streak beneath the wheels of the van. My fingers are gripping the steering wheel again.

'No,' I say. 'They were both killed in a coach crash. It was the M62 one in 1974. Have you ever heard of it? It was quite a big news story at the time.'

'Oh, no. I'm sorry, I haven't,' says Melissa, sounding genuinely sad for me, which is touching. 'That's awful. How old were you?'

'Nineteen,' I say with a wistful sigh. 'I sometimes think it was the turning point of my whole life.'

'I'm sure it was,' says Melissa quietly. 'I'm so sorry.'

I don't want to get stuck in the past. Dark times should stay in the background, where they belong. I force brightness into my voice. 'We all have our crosses to bear, don't we?' I say.

'You got that right,' says Melissa, her face turned to the window again.

We drive in silence through several villages, which probably look quite picture postcard in the daytime. I picture Melissa, myself, and Tilly having a ploughman's lunch in the garden of a pub we pass. It is on a corner, so well lit. The building is a long, low cottage style, whitewashed and quaintly uneven, with baskets of flowers tumbling from under a thatched roof. It's still too dark to see the colours, but I imagine them to be intense beacons in the daylight. The thought brings an unaccountable joy to my heart.

Everything feels more colourful now. More real.

It's somehow as though I have been asleep for years and now I am properly awake. When did I fall asleep? Maybe since I gave up my hopes of being a mother? Or when I was finally free of Terry? 'You've an old head on young shoulders', my mother used to say. I think she meant that I was more mature than other people my age and not given to outbursts of temper and heat, even as a teenager. But now … I feel as though my nerve endings are zinging with some delicious excitement and the thrill of this odd challenge. Melissa and I are closer than we have ever been. A bubble contains us as we drive along these roads, a bubble only marred by the presence of what we are carrying. But one which brought us together in the first place. For a second I feel almost tender towards that young man.

The darkness is now just a bruised lilac tint at the horizon. This capsule of contentment won't last. It can't last. A terrible fear clutches at my heart at returning to normal life and just for a moment a dangerous but delicious thought flashes into my mind.

It would be so very easy.

All it would take would be one slight shift of the wheel and all our problems would be over. We could leave it all behind. Together …

Of course, I do no such thing.

The band of light at the edge of the sky is starting to thicken now. There is a pearliness to it that makes things seem especially vivid along the side of the road.

The road begins to rise to the crest of a large hill. Around us lie fields topped with skeins of mist like bridal veils and there is a sweet little castle on the horizon. Once again I imagine that we are going on holiday.

I've had to put the windscreen wipers on now though and their swish and thump is hypnotic. I'm trying to concentrate but it's cosy – almost. Womb-like. As though Melissa and I are curled together in its embrace, twins joined by adversity. The *thump-swish-thump-swish* sound is almost like a heartbeat …

'Hester?'

Alertness blasts through me like the blare of a horn. Did I almost drop off? Thankfully, Melissa doesn't seem to have noticed.

'Yes?' I say, when I find my voice.

'I think we're nearly there. We have to take the next turning.'

I stretch my fingers on the steering wheel and frown as I peer through the smeary windscreen.

We're almost there.

There is work to be done. But Melissa and I, together, well, we're a good team.

MELISSA

She knows now that the moment for confession has gone. She meant it, for one wild and crazy moment, she really did. But Hester is right. They have to see this through now. Thank goodness one of them can be so clear-headed.

As countryside passes unseen beyond the van's black windows, Melissa ponders all the ways they could be caught. They have left a trail of breadcrumbs, should the police come looking.

The van will have appeared on countless CCTV cameras by now and Automatic Number Plate Recognition technology would lead the police straight to Hester's door, as she said. Then there is the whole AA business. And every inch of Fleet Services will have artificial eyes trained on it 24 hours a day.

All this is without the digital trail she has left at home. Melissa remembers how she looked up Scarrow Hall on her MacBook and then printed off various maps from Google. Even if she deletes the browser history, this information could easily be dredged up by people in the know.

But the crucial part is that they'd have to be looking in the first place. Melissa worries at a fingernail and then, tasting the thick chemical resin there, pulls her hand away and lets it rest in her lap. Yesterday, a lifetime ago, she had that done. It's insane that this can be a mere twenty-four hours later.

Her mood seems to ricochet like a power ball between two hard certainties: one minute she is certain she will be in handcuffs within a week, and then she is filled with wild belief that they really might pull this off.

Melissa glances over at Hester, who is peering intently through the windscreen. She thinks about when they first met. How can they have ended up here on this road, with Jamie's dead body a few feet behind them?

Tilly was a grumpy baby and it seemed like there was one drama after another as she grew. She was forever coming down with some bug or other, needing ear grommets, or falling off a bike and smashing her front teeth.

Melissa wondered now whether she herself had been a bit depressed in those days without realizing it. She wanted to claim it was her own mother's fault for never showing her how it all should be done. But really she knew that deep down she didn't feel that she deserved to be a mother. Mark had pressurized her into having a baby in the first place and secretly she had hoped it wouldn't happen. When it did, she loved Tilly in a way that frightened her and made her feel entirely inadequate to the task.

Hester used to take Melissa off for the afternoon sometimes and it was a godsend at the time. Tilly would come home covered in flour, or glitter (sometimes both) that Melissa would be hoovering up for the rest of the day, but at least she'd had a rest and some headspace for a few hours. She was grateful.

But, she remembers with a disquieting feeling now, Hester would go that little bit too far. There would be undermining comments here and there about Tilly's clothes, or what she was eating. Or she would buy her things that Melissa didn't want.

An uncomfortable memory floods back with sharp clarity now. Once, when Tilly was about three, she had come home from an afternoon at Hester's with a *haircut*. It was only a trim, but Melissa still remembered the hot, explosive feeling it had triggered inside her. When she had taken Hester to task about it the other woman had seemed baffled by Melissa's reaction.

'But it was falling in her eyes,' she'd protested.

When Tilly started full-time nursery Melissa had managed to work herself free of the bond. They'd coexisted at a perfectly workable distance since then, apart from Hester occasionally trying to engage her in some boring issue relating to residents' parking, or bins, or whatever.

She'd fantasized about walking away from her life, just leaving it all behind, in those difficult days of early motherhood.

It wasn't as though she hadn't done this before.

When Melissa began her new life and was no longer Melanie, she had been living with a man called Laurie, a thirty-nine-year-old lecturer at an FE college. She'd met him in the pub where she was a barmaid. He taught drama and seemed impossibly sophisticated to Melissa. Laurie taught her how to smooth her vowels and how to appreciate wine; he showed her that a diet of Haribo, Marlboro Lights, and Morrison's tuna and sweetcorn sandwiches was not going to keep her healthy long-term. He cooked punishing bean stews that gave her wind for days instead. Laurie had even got her reading a bit, filling in the vast gaps in her education with an eclectic mix of left-wing pamphlets, documentaries, and books by Ian McEwan or Martin Amis.

The end with Laurie had come suddenly. One day, Melissa had woken up in the morning feeling a little sore from some rather joyless sex the night before (joyless for her, at least). She'd gone into the kitchen to find Laurie had left a pair of socks poking out of the trainers on the mat by the back door. They hung like flaccid banners, draped over the ugly, unfashionable shoes and she'd felt such a wave of contempt that it had brought bile into her throat.

There had been no prior planning involved.

She'd simply gone to where he kept a pot of emergency money in the back of a kitchen cupboard and extracted the £110 in there, along with his credit card.

It was as easy as that. And without a backward glance, Melissa had walked out of his life.

She had gone straight to the nearest hairdresser and had her distinctive hair dyed blonde. Then, using the credit card for the last time, she acquired new clothes and went to one of the bars where city traders hung out. And then she'd met Mark and her life had changed all over again.

But she had never experienced a feeling as intoxicating as that moment in the early morning when she'd clicked the door to Laurie's flat in Crouch End and walked down the deserted street, bag slung over her shoulder and a lightness in her step.

She remembered a fox had slunk onto the pavement before her, all furry angles and sharp musk. She'd gazed into its golden eyes. It felt as though the world belonged to the two of them: wild, free spirits on the move.

Glancing up, she recognizes the name on the sign.

'Hester?' Her voice seems loud and unnatural in the small space.

'Yes?' says Hester.

Melissa takes a deep in-breath. 'I think we're nearly there. We have to take the next turning.'

They pass cottages whose thatched brows seem to glower at them in disapproval. Melissa gets the strange sensation that they will never leave these narrow roads. They will simply make endless circles, the three of them, forever. Two women and a dead man.

She chews her lips, trying to focus.

The light has come at last but the misty rain in the air gives everything a hazy look. They might as well be looking through Hester's net curtains.

Eventually they spot a narrow country lane they must have missed the first time and Hester slows so they can peer at the sign. Fittingly called Watery Lane, it is lined with such dense tree coverage that it has an ominous, tunnel-like look. It seems like it will suck them inside and simply close over, never letting them out again.

Melissa feels a stab of hot fear as Hester turns the van down the lane.

It soon narrows to a single track. City driver that she is, she begins to fret about cars coming the other way, even at this hour. And could a country house have such an inhospitable and narrow road leading to it? It's all hopeless. They will never find this well. And even if they do, they will never get Jamie's body into it. She might as well find the nearest police station and get it all over with.

'Oh Melissa, are you all right?' Hester's voice is shrill. Flustered, Melissa raises her hand to her face and finds it damp. She must have been crying again, or maybe it's just the tiredness making her eyes so watery. Everything feels ever more blurred. It's raining quite hard now and the windscreen wipers on this old pile of junk are only smearing the wetness around rather than clearing her view. Outside is an Impressionist painting of green and brown smudges.

'Yeah,' she sighs. 'I'm okay, I'm just—', then, 'oh, stop here!'

The car slows to a crawl and the two women peer at the battered sign in the shape of an arrow at the side of the road.

Sca ow H ll and River, it says in long-rotted letters, like a gap-toothed smile.

Adrenaline thrills through Melissa once again and she is suddenly more alert than she has felt since Fleet. It looks as though they are almost there.

Melissa looks at Hester, who meets her gaze with wide eyes that somehow convey excitement more than fear.

Why is she helping her?

Mark used to joke that Hester had a crush on Melissa, which

was silly and untrue, she was certain. He'd come up behind her, whispering in her ear, until she couldn't stop herself from collapsing into giggles and batting him away.

'Just imagine, you could strip off those thick tights and find the wonders beneath,' he'd say, and put on a high-pitched, old-lady voice in the throes of passion. 'Oh Melissa! Melissa! Go down on me!' Melissa had ended up squealing in horror and chasing him around the kitchen, slapping him with a tea towel.

But despite what Mark says, Melissa believes this assessment of Hester was off the mark. She is essentially a bit of a lonely, odd old fish and she genuinely likes to be helpful. If there had been something a little cloying and unwelcome about her constant offers to help, maybe that was Melissa's fault.

Yet she is a strange little woman. A bag of nerves about driving on a motorway, but she can walk into a room and see a man with his skull caved in before calmly emptying her freezer of cool packs to keep him fresh. Horror rises in Melissa's chest again. She longs for coffee. She longs for it to be over.

The silence hangs between them as the road widens again. They pass fields of rapeseed flowers that blaze violent-yellow in the dishwater light. Another sign directs them to *The House* and *RIVER*. As they drive down a rutted road that causes the van's suspension to groan and protest, she believes she can almost feel the thump and slide of Jamie's wrapped body moving around in the back.

Soon they reach a small, picturesque gatehouse with turrets and leaded windows that seem to eye them beadily. Engine humming, they sit in silence and look at the tall wrought-iron gates next to the gatehouse, which bar the entrance to a gravel driveway sweeping into the distance. It curves through some trees and the house can just be seen: a pale stone mansion criss-crossed with scaffolding. It looks oddly cowed and lonely despite obvious recent attempts at repair.

'Did your husband ever say how he got to where that picture

was taken?' says Melissa now. Her mouth is dry and her tongue clicks unpleasantly against the roof of her mouth.

Hester shakes her head.

Panic begins to hum inside Melissa again. Something is very wrong about all this.

The *Forgotten Dorset* website had given the strong impression that this place was a ruin. There was no mention of scaffolding, which suggests people are doing the place up. There was no mention of *fucking gates*.

'Oh dear, I think we had better move on!' says Hester now.

'What? Why?' Melissa looks wildly around.

'Is that a security camera up there?'

Melissa's gaze jerks up to where Hester is pointing a shaky finger. The all-seeing, anonymous eye mounted on the top of the gatepost does a small shift towards them.

'Let's go!'

She slams her hand on the dashboard and Hester gasps before pulling slowly into the lane again.

They drive along in silence for a few minutes before Hester clears her throat again. It is obvious she is trying to appear strong but her voice seems unnaturally high when she speaks.

'Maybe it's only the River that is open to the public?' she says. 'We should keep looking because the well might be entirely separate from the house. A leftover from another time, perhaps.'

Melissa says nothing but she is a little comforted by these words. Less than a minute later she sits up straighter in her seat.

'Hester, look! I think that's it!'

She slaps the wheel in the flush of exhilarated relief. There is a pale stone well, covered in a filigree of green moss, with a rotted wooden top coming up ahead on the right.

'Yes, yes, I think you're right!' trills Hester, giddy too.

The van comes to a stop on the opposite side of the road, next to a patch of woodland. A small neat car park is empty. Sparse silver birch trees shine in the gloom.

Then Melissa sees something that makes her cry out.

'Shit! Look! There's someone camping over there!'

Sure enough, a battered old tent sits only feet away, its shabby khaki almost camouflaged among the woodland palette.

Hester doesn't attempt to move on. Instead she begins to climb out of the van.

'Hester! What the hell are you—?'

The back of the van opens with a dull thunk, cutting off her question. Melissa breathes in sharply. The door closes again and she sees Hester scurry over to the well with a black wrapped package. Her stomach shivers. *The pestle.*

Hester drops it inside and turns with a triumphant expression before hurrying back to the car.

'Thank you,' says Melissa quietly, as she climbs back inside and starts the engine again.

Soon, they come to a clearing. The silvery expanse of river can be seen just beyond the fringe of trees ahead. Melissa turns off the engine. They sit in silence for a few moments, listening to the cooling tick of the engine and the grim tattoo of rain hitting the roof. It's like the very soundtrack of hopelessness. Despair seeps through Melissa along with the sleepless night chill.

'What are we going to do, Hester?' She badly wants someone to take over now, to tell her what to do.

'Well,' says Hester, carefully, 'there is a very deep river here. I think we're going to have to find a good spot and use the resources we have available. It's not ideal, but there we have it.'

Melissa darts a surprised look at the other woman. As usual, there is something very slightly *off* about her choice of words. It's as though she never really learned the exact rules of conversation, Melissa thinks, but she is too desperate and tired to analyse this any further. She would accept just about any instruction at this moment.

They get out of the van. Melissa pulls her hood up in an attempt to ward off the damp fingers of early morning air that creep around her neck. Bringing an actual coat seemed like an impossible feat of organization at midnight. How she wishes now she had thought about it properly.

The dog jumps out and starts sniffing around excitedly near the van before circling and lowering its back end to the ground. The resulting smell makes Melissa step back and cover her face with her hand.

'Oh poor Bertie,' coos Hester. 'His bowels aren't what they used to be.'

Melissa says, 'You know it can't come with us?'

Hester doesn't reply. Face tight, she roots in her handbag and pulls out a black, bulging rectangle. Of course Hester would have remembered a raincoat, Melissa thinks bitterly.

'I'm quite aware of that,' Hester finally replies. 'And he is a *he*.' She pats the seat. 'Come, Bertie.'

The dog returns to the van, lowered head and drooping tail beaming resentment as *it* jumps onto the seat.

Melissa stares at the small, bustling woman in her Pac-a-Mac as she closes the door of the van and looks around, mouth primly pursed.

'Hester?' she says, unable to stop the words from rising up.

'Yes?' Hester's small chin tilts. Her dark brown eyes are wary.

'Why are you helping me?' says Melissa. 'What's going on here? You didn't have to get involved in any of this. *Why?*'

Hester's eyes flare bright like a cornered animal's as she stares back at Melissa.

A wood pigeon in the trees gives a lonesome coo.

This could all come crashing down now, thinks Melissa. *She's going to back out.*

Her hand moves instinctively towards the phone in her pocket. *End it. It can only get worse. End it.*

Then Hester gives a short, surprising laugh. 'Because we are old friends, aren't we?' she says slowly, enunciating each word carefully. 'And you need me. You couldn't have done this without me. Isn't that what friends are for?'

There is nothing wrong with the ordinary words yet everything is wrong with them. Hester's smile, so triumphant, seems almost vulpine and Melissa has a bizarre mental flash of Hester coming close and then, of all things, actually licking her face. It's ridiculous and surreal and she starts to laugh. She knows this is an inappropriate response and it's making her urge to pee even worse.

She's plainly going crazy. None of this is Hester's fault. All she has done is to help her.

'Are you all right?' Hester eyes her, sharp now.

Melissa wipes her face with her hand. 'I'm sorry. Yes, I'll be fine. Let's go, shall we?'

The two women start to walk down to the bank of the river. The rain has eased into a fine aerosol-like mist. The need to pee is now so urgent that Melissa has to do the pelvic squeezes she learned during pregnancy. Her groin aches with it as they reach the river.

Gunmetal-coloured water churns and moves like an oily length of cloth before them. It will be so cold in that water.

She blinks, hard.

'I bet it's a lovely spot in the sunshine,' says Hester.

Melissa fights an urge to say, 'Don't you understand? Don't you know what we're doing here?'

'So what sort of place are we looking for?' she says instead. 'The water will have to be deep, won't it? Can we be sure that he won't … float?'

Hester smiles, showing small white teeth like a child's. 'We'll have to put some rocks into the wrapping, won't we?' she says patiently.

Melissa nods. Something is happening inside her. It would be so easy to give up. To switch on her phone, dial the nines and wait for the consequences. Would it really be worse than this?

'This way!' calls Hester, cutting through her thoughts. Her chipper tone chimes out.

Melissa hurries after her and then sees what Hester is gazing at, a triumphant expression on her face.

156

HESTER

It's as if my prayers for a dose of luck have finally been answered.

A little further down to the left the river narrows slightly and a curved brick bridge straddles the water. If we can get to the very centre, then this would surely be the deepest part? It strikes me as an eminently sensible idea. But Melissa doesn't seem to match my enthusiasm. She has been looking very strange over the last few minutes. I wish I could open up the top of her skull and see into her thoughts.

'How on earth are we going to get him up there?' she says. 'What if someone is watching from the other side and sees us?'

I really could do without the endless negativity. I gather all my inner resources and briefly squeeze my eyes closed, wishing she would remember that we are both tired.

That I am the only friend she really has, when it comes down to it.

'Melissa,' I say, tolerantly. 'It's unlikely that anyone will be out at such an early hour in this weather. And we're going to just have to drag it – *him* – aren't we?'

Melissa shrugs, like some sort of moody teenager. I can feel the foundations of my considerable patience begin to shake.

I can't do this alone. She is the one who has created this mess

157

by allowing that man into her house in the first place. I had to help her clear it up.

Frankly, I think it's time I stopped being such a doormat. It's always been my problem. I let people abuse my kindness. Just like Terry did with his endless wheedling demands to be 'loved'.

Why do people have to be so difficult? Things are going to change when all this is over. Melissa has to understand that we are equals.

'We're going to have to work together. I suggest you put a brave face on things and we just get on with the task at hand.'

For a split second all I can see is Tilly in her expression. Then she colours, swallows visibly and looks at the ground.

'I'm sorry,' she mumbles. 'I'm just sick of this whole thing, that's all. I want it to be over.'

'So do I! Come on. Let's get on with it. I think we should use the loading trolley again, don't you?'

She nods grudgingly. It appears that gratitude for the various helpful ideas I have come up with will not be forthcoming.

No matter. There is plenty of time for all that. The rest of our lives, in fact.

I just have to be patient.

The path to the bridge is muddy and studded with small stones. It is going to be extremely difficult to wheel the trolley, which is only slightly smaller in length than the cargo itself. The bridge is made from very knobbled, uneven brick. It is steeply curved, to make things even more complicated.

But there is no point complaining. This has to be done.

Silently, we trudge back to the van. My knee is really quite painful now and my back throbs miserably. I feel a little sick and my eyes prickle and sting with sleeplessness.

I've already decided that I am going to treat myself to all my favourite things when I get back. I will lie in the bath for hours then have a wonderful sleep. When I get up it will be a new day.

Maybe I will see if Melissa would like to go out for breakfast somewhere. That's a lovely thought and I picture us hazily in some café, me drinking tea and her with that complicated coffee she likes. We will eat pastries and maybe read the papers in companionable silence.

But first there is this.

When we open the back of the van we are silent for a moment. Even I am a little cowed to see that the body is positioned at a very strange angle; the foot end trapped under the decorator's trolley. I suppose it must have moved about in transit. Unfortunately, some of the plastic wrapping has come undone in the process.

His face is clearly visible. I look away but Melissa lets out a little cry and begins breathing noisily, almost panting.

I knew she would make much more of a fuss than I would. With difficulty, I crawl into the back of the van and yank a piece of plastic sheeting over his head, trying to tuck it in. But I don't manage to do it in time to prevent a glance of what lies beneath. His skin has taken on the waxy pallor of cheap cheese.

Melissa makes another funny little sound. I glance at her and see she is biting down on her hand, eyes huge and shining.

'Melissa!' I say sharply. 'Get a grip. This is no time to fall apart! Come up here and help get this onto the ground.'

Still making small noises deep in her throat, she clambers into the back with more grace than I managed and then presses herself back against the wall. She stares down at the wrapped body and a few tears snake down her cheeks.

'*Focus*, Melissa!' I say. 'We are almost on the final straight now! We can do this. I know we can! But we need to work together.'

She gazes at me and swipes a hand under her nose, her nod almost imperceptible. I must remind myself of the great stress she is experiencing. This girl simply isn't as strong as I am. I didn't even know how strong I was until today. As I glance down again at the bulky shape in its opaque plastic, I offer a little prayer of thankfulness to the man himself for giving me this gift of self-discovery.

Together, we haul the body to one side so we can get the trolley down onto the ground. It is very heavy and, when Melissa climbs down and takes the far end, I accidentally lose my grip and it pushes into her tummy.

She swears viciously and repeatedly. This is a very bad habit and I sincerely wish she would stop doing it.

'Are you all right?'

To her enormous credit, she doesn't complain further, just nods, tears slipping down her cheeks, unchecked now.

Once the trolley is flat, we push and pull until the body slips off the edge of the van's interior and lands, somewhat awkwardly, across it. I am interested to see that the effects of rigor mortis seem to have worn off and a certain floppiness has returned. Although I had been hoping for this, it strikes me now that it would actually have been helpful had we been able to prop him up vertically and push the trolley that way.

Then we huff and puff, push and pull, until the body is sitting upright on the trolley, back against the handles. Melissa is very red in the face and her eyes shine with fear and exertion. She looks very pretty, despite everything. A hank of bright hair has come undone from her ponytail and my hand itches with a sudden desire to gently tuck it behind her ear.

Being the taller, younger, and stronger of the two of us, Melissa takes the job of pulling the trolley backwards. My job is to try and prevent the man from falling off. He keeps slumping to the side.

Honestly, it feels as though he is deliberately trying to make things difficult for us.

We inch along, making the very slowest of progress. Every time we cover the slightest distance, the trolley catches on a stone, or the man starts to fall to the side again. Looking out for rocks, we only find a couple that would be of any use. I wish Terry's van still held some full paint cans. They would have done the job nicely. But as I said to Melissa, what other choices do we have now?

To make things more difficult, the rain has become heavier. It's that miserable, mizzling sort of rain that chills you to the core. I find myself thinking, 'I'm too old for this,' and then realize the idiocy of such a statement. As if there would ever have been a right time for dragging a dead body into a river! It's quite comical.

Then I wonder if I am going a bit mad because of all this. But that's not it exactly. There is something else. A strange sort of … happiness.

Despite the risk of being caught, despite the exhaustion and the wet clothes clinging to my cold skin, despite my grumbling tummy and the desire for a cup of good, strong tea, I feel more alive than I have for years. I'm aware of my body in a way I'd quite forgotten. It's as though I have shed ten years since yesterday when I was baking those scones.

It's Melissa who has brought me back to life. I glance gratefully at her as we trundle a painstaking foot forward but then I see her face is now scrunched in discomfort.

'What is it?' Alarm flares in my chest.

'I'm sorry,' she whispers. 'I'm about to wet myself. Can we stop for just a moment?'

I sigh. Sometimes Melissa is a bit like a child.

'Well, can't you hold it in?'

'I'm sorry,' she breathes again and gently drops her end of the trolley before shuffling off into the trees.

The cumbersome plastic larvae immediately slumps sideways and I am suddenly quite overwhelmed with irritation. *Bloody man*, I think, even though I don't normally use language like that. Muttering to myself, I try to heft it back onto the trolley but it's too heavy for me and I have to leave it lying at that odd angle.

I look around, wiping rain away from my face. Thank goodness for my Pac-a-Mac, although inside it, I feel chilled and clammy at the same time.

Where *has* Melissa got to?

I spot her coming through the trees then, shoulders hunched and arms folded across her chest. She looks cold and young and, well, quite lovely.

Looking up at me her eyes go wide and she makes a frantic flapping motion with her hands. I turn round slowly to see what she is looking at and horror fills my veins.

Our camper is awake and heading this way.

MELISSA

The man's eyes are trained sleepily on the ground. Dressed in scruffy jeans that hang somewhere around his hips, he has the bow-legged slouch of a man still under the influence of something. Yawning widely, he lifts his grubby t-shirt to scratch a pale, hairy belly. White earbud wires dangle through ginger-blond dreadlocks.

Hester darts behind a tree with surprising grace. But Melissa can clearly see Jamie's wrapped body, right-angled half off the decorator's trolley.

Her senses are cranked up painfully high. The dripping of rain through the trees fills all the space inside her skull; the green of the woods is too bright. Her own sour sweat and fear are choking her with their stink.

Somehow, the man still hasn't seen them. Reaching the river-bank, he unzips his fly then pees, simultaneously letting out an audible fart. Briefly looking up at the river, he turns back the way he has come and trudges back in the direction of his tent.

For several moments Melissa remains rooted to where she stands. Relief begins to pump through her veins, sweet as balm. But it is short-lived because this must surely herald the start of the day for the crusty camper. He might even be about to start packing up the tent.

She hurries to where Hester crouches behind a tree, her face drawn now.

'We have to hurry,' says Melissa in a hoarse whisper. 'Help me get him back onto the trolley and let's *go*.'

Hester says nothing, but nods in agreement.

Melissa squats down next to Jamie's slumped torso and tries to grasp the loose plastic to haul him back onto the trolley. Hester ineffectually pushes at his head but, within a few moments, he is more or less ready to be moved again anyway.

Renewed fear gives Melissa the strength to move faster now and the trolley bumps and rolls along the rough forest path alongside the river.

When they get to the foot of the bridge they both stand straighter and scan all around to see if anyone is within sight, either here or across the river. But all seems to be clear, and together they begin the laborious business of pulling the burdensome trolley up the uneven brick of the bridge.

Melissa is bathed in sweat and her rain-sodden hoodie feels as though it is twice its usual weight. Her legs shake with exertion and muscles in her shoulders scream and cramp. She's baring her teeth as they hit a section of brick that sticks up and catches on the trolley wheels.

'Come on you fucker,' she hisses.

Registering the prim look from Hester, she thinks, *Just say something. Try it. See what happens.* The thought of tipping Hester over the bridge and watching the water seal over her head shocks Melissa. She briefly wonders what she is turning into.

Gasping with exhaustion, the women stand at the apex of the bridge and gaze down at Jamie as though a solution to the next impossible thing will magically present itself. He looks so big and heavy. Far too solid and large to be lifted and put into the water.

'Okay,' says Hester, breathing hard. 'We have to get it upright and then we can tip it over.'

It is illogical to mind, but Hester has been doing this all night; referring to Jamie as though he is nothing but an inconvenient parcel. She calls her fucking dog 'he' but an actual human being is treated like ... nothing.

That plastic shroud contains a person. A person she tasted and touched just last night. Someone who once made her laugh so hard at his impression of Kathie's Glasgow accent that Coke had squirted out of her nose.

Regret pounds inside her with a sickening, steady beat. *You killed him. You killed him, you killed him ...*

Wordlessly, the two women haul the bulky body into an upright position. Melissa's muscles shriek but, thanks to all that Pilates and yoga she filled her empty days with for the last few years, her body is stronger than she thinks. Soon Jamie is slumped against the wall of the bridge. Pushing hair soaked with rain and sweat from her face, Melissa looks around. If anyone was watching, if the police suddenly swarmed through the trees, she would still push Jamie into the water. Events now are a runaway vehicle that can't be stopped. Forward motion is the only thing possible.

'Right, when I say so, heave him forward and over, okay?' she pants.

Hester nods, cat's bottom mouth drawn tight.

'One, two, three—HEAVE!' says Melissa.

Jamie topples forward and then slithers impossibly fast into thin air. There is a loud splash and the two women peer over at the water as one. Jamie bobs and floats in the fast-moving water then drifts sideways towards the riverbank, where he rests against the reeds, trapped.

'Shit, no!' whispers Melissa, sleeved hands covering the lower half of her face. 'He's not heavy enough to sink! What are we going to do?'

Hester is muttering quietly to herself and Melissa realizes she is praying. They watch as the body moves with agonizing slowness, bobbing and twisting at the side of the river. Then water starts to seep inexorably into the plastic sheeting and the women watch breathlessly as it begins to sink. But first it turns over and some of the sheeting works free so that Jamie's entire head is exposed.

'Oh, Jesus.' Melissa feels tears and nausea rise at once at the filmed eyes that gaze up at them in the grey-doughy face.

'I'm so sorry, Jamie,' she whispers and feels Hester's sharp gaze on her. 'I'm so very, very sorry.'

She can't move from the spot now and doesn't even notice that the rain has stopped. She doesn't see that the sun is breaking through the clouds. A swathe of gold brightens the stretch of river ahead and the air is suddenly suffused with birdsong.

Jamie takes one last, almost lazy, roll in the water and then he is gone.

HESTER

I am very keen indeed to get away from here but Melissa is staring down at the water as though this was some sort of official burial. I even wonder whether I should offer to say a few words. But I quickly decide against this. She is upset and we are both very tired. For the first time I have the thought that she might have wanted to *save* that man.

I do hope she isn't going to be consumed by the guilt. I hate to see her looking like this. There is really nothing to be gained from feeling like that.

She stares down at the water and, although she isn't crying, she seems to have aged since yesterday. No doubt I have too, but I have less to lose.

'Melissa?' I say gently and touch her arm. She flinches, as though she has been scalded, and regards me as though I am a stranger. 'I really think we should go, don't you?'

She nods dumbly and swipes her face with the sleeve of her jumper.

'I'm still okay to drive,' I say hurriedly.

She doesn't even protest.

In the van, I put the heater onto its maximum setting, but at first it just blows icy air into the cabin, so I turn it down again. We

167

can't leave straight away because the windows are fogged and it always did take a long time for them to clear. I remember Terry used to complain about it all the time.

Oh Terry, what would you think of me now? I wonder and get rather a thrill from this thought.

It really is unpleasant in this van. I'm never going to be able to see unless these windows clear. With a huff of irritation, I wind down the side window and then emit a small shriek because the man we saw a little while ago is standing right there, inches away.

He peers in at us. All we can do is goggle, mouths agape.

His eyes are an odd gold colour, like a cat's. A tufty beard sprouts from a long chin and a hand-rolled cigarette dangles from his lip. He sucks on it and a strange, sweetish smell drifts into the car.

I don't think I have ever been at such a loss for words. Is it all over for us? Did he see what we did?

I force myself to act normally and try to move my resisting mouth into both words and a faint smile.

'Morning,' I say.

At the sound of my voice, Bertie, who had been sitting on my lap for a short cuddle, pops up and greets the man with a fierce wagging of the tail.

'Good morning, ladies,' the man says in a surprisingly well-spoken voice, albeit one that is a little slurred. 'And look at this little fella! May I stroke him?'

The way he speaks simply does not match his scruffy, hippy appearance. I would be checking my purse was still in my bag if I ended up next to this young man on a bus. I nod, stiffly, and he reaches in a bony white hand, with about ten leather bracelet things around a thin wrist, to stroke Bertie's head with surprising gentleness.

'What's his name?' he says, cooing at my delighted dog, who turns onto his back in order to receive more love.

'It's Bertie! I think he likes you!' I say, brightly, although I fear I may be a tiny bit shrill.

I glance at Melissa. She is focused on the man with the rictus

168

expression of someone in pain. I feverishly search my brain for some form of explanation for why we are here. But what possible reason could there be?

'Good to see someone else here,' says the young man, taking the cigarette between his thumb and forefinger in a way that also ill-fits his rather plummy accent. He takes a deep drag and blows the smoke out in a pungent gust that makes me cough. 'Some of the best fishing in Dorset here, if you know where to look.'

'Yes, I believe so,' I say weakly. I still can't think of any reason why we would be sitting in this car park at 6.30 in the morning.

'We've been visiting family,' I say in a gush. 'Thought we'd have a break and admire the river.' I'm cringing as I say this.

To my enormous surprise, he holds out the cigarette towards me.

'Goodness, no thank you!' I say with a small laugh. Imagine the germs, even if I did smoke.

To my astonishment, Melissa's thin, pale arm snakes past me and she takes the cigarette from the man, still without saying a word. She takes it to her lips and draws deeply, then does it again, her eyes squeezed tightly shut.

I can't believe it has taken me so long to understand what is happening. Really, what is Melissa thinking? Not only has this young man seen us, but her DNA is now all over that marijuana cigarette.

I clear my throat loudly.

'Well, we had better be going,' I say, trying to remain cheerful-sounding even though fury is coursing through me like the hot drink I have been craving for hours.

Melissa hands the nasty thing back to the young man and smiles weakly as he grins at her.

Honestly.

'Bon voyage,' he says. 'Oh and one other thing ...'

My breath catches. 'Yes?'

'Your rear light is smashed. Did you know?'

'Yes,' I say on a long out-breath of relief. 'I plan to get it seen to when I'm home.'

'Good idea,' he says. 'The filth'll pull you over for that.' And with this he slaps the roof of the van, making us both jump. Then he swaggers off, drumming out some unknown rhythm on the leg of his baggy jeans.

Melissa scrunches sideways in the seat, her back almost facing me. It feels as though she is trying to get away from the interior of the van, but maybe that is just the tiredness showing again.

Wordlessly, we drive out of the car park and onto the narrow road that runs past the big house. I think she is trying to sleep but when we reach the main road, I crane my neck to look and see that her eyes are open. She stares glassily ahead like a very tired, beautiful doll. Her pale skin is shadowed under the eyes and I get the odd notion that I would like to press my fingers there to cool and soothe her. This flusters me because it's such a strange thing to think. I give myself a little shake and try to concentrate on the road.

It is difficult though, as sunlight spears through the windscreen and jabs my eyeballs. I pull down the sun visor but it only helps a little bit.

The traffic is much thicker now, of course. I find that I can just about cope if I stretch my eyes wide and blink as much as possible. But the truth is that any exhaustion I felt before is nothing to what I'm experiencing now. The thought of reaching the M3 makes all the adrenaline that has sloshed around my poor body all night curdle like stale milk. I'm really not sure that I can go any further without a nap.

But how will I break this news to Melissa? She might insist on driving and that frightens me even more. I clear my throat and decide to brave it.

'I really am very tired, I'm afraid,' I venture. 'I'm not sure either of us should be driving unless we can have a small rest first.'

'Yes,' she says, to my astonishment. 'I think we should stop at

170

the next services and see if there is one of those Travelodge Inns or whatever they're called. Even if it's for a few hours. I want a shower.'

It's all I can do not to exclaim. I never expected her to agree. But I'm not sure it will be that easy.

'The only thing is, I'm sure we'll need some sort of identification to check in. And that's not a good idea. And also, what about Bertie? I can't leave him in the van.'

I'm mulling over this conundrum as the first sign for the dreaded M3 appears ahead. Melissa yawns noisily before replying in a strangled voice.

'Look it's not the bloody Ritz,' she says. 'It's the sort of place salesmen go for a quick afternoon shag, so I'm sure it will be fine. And you can sneak the dog in under your coat or something.'

Wincing at her terminology once again, I say nothing and Melissa speaks again.

'I am so desperate to *wash*. I feel so—'

She doesn't finish but starts to scratch both her arms at the same time, surely hard enough to be sore. It's as though she has insects crawling on her, the way she's doing it, and my badly behaved imagination immediately throws a horrible image of maggots into my mind. Then I see that man, Jamie, with maggots coming out of his hollowed, sightless eye sockets and my mouth fills with saliva.

Oh dear, I must *not* be sick. I breathe slowly, in and out, in and out, until I have to focus on getting us onto that motorway again. Bertie is whining a bit now, which is very out of character for him. He must need to go again, and he isn't the only one. Melissa may have been happy doing that in the woods but it's not something I would ever contemplate.

I indicate right and turn down the slip road to the motorway. The traffic is quite heavy, even though it is so early, and I blink hard, forcing myself to be awake and be alert.

Thankfully, the services are only about half an hour away but

I do feel every second of the journey. I cling to the slow lane as cars thunder by. At one point a lorry comes so close to our bumper in the side mirror that I am sure we will crash. But with a flash of lights and a rude blare of the horn, the lorry passes, and I can breathe again.

When the sign for the services appears it feels like a beacon of light on a dark night, even though it is, of course, a sunny morning now. But it is as if I have been holding my breath the entire time I have been on this road. I'm a little nervous about whether we are going to get away with booking a room as we pull into the car park of the Travelodge and I'm still fretting about the Bertie issue. But I don't mind admitting that it's just a tiny bit exciting too. I know it's not, as Melissa put it, 'the bloody Ritz', but it's still a hotel.

I must say, there is something pleasing about hotels. It's the sensation of everything laid out specially just for your use, from the tiny soaps, to the chocolate on the pillows at the better establishments. I have quite a collection of shower caps and sewing kits at home.

And yes, if someone had said to me just thirty-six hours ago, 'You and your old friend are going to book into a hotel together after having the most extraordinary day and night of your life,' I probably would have told them they needed to lie down in a darkened room for a while.

I can add this one to the very long list of new experiences I have had since yesterday.

When we have parked, I realize I had better try to tidy myself up a little.

I would have expected Melissa to want to put some make-up on because she is usually immaculately turned out. But she doesn't seem to have any interest in this until I point out that we ought to make the effort to look respectable.

Using the mirror in the sun visor, I try to tidy my hair. After a short pause, Melissa gets out her make-up bag and applies some foundation and eyeliner, listlessly gazing into a small mirror.

'Want some of this?' she says, offering the bag towards me, and I shake my head. I've never really known how to apply it, is the truth of the matter.

'C'mere,' she says and leans over to cup my chin in her hand, to my great surprise.

She starts to smudge foundation under my eyes. 'Keep your eyes closed,' she orders, and I obey as she slicks on some mascara.

When I'm allowed to open them, she regards me closely. 'You should wear make-up, Hester,' she says. 'It suits you.' Her admiration warms me like sunshine. 'Let me sort your hair now.'

I close my eyes as she teases and smooths my hair. It's all I can do not to sigh with pleasure. It reminds me of my mother's touch, in some ways, but it's different in ways I can't explain. I feel a little bit tingly when she says, 'There, you'll do,' in a tone of satisfaction and sits back in her seat.

I feel quite chipper as I get Bertie out for a quick widdle and then pop him back inside the van. He protests and barks, which is quite out of character, so I do hope he isn't going to make this even more difficult. We walk slowly over to the entrance of the Travelodge.

It's a low cream-coloured building with the distinctive black, white, and blue flag hanging over double doors. There are a couple of cars in the car park and, as we approach, a family come bustling out.

The mother is grossly overweight and has one of those faces that could mean she is anywhere between twenty and late fifty. She has a clinging vest top in bright pink with the words 'Too Hot to Handle'; a football-like bust wobbles beneath.

The man is equally overweight – a great bull of a man – and yet two beautiful children of about four and six bounce along behind them. A boy and a girl, they both have blonde curls, cherubic faces with wide blue eyes, and skinny arms and legs.

They are perfect.

It never ceases to amaze me that human gargoyles can produce delightful offspring. It's so terribly unfair. I start to wonder what would have happened if Terry and I had mixed our gene pools.

A terrible picture comes into my mind then: the waxy look of his skin as he lay in the water, eyes open and sightless.

Typical of him to try and make me feel guilty when I am feeling so tired and vulnerable. Sometimes my subconscious likes to play tricks.

I must get a grip of myself.

The woman catches my look as we pass. She stares at me in a vaguely belligerent way through unattractive red-framed glasses.

We walk over to the reception desk, where a girl of about twenty sits, quite obviously texting on her phone.

She has a small pinched face that is almost orange with thick pancake make-up. Her eyelashes are clogged with gloopy mascara and her eyes are slightly bloodshot. Coming to the end of the night shift, I imagine, which hopefully should mean she is more pliable. Her name badge says her name is Leanna.

Melissa had insisted that she 'do the talking' as she put it, so I simply smile at this Leanna as she casts her eyes over us both in a desultory fashion.

'Hi,' says Melissa in a low, friendly voice. 'We need to book a twin room, please.'

Leanna taps a screen.

'How long will you be staying with us,' she says. There's no question mark in this monotone voice.

We had already agreed that we would book for a day, as it was unlikely there would be a rate offered for anything less.

'Just for one day, but we'll be gone in a few hours,' says Melissa, her voice warm treacle. 'My friend and I just need a shower and a nap.'

She really does speak so nicely. And it feels *good* to be called her friend again.

Hearing her say these words, I really have no regrets about any of this either. None of it.

'If I can take a credit card,' says Leanna, who hasn't made eye contact the entire time we have been here. If I were her boss, I would be sending her on a customer care course *toute suite*.

Melissa leans on the counter and bends toward Leanna in a conspiratorial way.

'We'll be paying in cash.'

'Fine,' says Leanna, stifling a yawn. 'But I'll need ID. If I can get something like a driving licence then I can book you in.'

We exchange brief glances. This is exactly what I feared would happen. It is a little typical of Melissa to be clueless about this sort of situation. She, no doubt, stays in such lovely hotels usually that she expects an establishment like this not to care. But it's a chain, isn't it? A successful one too, which will have its own practices.

Someone else has come into the reception area now. It's a tall man in his forties, with a mop of reddish curly hair and a neat, pointed beard. He has a wheeled case and keeps yawning and rubbing his face.

Melissa clears her throat.

'The thing is, Leanna, we both had our purses robbed last night in a pub. It's lucky that I had some spare cash hidden in my bag. We've reported it and everything … the police said there'd been a spate of thefts like this in, er, where we were staying.'

Leanna looks up and meets Melissa's eye directly for the first time. Her cheeks flush, and she blinks furiously.

'I'm really sorry, but I will need some sort of guarantee if you're to book a room. It's the rules. My boss will kick off if I make a booking without a registered card of some kind. And anyway, the computer won't even allow me to book the room without that. It can't actually be done on our system.'

I am quite aghast. This really is a problem. I hear a very large sigh gusting from the man waiting behind us then and embarrassment prickles over my skin.

Melissa's eyes are filled with storm clouds now and electricity seems to spark around her. I fear she has finally reached her limit. But she must not lose her temper now, not when we have got so far.

'Are you sure there is absolutely nothing you can do to help us, dear?' I interject, smiling hopefully at the young girl, whose jaw is set mutinously. I sense her toes digging in under the desk. This person is not going to budge.

'Can't be done,' she says and then, 'Sorry.'

Never has that word been less meant than now. She pretends to tidy her desk, which quite clearly contains almost nothing but a magazine and a few plastic coffee cups. Her eyes remain cast down, her cheeks now crimson.

'For God's sake, love,' says the man behind, suddenly, in a northern accent that pronounces the endearment as 'loov'. 'Let them book a room on my bloody card. I've been driving all night and I just want to get my head down.'

Leanna looks uncertainly from the man to Melissa and then to me as he comes to the counter, noisily clattering his small case, which has a resisting, squeaking wheel.

'Well,' she says uncertainly, 'I suppose there's no reason why I can't do that if you are happy to do it.'

He glances at us and nods. He's quite handsome, if you like the big ginger type of man. Sort of like Henry the Eighth in his slimmer days.

'It's fine,' he says. 'You don't look like you'll cause too much trouble.' He winks at Melissa, who laughs and thanks him profusely.

I hope it's only me who notices how unnatural and high that laugh sounds as I add my own thank you.

A few minutes later, our knight in shining armour disappears into the lift, while Melissa is given the key to our room: a credit-card sized piece of plastic.

Loudly calling out that I will just go and get something from the car, for the Unlovely Leanna's benefit, I make my way back

176

out into the violent daylight for the next, difficult, part of our plan: getting Bertie past that young martinet.

I open the van and a heinous smell greets my nostrils.

'Oh *Bertie!*'

He lays his head on his paws, ears flattened. His tail thumps slowly but his eyes beam shame and fear of rebuke. I put my hand on his head, fighting back my disgust.

He's a very sensitive boy and all this travelling must have gone to his tummy.

I realize now how very quiet he had been since we left the riverbank. The poor animal must have been feeling quite poorly.

I hunt in my bag for antibacterial wipes and do my best to clear up the wet offering on the seat. Thank goodness there isn't very much of it. I manage to get it all cleaned up, while Bertie watches me gratefully. I toss the soiled cloths in a bin and then clean my hands.

I have a very strong stomach. It is one of the very unfair ironies of life that dirty nappies and sickness would not have bothered me one iota. The way some mothers complain about their children's natural bodily processes, you would think they were nurses in a field hospital at the Somme, rather than people who have been privileged enough to become parents.

Still, no point thinking that way now. I must get to Melissa.

'Right, boy,' I say to Bertie, wrapping him up in my cagoule. He wriggles and kicks and tries to get free. 'Bertie!' I have to speak very sharply to him then. 'Mummy needs you to be very good and very still!' I have no alternative but to tap him hard on the nose, which hurts me much more than it hurts him. With a pitiful whine, he rests his head on my arm and I flap one of the sleeves over to cover his head.

I peer nervously at the desk as I walk in but Miss Leanna isn't there and the desk is empty. Another piece of much-deserved luck.

No one is in the lift either. Things are really starting to look up.

We will rest and then begin the day with clear heads.

I allow myself a little smile as I make my way to our room.

MELISSA

Hot water runs over Melissa's lips, her mouth a square of anguish. She has to press her hands against the plastic wall of the tiny shower cubicle to stop herself from buckling at the knees. Sobs rip through her, hard like birth contractions, and their force begins to frighten her a little.

When the crying finally peters out, she stands with water running over her face, eyes jammed tight shut. But she can't stop seeing that lifeless face and his body bobbing and twisting until the grey, cold water finally swallowed it up. Then she pictures his triumphant expression as he moved beneath her last night, his chest damp, hot, and hard under her hands. Filled with life. And that's even worse.

The acid rises up without warning and she shoves the glass door open, stumbling out of the still-running shower just in time for the vomit to splash into the toilet bowl. There's hardly anything to come up and her stomach heaves another two or three times until she knows she is spent. Miserably, she flushes the toilet and turns off the shower.

She longs for a toothbrush to help cleanse the foul taste from her mouth and thinks it doubtful you can get one from Reception in this sort of budget craphole. Miserably, she cranes her neck and lets tap water run into her mouth. Her neck aches and her back aches and her head feels as though someone has filled it with wet sand and then given it a few kicks.

How did she end up here? It feels as though some kind of whirlwind began in her kitchen last night that scooped her up and delivered her here without her really meaning any of it to happen. But an unforgiving little voice in her ear tells her she let it all happen. She was a willing participant. She can't blame anyone else for this.

It's only now she realizes there is a sound coming from outside the bathroom: a gentle knocking. *Oh God, Hester*, she thinks. How long has she been in the shower?

Wrapping the thin, inadequate towel around her body she hurries to the door. Hester almost falls in, wild-eyed, clutching a wriggling package that's presumably full of dog.

'Goodness!' gasps Hester. 'I've been out there for ages! Didn't you hear me, I was ...'

She seems to bite off the end of her sentence as she takes in Melissa's appearance. Her cheeks flush hard and she drops her eyes. The dog bursts from the package and lands four-footed on the floor, where it begins to sniff about excitedly. Melissa flinches when its nose touches the bare skin of her foot.

'Oh you poor girl,' says Hester, still avoiding her eyes. 'You've been crying. Are you all right?' She is still blushing fiercely, which Melissa has never seen before. One of her hands drifts up towards Melissa's naked shoulder, a little shakily, and Melissa finds herself stepping back as she nods. *Please don't hug me*, she thinks, knowing that any kindness like this will cause her to split at the seams.

'I'm fine,' she says croakily, her throat dry and sore from sobbing and sickness. 'Really. I just need to rest for a while, that's all.'

Fervently hoping Hester won't want to have some sort of post-mortem of events, Melissa crosses to the furthest single bed and reluctantly puts on her knickers and bra again.

This probably shouldn't matter because she feels as though she will never be truly clean again, anyway.

Even though Jamie's body was thrown in the water, she feels as dirty as if she had dug a grave with her bare hands, soil blackening her fingernails and working into the creases of her skin. She stares at her hands now, as if looking for the evidence and, thank goodness, the practical girl inside her comes to the fore and tells her to cut the Lady Macbeth stuff and get a grip on herself.

Suddenly aware that Hester's eyes are on her, Melissa looks up and then, flustered, puts on her t-shirt, jeans, and socks. Finding a comb in her handbag, she drags it through her hair and then lies down on the single bed, facing the bathroom.

'Do you mind if I draw the curtains?' says Hester quietly.

Melissa shakes her head on the pillow. There's a swooshing sound and blissful darkness enfolds the room. At least there are proper blackout curtains here. Melissa closes her aching eyes.

Hester gives a little sigh and mutters to the dog, which is no doubt in the bed already. There's a creak as the other woman lies down.

Even though exhaustion presses down on her, pinning her body to the bed, Melissa's mind is clearly not going to allow her the rest she craves. Instead, it presents her with an HDTV-quality flicker book of images she doesn't want to see: Jamie's lifeless eyes staring up at her; the heft of his body as he slumped sideways on the trolley. The jammy mess in his hair and the *crump* of his face hitting the tiled floor. Jamie standing on her front doorstep; Jamie gently flirting with Tilly.

Tilly.

Scrabbling to a sitting position, Melissa fumbles to the side of the bed for her handbag and the phone inside.

She hadn't even thought about her daughter for hours. What kind of mother is she? Her iPhone comes to life and shows that she has five messages:

Tilly, 11 p.m.: 'Going 2 beach with Stacey and co in morning. C U pm'.
Mark: 'Hold-ups with filming. Sorry. Home early Weds. Mx'.
And then three from Saskia:
'How U feeling hon? Sxxxxx';
'Making most of Nate doghouse. Currently weeding garden LOL!';
'Hope sleep sorted you out. Call me? Sxxx'.

Weak with relief that there hadn't been an emergency, Melissa taps out quick messages to all three and then flops backwards on the bed.

'Everything okay?' Hester sounds sleepy and hoarse.

Melissa is suddenly overcome with a wash of pure loss.

She doesn't deserve any of them anymore.

Staring up at the ceiling in the gloomy light, she hears the distant hum of the motorway and the rustling of Hester in the other bed. The dog gives a sleepy little *woof* in its dreams.

'I don't know, Hester,' she whispers finally. 'I'm not sure any of it will ever be right again.'

There's further movement and she turns over to see Hester is now facing her. The dim lighting highlights the lines on her face. The other woman looks old and exhausted. A fresh stab of guilt assails Melissa. She should just have called the police and tried to make the self-defence story work. At least then Hester wouldn't be an accessory to a crime.

'Oh God, what have I done?' she says, turning to let the tears soak into her pillow. The bed compresses next to her; she feels the gentle touch of the other woman's hand on her shoulder, gently patting, and then stroking her hair. It helps. Comforting her like the hand of the mother she never had.

She didn't think she had more tears to spare but Melissa sobs, her shoulders shaking.

Hester says, 'there, there, darling, there, there,' over and

181

over again, so softly it's only just possible to hear her.

After a while, Melissa turns the other way and grabs some tissues from the box on the side. Blowing her nose with a damp honk, she gestures to Hester to make room for her to get up. Hester moves back to the other bed and they sit, knee to knee.

Melissa toys with the damp tissue, twisting it round her fingers. It quickly starts to break up, sending dandruffy flakes to the rough carpet.

'I'd do anything to turn the clock back,' she murmurs, meeting Hester's eyes at last. 'Really. Anything at all. I never meant to kill him.'

Hester gives another vague 'shhh' and pats Melissa's knee.

'God, I'm a *murderer*, Hester,' she says and more tears come. She buries her face in her hands again. It is intolerable. The guilt will drown her, she feels. 'I killed a person!'

'No, no, no,' says Hester in a soothing tone. 'You're not. No.'

Melissa knows she is making meaningless sounds to comfort her.

'But I *did* though! I hit him!'

No one would ever understand that she hadn't really meant it. It had been one white-hot second of rage. How could such a small implement do so much damage?

'You just don't understand,' she whispers. 'You don't know what *really* happened.'

Exhaustion, guilt, and fear seem to mix and expand inside her like bread dough. They fill her stomach and her throat. She can't breathe.

Melissa stands up, gasping, crying, and begins to slap at her own head.

'Melissa!' Hester's voice comes from far away. 'Stop it now, you're frightening me! Try to take slow breaths!'

And then Hester is right there. Her eyes catch the small streak of light filtering into the room through the curtains like tiny candle flames. She grips Melissa's wrists in her small, dry hands.

'No, *you* don't understand, my darling girl!' Her voice is clear now but too loud.

'You are not alone,' she says. 'I keep telling you that. You never have to feel alone again. I'm here for you, Melissa.' Melissa is aware of quickened breath, which comes hot against her cheeks. 'I helped you … I …'

Melissa nods and mumbles 'thank you' because she can't think of what else to do or say and manages to peel her wrists from Hester's grip. She wants to curl into a ball and disappear. She sinks onto the bed and curls into a foetal position, her back to Hester. She feels the light touch of the other woman's hand as she begins to stroke her hair again.

PART THREE

HESTER

Sitting back on the bed I let out a small sigh of satisfaction at a job well done. I regard the three piles of clothes on the bedroom floor and think I should have done this years ago.

The three bundles are: keep, bin, charity shop. The throwaway pile is by far the largest; a teetering mountain of fabric in various faded hues. I will struggle to fit it all into two bin bags.

I have been going at it all morning and I am sorely in need of a cup of tea. This has been hard work. And not just of the physical variety.

Seeing particular garments again has been so poignant. I reach out to finger the tartan skirt that my mother used to wear to parties, the material now limp with age. I used to bury my face in the soft billowing flare of it when I was small and it was so wide and swishy I couldn't get my arms all the way round.

I wish there was some residue of her perfume here but, like her, it is long gone. With regret, the empty bottle of Rive Gauche has been added to the dustbin pile.

There was a time, after I lost them both, that I would dab that perfume to my wrist, just as she did. I would wonder how my pulse could still throb with life when hers had simply … stopped. Crushed in a tangle of metal at the side of a road.

I hoped the pipe smoke aroma might have lingered in Dad's suits too, but there is no trace now. What's more, the moths have had rather a field day. I hold a mustard tank top I don't remember to my nose and take a sniff, but only breathe the musty, sweetish smell of neglect.

Yes, this morning's work has been a little melancholy but perhaps it has been therapeutic too. Terry used to grumble about the wardrobe in the spare room being taken up with all these old clothes, claiming he could find a use for the space. I stood my ground and he eventually realized that I wasn't going to budge. But now I am the one deciding that my house needs to 'get with the times'. It's time I 'moved on' as they say.

Terry's things went long ago, of course. I have already had one clean sweep, in a manner of speaking.

Time for that cup of tea.

I have one more look around at the fruits of my industry, picturing what the room will look like when I've had it decorated. I can't remember the *exact* colour of the walls in Melissa's spare room, having not been in a fit state to appreciate it when I slept there, but I did like that shade. It was so calming. I will have a look next time I am around. I have already invested in some cushions to put on the bed and I think this room is going to be quite transformed.

I don't know where the summer weather has gone. The sky outside my window is dishwater grey so I snap on the overhead lights as I make my way downstairs, humming 'Summertime' as I go. I've always loved that tune.

Flicking on the kettle in the kitchen, I wonder what she's up to today. Maybe I should knock up a Quiche Lorraine for her to have tonight; something nice and easy. They could have it with a salad. Although last time I was round, I did notice the pasties I'd made were sitting, untouched, in the fridge. You would think Tilly and Mark would be eating them, even if Melissa isn't that hungry.

I can't help a small smile when I think of how surprised Mark was to see me there, drinking tea and chatting, in the first few days after … Dorset. He couldn't have looked more taken aback if the Duchess of Cornwall had appeared at the big stripped pine table, helping herself to a homemade macadamia cookie. Ha! It was a challenge to keep the gleam of satisfaction from my eyes.

I asked him some questions about the progress of his television programme and he was polite but obviously dying to get away. He kept shooting puzzled looks at Melissa, but she had her head down and was once again attacking her kitchen surfaces with cleaning products. She does this far too much, this excessive cleaning. They should all, and especially Tilly, be exposed to at least some germs, in order to build up immunity. Maybe I'll find something on the internet, now I'm a 'silver surfer', and print it out for her.

I pretended I was interested in his silly programme, but I have my own reasons for avoiding that sort of subject matter.

Terry found the trips to the fertility specialist quite excruciating. The doctor we saw certainly wasn't like Mark, with his shiny good looks and smiles. No, he was an old school consultant with horn-rimmed glasses and an imperious manner. Terry tried to joke about the squalid little side room with its mucky magazines and plastic beaker but I didn't want to hear about any of that. I just wanted some answers. And I got them.

Terry's sperm count was very low. He'd blushed and looked very uncomfortable when this was revealed, as though his stupid pride was the most important thing! Age was part of it, but the specialist explained he was just 'made that way'. There was nothing technically wrong with me, but I was the wrong side of thirty-five and that didn't help.

This seemed so very cruel, when our local high street was – and still is – jammed with hi-tech buggies pushed by women who are no spring chickens. There was a time when every single one of them felt like a painful rebuke.

When things reached their lowest ebb for me, I considered going out to some bar and having intercourse with any old man who looked fertile (although quite how I would have assessed that, I'm not sure). I got as far as looking at the sluttish dresses and high-heeled shoes they sell in that cheap Turkish shop by the bank.

Women in films are always doing things like that, aren't they? They sit in bars and wait to be approached. But I think this may be more of an American phenomenon. The Feathers pub doesn't look like the kind of place a woman like me would stand out. There was also the possibility that I might run into one of Terry's friends, or even Terry himself.

So I gave up on that idea and my longing and love turned into a cold, hard stone in my chest. It was his fault. Not mine. My life could have been different. I wouldn't have had time to get mixed up in Melissa's problems if things had happened as they should.

Sighing, I swirl the teabag around in the cup. As the water stains russet brown, I find my mind drifting back to Melissa's appearance when I saw her yesterday. She has definitely lost weight, which is a concern. And don't get me started on the hair. I can't even think about that without getting upset.

I have had moments, it's undeniable, when I have thought about easing her burden. What good would it do now though? What's done is done. I've never thought there was much point in looking backwards.

But I can't seem to stop bad thoughts from spiralling. I sometimes picture myself walking into a police station and announcing to the desk sergeant in a clear voice that I wish to report a murder. I can picture it all so clearly.

The neatness of it pleases me. I have nothing much going on

in my life, after all. Only Bertie would really miss me. I can't imagine prison is that bad. It's all televisions and activities these days anyway; more like a holiday camp.

But I hope it won't come to that. As long as Melissa can stay strong.

MELISSA

Her hand strays to the back of her neck, where newly exposed skin meets the tufty roughness of her hair. She can't seem to stop worrying at this spot. There's a strange sort of comfort in pulling it, tweaking, until it hurts.

Mark's mouth was a perfect 'O' of shock when he saw what she had done to herself. Melissa mumbled something about it being 'better for the summer' but she was aware her husband thought she was going mad.

It hadn't felt like madness, the evening she had started to cut it with the kitchen scissors. It seemed necessary and right. She wanted the Russian girl's hair *out* and away from her. It didn't belong to her. She had no right to it. It needed to be *gone.*

Hacking away, she had watched the hair pile up on the table in front of her; the translucent plugs queasy reminders that these soft tresses had grown on another, poorer, woman's head. When she had finished, she stared at it for some time before bundling it up and almost running to the bin to throw it inside. Then she'd poured another glass of wine, filling it so high it slopped over the rim, and gone to watch television. She didn't care what she watched these days. Cookery programme, drama, documentary … it didn't matter. It just helped her to stop seeing Jamie bobbing about in that icy water. For a short time, at least.

But Tilly's reaction the next morning prompted Melissa to go to a salon in Kentish Town to have it tidied up. She'd looked almost tearful and Melissa experienced a twinge of regret.

She couldn't face her usual place. This salon, Hair by Jayne, was small and tatty and doing a bustling trade with chatty, elderly women having perms. She asked the stylist just to 'make it look better, I don't care' and studiously avoided eye contact and conversation until it was done.

Now as she leaves her bedroom, she pulls the belt of her dressing gown around her narrowing middle. She hasn't been able to face food, telling Mark and Tilly that she has been hit by a virus. Which doesn't explain the hair.

Or why Hester is suddenly in her kitchen, seemingly all the time.

In the first few days after that horror trip to the river, she tried to convince Hester that she was too sick for visitors. But Hester had chirped, 'Nonsense, you just need a rest! I'll be back later with something home-cooked!' and bustled off home. She came back later with a shepherd's pie that Tilly said tasted 'kind of weird'. It lay congealing on the side until Melissa had guiltily gouged the fatty, solid mass of it into the bin.

Hester made old-fashioned so-called 'comfort food', but it didn't offer much in the way of solace. Devoid of even garlic, chilli, or coriander, it wasn't the kind of thing her family was accustomed to eating. She was secretly glad Tilly was as fussy about this as she was about Melissa's more adventurous cookery.

Hester came back with something else, Melissa forgets what, a day or so later. She had breezed in and sat down at the kitchen table as though nothing had happened there. As though they were normal neighbours who hadn't hefted the lumpen weight of a dead man onto plastic together. As though Melissa wasn't a murderer and Hester an accessory.

Every time she saw Hester, she felt even worse. And resentment towards the small, fussy woman was beginning to spread like a poison inside her. What would have happened if they had just called the police? It was Hester who had really come up with the bulk of the plan. She had been the one who first suggested getting rid of the, of *Jamie's*, body. She had suggested the place in Dorset and insisted on driving them there.

She had been so eager to help. Such a good, concerned neighbour.

Mark had asked why Hester was suddenly coming round to their house with gifts of food. 'I mean, you don't even like her!' he said.

'I do!' Melissa had protested feebly. 'We've sort of ... reconnected.'

Mark made a frustrated sound she couldn't interpret and left the room.

Melissa walks down the stairs on wobbly legs. She knows she must try and eat something.

Tilly is still asleep at midday, Mark at the hospital.

In the kitchen she makes an espresso and then takes it to the table, where she opens her MacBook and goes through the secret ritual she has done every day for the last week and a half.

She is itching, as always, to Google, 'body found in Dorset river', but forces herself instead to browse Dorset local news sites. If anyone wants to know, she will say the family is thinking of buying a holiday home there and she is interested in learning about the area. As subterfuge goes, it is pathetic. Yet still she scrolls through pages of stories about car accidents and robberies and primary school children winning prizes before deleting her browser history.

Still nothing.

In some ways she would feel better if his body turned up. Waiting for disaster to fall is eating at her like a malignancy. She forensically analyses the many reasons the police might come to her door in the middle of the night, every night. It seems her brain is to do this, rather than sleep, between the hours of 1 a.m. and 4 a.m.

There's a sound at the French doors now and Melissa slams down the lid of the laptop and rises to her feet in one movement, heart pulsing in her ribcage almost painfully.

Saskia peers in, framing her face with the curve of her hand. She mouths, 'Let me in!' before doing some comedy rapping with her fists on the glass.

Melissa tries to smile but her cheeks are too stiff; her whole face feels rigid. She has been avoiding Saskia, citing stomach flu that started around the time of the party. But the sight of her now causes a shift inside Melissa. A need for human comfort swells inside her. She hurries over and opens the door.

'What the fuck, Lissa?' says Saskia.

Then she is holding her because Melissa is suddenly sobbing into her warm, spicy-scented shoulder. She is much smaller than her friend, and Saskia's arms envelop her now as she emits worried little 'ssh' sounds.

Melissa tries to laugh and pulls away after a time. Her face is blotched and puffy with tears and exhaustion.

'God, I don't know where that came from,' she says, trying to inject normality into her tone. 'I've been a bit under the weather. I'm sorry.' Her voice bubbles with mucus and she goes to get kitchen towel from under the sink, before honking loudly into it.

Her friend regards her carefully.

'What's happened?' says Saskia quietly. 'Is it Mark? Has he done it again?'

For a moment Melissa is utterly confused. Done what again? Then it comes to her and she can't help the bitter laugh that forces its way out. She experiences a sharp stab of nostalgia for the time when this was the worst of her worries.

'Ah, no, no, nothing like that,' she says feebly. 'Look, have a seat. I promise to stop blubbing now and I'll make you a coffee.'

'I don't want coffee,' says Saskia, taking her sunglasses off her head and sitting down at the table. 'I just want to know whether you're all right. We've barely spoken for two weeks.'

Melissa sits down opposite and tries to look at her friend. Saskia is staring at her, eyes gentle but appraising.

She can't think of anything to say.

'Okay,' says Saskia, 'Are you at least going to explain the chemo haircut at any point?' she says. 'I wasn't going to say anything but it's a bit hard to miss.'

Melissa is surprised at the laughter that froths up from inside. She can always rely on Saskia to cut through the bullshit and she feels a deep thud of love for her now, like an ache.

Just be normal, she tells herself. You can do that. Pretend you can do it.

'It's bloody awful, isn't it?' she sighs, patting the back of her head. 'I don't know what I'm going to do. I just fancied a change. But … it went a bit wrong.'

'I'll say,' says Saskia. 'Here, let me.' She pulls a scarf out of her handbag. It's chiffon, patterned with thin grey stripes on a mustard background. She comes over to Melissa and expertly begins to wrap it around her head. The gentle touch of her fingers is a comfort that makes Melissa want to cry again so she squeezes her eyes shut for a moment, willing herself to keep it together. Saskia finishes with a knot and stands back with a look of satisfaction.

'There you go. All you need is a pair of shades and an open-topped car and you'd give Grace Kelly a run for her money.'

Melissa smiles back gratefully. 'I'll take your word for it.' She has to swallow a fresh wave of tears and forces normality into her voice. She is suddenly desperate for Saskia to stay. 'Look,' she says, 'are you sure you don't want a coffee or anything?'

'No, it's too muggy for coffee.' Saskia walks to the fridge and opens it, looking for one of the many Diet Cokes she drinks each day.

'Christ, what's all this?' she says with a laugh. 'You auditioning for *Bake Off*?'

Melissa tries to think what's in there. Pasties, a quiche, some sort of apple pie. All from Hester. There is no point in lying. Saskia knows she would never cook this sort of food.

'No,' she says, slowly and carefully. 'It's, um, it's all from Hester.' Her stomach seems to crawl with ants. She silently begs Saskia not to question her any further.

'Really?' says Saskia with ease, opening a can with a sharp *fssht* before sitting back at the table and taking a long drink. 'Why's she doing that all of a sudden?'

Why? How can Melissa possibly begin to answer this question? She feels paralysed by its intricacies.

Saskia sighs and speaks again, saving her from having to answer. 'Gawd, has she forgiven us, do you think?' she says. 'Honestly, bloody Nathan! I still can't believe he did that to her of all people.'

Melissa smiles and looks at the table with a shrug. She can't think of a single thing to say. Her mouth has become dry and her knee is shaking. She has to place her hand on it to stop it from banging against the underside of the table.

But Saskia isn't going to let this go. 'So come on,' she says. 'Seriously, I'm curious. Why is she suddenly back on the scene? Didn't you manage to get shot of her a few years back?'

Melissa hesitates. She imagines, just for a moment, the sweet relief of unburdening herself.

'Well,' she says with care, 'we just started talking again, I suppose. She's not so bad really.' *Please, Saskia, stop*, she thinks. She wants a moment's peace from Hester invading her head and her kitchen.

'Rather you than me,' says Saskia, making a moue. 'I think she's downright weird. Didn't she once suggest she moved in with you?'

The laugh that bursts from Melissa springs unnaturally loud

from the knotted ball of tension inside her but Saskia doesn't notice.

'No! It was nothing like that!' she says and then pauses. 'It was coming on holiday with us.' She covers her face with her hand as more laughter rises, unstoppably.

'Can you imagine?' says Saskia beginning to rumble with her distinctive husky giggle. 'You'd be getting into bed and she'd pop up between you to remind you to floss or something. Or, you'd just be getting down and dirty and she'd tell you off for making her lose her page in the *Reader's Digest*.'

Laughter cascades from Melissa. She can't stop it.

'Budge over, Mark,' Saskia speaks in a high-pitched, prim voice that is uncannily accurate. 'It's my turn to cuddle up next to Melissa tonight! You've had your go!'

'Oh *stop!*' Melissa manages to gasp through her hysteria. 'It's too easy to picture it!'

Tears trickle from the corners of her eyes. Her empty stomach aches but it feels so normal, so sane and healthy. The kind of thing non-murderers do. Melissa wants this moment to go on forever, despite the guilt that nips at her. Poor Hester. She can't help being so odd.

'But really though,' says Saskia as they start to settle down again. 'Do you really want *her* back in your life?'

Melissa stares down at the kitchen table and sighs heavily.

'Not really, no,' she says quietly. But it's not that simple, she thinks.

It is only now that she can admit to herself how suffocating she is finding Hester.

She is going to have to find a way to pull away from her if she has any chance of coming through this nightmare.

HESTER

I place my hand against the wall to steady myself. My legs are shaking. I'm winded, like someone has hit me in the tummy.

I was only coming round to see how she was. As I got to the French doors I heard Saskia's awful voice. Their conversation drifted out like dirty smoke. I feel it fill my lungs, choking and poisoning me.

Such cruel words. And the laughter. Openly *laughing* at me. I can't take it in. The vile friend isn't a surprise. She's nothing but a trollop. But Melissa? After everything we've been through. How could she speak about me like that? As though I were nothing to her? After what I *did* for her?

Some masochistic urge makes me want to stay and hear more but after they've purged themselves of their mirth, Saskia begins to witter on about her idiot man-child. I clench my hands so hard into fists my nails cut my palms. I picture her open mouth, with those big teeth laughing and swallowing all the air around her. Sucking Melissa into her orbit. Turning her against me. I imagine grabbing that thick, dark hair of hers and pulling it, pulling it until she begs me to stop. Oh yes, that would surprise you, wouldn't it, Saskia?

I have to get away from here. Stumbling a little, I hurry back to the garden gate and back towards my own house.

Bertie whines when I come back into the kitchen. He can always tell when I'm distressed. I pick him up and hold him tightly to my chest as I go into the sitting room and slump into my armchair. I feel as though I am a thousand years old.

We sit together, my little friend – my only friend – and I, stroking him until he falls asleep in my lap, his small chest rising and falling. I lay my hand on his warm, coarse hair and sit, immobile with misery.

The betrayal feels like cold mud sludging through my veins. When I think of what I have done for Melissa. She doesn't deserve a friend like me. I should have left her to sort that Jamie man out on her own. Ha! I'd like to have seen her dealing with things the way I did!

The pictures tumble into my mind now, so vivid I can almost smell her kitchen and feel its walls erecting themselves in a dreamscape around me.

When that bubbling sound drifted up from her kitchen floor, it gave me quite a start. I'd honestly believed he was already dead, as Melissa had said.

As I cautiously walked towards him I could see that he was looking right at me. A froth of spit formed and broke at his mouth. His lips moved the tiniest fraction as he tried to speak.

I stared down at him.

I couldn't make out what he was saying. It may have been 'help', I suppose. But my mind was racing. If I called an ambulance he could make a full recovery. But no one would have believed Melissa hit him as an act of self-defence. No one ever believes the victim of this sort of crime.

The thought of Melissa being led away in handcuffs was so

200

terrible, so entirely *wrong*, that I was suddenly quite resolute. I knew that I couldn't let it happen.

His eyes flared with hope when I sat back and regarded him.

All I could see in my mind's eye was his filthy ape-hands pawing at Melissa's soft skin, trying to soil and hurt her.

But it wasn't just that. It was the sight of him early that morning. Striding around in his underpants. So arrogant. As though he had rights over Melissa. As though he had a central place in her life. Calling me Grandma! And I've not even had the good fortune to be a mother.

And I suppose everything that had happened with that Nathan boy boiled up inside too.

Rage is meant to be hot isn't it? But it filled me with a cleansing white light – pure and cold. Shushing him gently, I placed my hands over his nose and mouth. Weakened as he was, he bucked and kicked but with little strength. Still, I had to press my torso down onto his face. And it seemed to go on and *on* … I closed my eyes, begging him just to let go, to accept things.

A powerful happiness coursed through me. At last, I thought, I can show Melissa what she means to me. And yes, I'll admit it; all the way through this I was seeing that other day in my mind, when I finally became free of the useless man I had married. There had been a delicious sense of freedom then too.

It is crossing a line the first time that feels like such a big step, you see. Once you have done it once, it's no distance at all. So I pressed down until it was over.

We all have dark impulses sometimes, I'm sure.

Melissa doesn't know what I did for her.

Well, I'm not going to let it go.

When I lift Bertie gently to the ground, he eyes me and thumps his tail happily before going back to sleep. My dear boy. He's the only one I can rely on.

I go into the kitchen and pick up the little shepherdess orna-
ment from the windowsill. I've always loved her blonde curls and
the tiny dog at her feet that reminds me of Bertie.

Her crinoline skirt is hollow and, underneath, Melissa's spare
back door key nestles there comfortably.

I set my alarm for 3 a.m. but I'm not really asleep when it beep-
beep-beeps into the darkness. I'm too stirred up to sleep. I'm
shivering, with nerves, with the chill of night but also, perhaps,
with a little bit of excitement as I slip on my dressing gown and
slippers and make my way out of the bedroom. Bertie wakes and
I whisper sternly that he is to stay. With an obedient little flick
of the tail, he lays his old head down again to sleep.

I switch on the garage light, smelling the old paint tins, dust,
and white spirit that still fill some of the shelves in neat rows.
Terry always did keep it very tidy in here. A draft curls under the
doors and I hear the wind bash against it, as though longing to
be allowed inside.

The shelf is high so I reach for the step stool I bought for Tilly
when she was too little to reach the table. It's a lovely thing: white
wood, with blue lambs and chickens gambolling around the
bottom. She used to love clambering on and off that step in my
kitchen. Such a sweet image.

Stepping onto the upper step of the stool now, my knees
complain and creak. I reach up to the shelf above my head and
push aside the box of nails and the pile of plumbing catalogues
I really must get round to throwing out.

Feeling around blindly in the space behind, my hand touches
the crackly plastic bag and I draw the item to the end of the
shelf and down. My heart always quickens when I do this.
Oddly though, it somehow gives me a feeling of strength and
peace.

Holding the wrapped object, I climb down and sit on the top
step. I cradle it in my arms, feeling the heft, the potential force

of it. I imagine the sound as it connected with hair and skull and swing it through the air, testing how it might have felt.

I won't unwrap it, because I am not wearing gloves.

I'm still not entirely sure why I kept the blood-and-hair-smeared pestle. Nestled in pieces of kitchen towel, it was placed on the side until I had donned some brand new Marigolds and was able to hide it away properly. I then took one of my spare ice packs and wrapped it firmly in another bin bag. I feel rather tickled by the image of myself throwing that other package into the well.

Some instinct told me I needed insurance.

The pestle's unpleasant residue is now a deep rusty brown. I can't face cleaning it (and why should I? I didn't hit the man with it, after all) but neither can I bear to carry it like this. I rip off a piece of the blue paper that Terry used to keep for wiping his hands as he worked on the van and wrap it around the pestle's base.

The night air is sweet and cold on my face when I open the back door. They lock that side gate at night, but luckily there is a piece of broken fence (which I have asked Mark to mend to no avail) that should be just about big enough for me to squeeze through.

I hesitate as I contemplate the damp grass and, taking off my slippers, I hold them to cross the garden. My heart pitter-patters a little bit but I am becoming adroit at doing things that intimidate me these days. The cold dampness of the grass under my toes makes me shudder.

The piece of fence comes away with difficulty and I squeeze through the gap, gasping as a nail snags my dressing gown. I extricate myself, grimacing at the aching in my knees as I manoeuvre myself to the other side of the fence.

I walk quickly across the grass, my toes scrunching in protest until I get to the French doors, where I slip my chilled, wet feet into my slippers again.

I have this all planned out but my hands shake as I turn the key in the lock.

Mark's car isn't in its usual spot out front. I don't want to run into Tilly, but I am banking on the fact that teenagers sleep like the dead. And Melissa, well, she's no stranger to sleeping pills. She told me herself.

The kitchen is bathed in the milky under-lights of the cupboards, along with neon slashes of green from the cooker and microwave. How typical of Melissa not to turn off energy-guzzling appliances at night. The room smells sharply of cleaning products with a very slight hint of cigarette smoke.

My eyes drag to the spot where the body lay and for a horrible second I think he is still there. I swear I can see a lumpy shape, black blood spreading across the floor.

But then the vision clears. I am just being silly.

I go to the ornate metal grate over the air vent in the corner of her kitchen. It's a quirk of these buildings. I have the same one.

The grate comes away easily and I place the object inside. It makes a metallic screech of protest as I push it back into place. I wait for a few moments, checking there is no sound coming from upstairs, before I get to my feet and dust myself down.

The strange thing is, now I am inside, I am not really afraid. I feel a sense of power, if anything. And I'm not ready to go home yet, to Bertie and my own quiet house.

My eyes stray then to the glint of Melissa's knife rack on the wall and I wonder how it would feel to use one of them. How hard would you have to push? Would it slide in easily, or would the muscles offer resistance? I imagine the soft gasp of pain and her eyes meeting mine. We would be united by death once more.

Something frantic inside me stills.

Then I am a little shocked at my own imagination. I am a good person and there has been enough violence. I will get my own back my own way.

I'm a small, slight woman and in soft slippers I make no sound as I ascend the staircase. I watch each foot press onto the stair as I rise, acutely aware of the smooth wooden banister under my hand. My nerve endings seem to sing and fizz like a broken fluorescent light. I am electrified with the thrill of this act. More alive perhaps than ever before.

I reach the landing and listen to the gentle sighs and ticks of the sleeping house. A dog barks somewhere outside. Not Bertie. It feels like a night-time companion.

I know which room is hers, of course. The door is pulled over, but not closed. I push it slowly and the door seems to gasp as wood rubs on carpet.

Stepping into the room, I pause and allow my eyes to adjust to the gloom. There is a sour sleep smell in the air, mixed with some sort of perfume I don't recognize. Hair products, perhaps. The curtains are heavy and at first I can't make out the bed. Then I see it and – after a second or two – the hump of her body beneath the duvet.

My heart begins to pulse and thrum in a pleasurable way as I pad on silent feet across the room. Melissa is on her side, her face a pale moon, hair a tangled halo on the pillow. I see a hand reaching out – bone-white in the dark, warm room – and realize it is mine. Snatching it back, I feel a little dizzy with the sense of my own power.

I could do *anything*.

Melissa makes a sound: a groan mingled with an unintelligible word. And where closed lids had been I am looking into the shine of her open eyes. I fancy I can see a tiny version of myself reflected in them. I don't move a muscle. She mumbles something in her sleep and closes her eyes again.

It's as I get to the bottom of the stairs on shaking legs that I hear the sound. Urgent whispers are coming from the landing. My heart seems to stop beating as I pad quickly to the kitchen door and try to dissolve into the shadows.

It's only now that I really think about what I am doing. How this might appear to others.

The voices are coming down the stairs now, getting closer.

I bunch the sides of my dressing gown in my fists and try to quell the panic inside me. I think I might be having a heart attack. My chest is tight and I want to *run*, run away from here, but I must be silent.

I *can't* be discovered.

'I didn't mean to drop off!' says a familiar male voice in a low, sleepy murmur.

There is a giggle. Tilly. 'I know! Me neither!' she hisses. 'But my mum would go mental if she found you here! Go on, go home.'

I move my head very slightly to the left to see Tilly pressing her body up against Nathan's. He slides his hand down her back. She is dressed only in her bra and knickers and he grabs and squeezes her bottom as though it is made of putty. I want to look away, but cannot.

'Call you tomorrow, okay?' he whispers and she nods and kisses him on the lips before opening the front door.

When the door closes, she runs back up the stairs, rather heavily.

I am feeling quite calm again now. I did the right thing, coming here.

A few moments later I am squeezing through the fence and back into the safety of my own garden.

All in all this has been a most useful neighbourly visit. I'm sure Melissa won't think so much of her friend when she discovers her son has been sleeping with her fifteen-year-old daughter.

And now I must get some sleep. Tomorrow, I have a busy day ahead of me.

MELISSA

Wandering the aisle of Wholefoods, Melissa sips from her Starbucks' cup, closing her eyes as the extra hot, extra shot latte suffuses her bloodstream. She has tied the scarf around her hair and is wearing make-up for the first time in a week. It feels, pleasantly, as though she has stepped back into her own skin.

Maybe having a prosaic, domestic problem to deal with has forced her back to normality.

But she is in no hurry to rush home to face her sulking, red-eyed daughter.

Stopping to look at the vegetables, she idly picks up an aubergine just because the taut, midnight skin is pleasing to look at. She places it in her basket.

It's always therapeutic, shopping in here.

The shelves are loaded with organic produce that is almost aggressively healthy and wholesome. Melissa pictures the mean little Spar at the end of the road when she lived with her mother. Newspapers, porn, sweets, tinned crap. Maybe a wizened banana or two and a sad collection of tomatoes that tasted of nothing but acid.

She belongs *here*, not there.

She wants all of it, from the sweet, scarlet tomatoes on the vine to the grimy potatoes designed to make rich metropolitan buyers feel at one with nature.

Tonight they will eat as a family.

Something has to change.

Hester was round early, before nine. Melissa realized immediately that the other woman's expression was cool and distant.

'I'm sorry to bother you,' she'd said, not quite meeting Melissa's eye. 'But when Tilly has friends staying until the middle of the night, could they avoid slamming your front door? It woke me up, you see, and I couldn't get back to sleep.'

Melissa smiled, awkwardly. 'I ... don't know what you mean. She didn't have anyone here last night.'

Hester coughed and her mouth twitched into a tight smile.

'Well, I'm sorry, Melissa,' she said stiffly, 'but I looked out of my window at around 3.30 a.m. and clearly saw that Nathan boy exiting your house. I do apologize if you didn't know about this ... relationship.'

Melissa felt a tumbling sensation inside. The little bastard ...

'Thank you, Hester,' she'd managed to say, in a controlled voice. 'I'll speak to her. And please accept my apologies.'

Hester had walked back into her house without another word. Melissa felt a flicker of relief. Maybe things would go back to normal between them now and they could resume the polite distance that had worked so well.

There had been a loud, tearful row with Tilly, who claimed her mother didn't let her do anything, but only cared about exam results. Melissa had half wanted to slap her, this ungrateful child who had no appreciation of her riches. Tilly was told her allowance was to be cut for the next month. When she went into her bedroom, she slammed the door so hard the house shook.

She knew the phone call to Saskia wouldn't be easy but it had taken even more of a sour turn than she had expected. Melissa should have known that the one boundary she couldn't cross was to criticize her golden son; apparently, they were 'only doing what young people do'. Melissa told her he was to keep away from her daughter, who was not going to waste her promising future on boys. The phone call ended frostily.

Unpleasant though it had all been, the events of the morning had forced Melissa to take stock. She'd felt lately that she was watching everything through a Perspex screen but now it was time to try and reconnect.

The focus must be on her family now. So they are eating together tonight, whether Tilly likes it or not.

Mark has promised he will be back by seven. Melissa isn't going to tell him about Nathan; a concession that Tilly accepted with mumbled thanks through the bedroom door. He doesn't need to know about this.

She is cooking a lamb tagine and can almost taste the warming cinnamon and ginger on her tongue. They will have a hazelnut meringue torte to follow; the raspberries are in her basket, dusky and beautiful, beaded with moisture that might be early morning dew rather than condensation from the chiller.

They will eat together and anyone looking in the window would see an enviable image: an attractive family unit, talking about their respective days and eating a delicious meal made from expensive, organic ingredients.

Half an hour later, Melissa opens the front door and comes into the hallway, which smells of polish and the fresh flowers she had delivered this morning. The cleaner came today and the oak floorboards gleam with warm, honeyed light. She takes a deep, satisfied in-breath and feels something approaching peace.

She's putting her keys in the little ceramic bowl that Tilly made in her first year at secondary school when she becomes aware of voices.

Coming into the kitchen now, Melissa comes to an abrupt halt.

Tilly is sitting at the table with a woman who is perhaps in her twenties. Melissa doesn't recognize her. She doesn't look like anyone Tilly would know, in her cheap sweatshirt with its flower design and her mousey hair pulled into the sort of harsh pony-tail that Mark calls a Croydon facelift. The woman looks at her with an open hostility that confuses her further. Melissa's eyes then shift to a movement on the other side of the kitchen.

A small girl with blonde hair in a straggly topknot is standing there. She stares at Melissa through bright blue, distinctively shaped, eyes.

'Hey Mum,' says Tilly, still slightly warily. 'This is Kerry ... and *Amber*.' She says the second name in a chummy children's television presenter voice.

'They're looking for Jamie. Any idea where he went?'

HESTER

I could hear the shouting quite clearly from my back garden.

Serves them right! I hope Melissa gives Saskia hell about it too.

But I didn't spend long listening. I had things to do.

I dressed carefully for the visit to the police station, putting on my smart blue Mackintosh even though the sky was leaden and the air thick with heat. I was rehearsing what I might say as I walked to the bus stop.

'I believe my neighbour has committed a terrible crime.'

Or:

'I saw my neighbour hiding something in her kitchen. I think it could be a murder weapon.'

Nothing sounded quite right.

But in the end, I never got that far.

I was mulling all this over when I spied a young woman with a child who looked rather lost coming up my road. She was a common sort of creature; puffing away on a cigarette right over the little girl's head, face all pinched up. Her large, rather doleful, eyes were framed by spider legs of gluey mascara.

Something about her manner caught my attention and I slowed

my steps. She kept looking at houses and then walking on a little bit, clearly searching for something. Or someone. The child was obviously tired, and I heard the woman snap at her in a way that wrenched my heart a little.

Getting closer, I studied the child, who seemed to be about four. She was on the chubby side, with thin blonde hair drawn into an unflattering topknot. When she spotted me, she stared with the wonderful lack of guile that all small children share. It took a second for me to realize that she had Down's syndrome. Poor little mite. Sympathy flooded my veins.

'Can I help you at all?' I said to the young woman, and she looked at me suspiciously before sighing and stubbing out her cigarette on the pavement. I nearly said something about littering but decided against it.

'I'm looking for someone who I think lives round here,' she said, with flat northern vowels. 'You probably don't know her.' She eyed me up as though she could possibly make that sort of judgement based on appearance.

'Well, why don't you try me?' I said politely.

She hesitated for a second and a nerve jumped in her cheek. I got the feeling that she was thrumming with tension inside and trying to hide it.

'She's called Mel,' she said grudgingly. 'I don't know her second name.'

She blushed hard, no doubt conscious that trying to find someone in a city the size of London with such scant information was a fool's errand.

But ... Mel? Could it be?

'I know a Melissa,' I said steadily, excitement flickering like a lit candle. 'Could that be the person you're looking for?'

She gave nothing away. But she looked exactly like someone Melissa wouldn't want as a friend. Something told me, pleasingly, that she spelled TROUBLE.

With a thrill of shock I realize she might be connected to that

Jamie character in some way. A sister? Melissa told me he had no ties, but it has to be possible I suppose. This would be very stressful for Melissa.

'Let me show you the way,' I said with a warm smile.

I walked her and the little girl all the way to the front door.

And now I am here, in the garden, hoping to overhear what might be happening next door but, frustratingly, she must have the doors shut.

I am running out of things to do when Bertie suddenly presses his nose to the gap in the fence and begins furiously wagging his tail.

The small, pale arm of a child worms through the gap and roughly taps the top of Bertie's head with a chubby flattened hand. As I get closer I hear a hoarse giggle. Bertie rolls onto his back for a tummy tickle.

Tentatively, I crouch down next to my dog and look through the hole in the fence.

'Hello,' I say gently. I can see a half slice of the little girl's face. She stares back at me with the one blue eye I can see.

'We didn't get properly introduced before, did we?' I say. 'This is Bertie and I am Hester. What's your name, sweetie?'

'Amber Mae Piper.' Her voice is monotone and a little loud. Then she says, 'I live at Flat 302, Burnside Estate, N9 2HJ.' She busies herself with patting Bertie again. I can see he is starting to tire of her rather heavy-handed affection but I'm very anxious that she shouldn't leave.

I am just trying to form another question when, unbidden, little Amber suddenly says: 'We are looking for my daddy.' She has that flat intonation I've heard before in people with this syndrome but it's her words that have caused my legs to wobble beneath me.

'Your … daddy?' I say weakly. Then, because I can't stop myself, 'What's your daddy's name?'

213

She doesn't reply but yanks a clump of grass from her side and tries to feed Bertie with it. Bored now, he has taken to licking his front paw with great concentration.

'Amber?'

The harsh voice blasting from Melissa's kitchen almost makes me fall backwards onto the grass. Amber's mouth turns down at the corners.

'Would you like to come and see Bertie again some time?' I say.

A beautiful smile lights up her face and she nods. And then, as though it was the obvious follow-up, 'My Daddy is Jamie Liam Cox.'

She gets to her feet and bustles away; a small washerwoman with chores to attend to.

'Bye bye,' I whisper. 'Bye bye, Amber.'

Back in the kitchen I slump into a chair and stare into space.

I haven't experienced much in the way of guilt about what we did. I know that's wrong of me, but there it is.

But everything has changed now. I never knew that young man was a father; rapist or not. What we did has had an effect on that little angel's life. I slump forward miserably, my head on the kitchen table. I begin to bang it repeatedly onto the plastic tablecloth, whimpering, 'No. No. No.'

My head hurts and my stomach turns over. I run to the sink and bring up the remains of my breakfast cereal.

I reach for a knife from my wooden block near the cooker and fling it at the far wall. It bounces off and lands with a defeated thud on the lino. I take another and throw it at the kitchen door, using all my strength and yelping a little.

It hasn't helped. So next I take a plant pot containing a small cactus from the windowsill and throw that at the same spot. Then the china chickens that belonged to Mum and then my wedding crockery. Then the china shepherdess.

214

Smash, smash, smash …

Finally, I sink into a chair and rest my head on my arms.

Everything is becoming muddled in my mind again. I have to remember that Jamie wasn't an innocent man. Didn't he try to force himself on Melissa? I wish I hadn't cared about that. I wish I had never stepped in and helped her as I did. It has brought me nothing but ingratitude and heartache.

Bertie gives a small cry. Looking around at my devastated kitchen it occurs to me that all I have is a small dog and a lot of unwanted memories. I thought I had a friend, but I was wrong.

I have nothing to lose anymore.

MELISSA

Spooning coffee into the cafetière, Melissa's hands shake so hard that dark grounds scatter over the stonework surface. She tries to scoop the mess into her palm but the kitchen surface is damp and the coffee streaks, reminding her of Jamie's bright blood smearing her floor tiles.

Her breath has become lodged in her chest and she has to force herself to suck it in and blow it out again. *Oh God*, she thinks, *please help me through this.*

The act of making coffee, heating milk and putting it into a jug, and then carrying all this over to the kitchen table feels like an overwhelming, momentous thing. How can she look this woman, Kerry, in the face?

If only Tilly hadn't been here, she could have denied ever having had Jamie visit them. Damn Tilly, she thinks and for a sickening, confusing second she hates her daughter.

Instead, she had pretended to look puzzled and said that, yes, Jamie had visited, but no, she had no idea where he was now.

She wanted to scream – 'Get out! Get out of my house!' – at the woman and her sweet little girl but Tilly was offering coffee and now Melissa is making the coffee and wishing the process took ten times as long as it does so she can think what to do.

216

When she comes to the table, too soon, to lay down cups, pot, and milk she can feel the young woman's eyes fixed hard upon her.

'Lemme see what Amber's up to,' she says in some sort of northern accent and moves to the kitchen door where she shouts the little girl's name.

Melissa and Tilly both wince, as though it were choreographed, and briefly meet eyes. Melissa keeps her expression blank and then watches Kerry as she stands there in her Primark clothes. She has olive, sallow skin and light-brown eyes and could be quite pretty, were it not for that tired patina of poverty and stress Melissa recognizes so well.

She has worked her whole life to scrub that look from her own skin. It offends her now that this person is here, bringing a tsunami of remorse in her wake.

'Aw, she's so cute!' says Tilly as the little girl toddles back into the kitchen. 'How old is she?'

'Five,' says Kerry like the word is a hard, unsavoury pip. 'But it's like she's younger.' All her sentences have this *rat-a-tat* quality. She is nervous and attempting to cloak it with aggression.

Amber becomes shy then and presses herself against her mother's side, turning her face away. She's holding a pale yellow muslin cloth of the kind Melissa remembers from Tilly's baby days. It's wrapped around her hand and as she sneaks her thumb into her mouth, she gently rubs her cheek with the cloth.

'Mind *out*, Amber,' says Kerry grumpily as she reaches for coffee, and then, as though she has been waiting for the right moment, she blurts, 'So are you 100 per cent sure that he didn't say owt about where he was going?'

Melissa pours milk into her coffee and shakes her head, keeping her focus on the cup. 'No, not at all,' she says.

Finally, she forces herself to look up and meet Kerry's eye.

She braces herself against the harshly appraising look and she feels heat creep, treacherously, across her cheeks. Flustered, she

217

lifts her cup and takes a sip of the coffee, which is far too hot and burns her mouth. She wants very much to cry.

'I dunno,' says Kerry gnomically and sits back, lifting her own cup to her lips. She takes a long drink and then continues. 'It's just that he told me he was coming here.'

'Oh?' says Melissa, too distracted to notice the bitterness in this statement. 'Well, Kerry,' she says, 'I'm afraid I can't help you. He did come here and I let him sleep in the spare room because we were having a party that night.' *God*, she thinks, *why am I giving all this detail? She doesn't need to hear that.*

A sudden image of Jamie's muscular back and taut, rounded buttocks as he got up in the middle of the night floods her mind and she forces more unwanted coffee down.

'We talked about the past a little bit and then in the morning he got up and left. And that's really all I know about it.'

The young woman opposite blinks and, to Melissa's total horror, swipes at a tear that brims over her eyelids.

'It's just, Amber's really missing him, and I don't know what to tell her.'

Tilly's head swivels to her mother. She is shocked and not a little entertained by all of this. Amber is wriggling and Melissa gives her daughter a meaningful look, cocking her head slightly towards the door.

'Hey Amber, shall we go and find something to watch on telly?' says Tilly. The little girl unpeels herself and smiles angelically.

'I like *Peppa Pig*,' she says in her flat voice.

Tilly, who had always longed for a younger sister, holds out her hand and Amber takes it easily. They leave the room as both women watch.

'Look, Kerry,' says Melissa in a low voice. 'I'm really sorry that you can't find Jamie but it's really nothing to do with me. I was very surprised that he turned up here and …'

'Were you now?' says Kerry in a hard, accusing tone, swiping angrily at her face.

218

'Well, yes, of course,' says Melissa, confused. 'Why wouldn't I be? I hadn't seen him in years.'

'Yeah but you were dead close as kids, weren't you? That's what he told me, anyway. He reckoned you and him had some kind of *special bond*.'

She emphasizes the last two words and Melissa sees, with a clarity that punches her in the stomach, that this young woman loathes her. Jamie has clearly exaggerated a past that Melissa wanted wiped out of existence, burnishing it with gold.

She swallows, sure that her heartbeat is echoing and booming around the room now. 'I think he has exaggerated things a little bit,' she says, her mouth suddenly dry. 'We were in care together for a relatively short time. I've honestly barely thought about him since.'

Kerry looks up, stung, and Melissa sees that she is only making this worse. She doesn't want Jamie to have been close to Melissa. But for Jamie to have no value in Melissa's life hurts her pride in some complicated way too.

'What I mean is,' she says more gently. 'We knew each other briefly at a very difficult time in my life. Can you understand that I don't really want to revisit that period of my childhood?'

Kerry barks a short, harsh laugh and looks around at Melissa's kitchen. Melissa knows exactly what she is thinking. *Stuck up cow with her four-by-four in the drive and her kitchen that's bigger than my whole flat.* Probably. Something in her hardens. She was once a Kerry. And she's worked for this. She's Melissa now and she's buggered if she's going to sit here and feel guilty. About that, anyway. Her stomach contracts.

Tilly comes back into the room chatting to Amber, who is holding her hand and looking up at her with open interest. Melissa feels herself free-falling. Oh God, that little girl had a daddy. And that daddy is now bloated and dead in a river in Dorset.

Kerry is getting to her feet.

'C'mon, Amb,' she says. 'Time for us to go.'

Amber makes a moaning sound. 'Mummy we stay. Tilly going to show me her room.'

'I said we're going!' snaps Kerry and everyone flinches. The little girl moves to her mother, her eyes downcast.

Tilly looks at Melissa, aghast at the other woman's harsh tone. Melissa makes a movement to indicate that it isn't their business.

She knows what her daughter is thinking but Melissa can see that Amber is a perfectly adequate mother. It's evident in many ways that this little girl is loved and cared for. Kerry is simply a woman who has no power over her circumstances, that's all. Tilly can't begin to imagine what that feels like. Melissa has been on the sharp end of bad mothering, and she knows the difference.

By the time they reach the front door, Melissa is able to be almost upbeat in her hopes that they find Jamie soon and that she is sorry Kerry had a wasted trip. There's a soaring euphoria that they are almost out of her house.

'Hang on a minute.' Kerry roots in her handbag and emerges with a flyer for a hairdresser and beauty salon. She finds a broken Bic biro in the bag and begins to scribble on the paper, the pink triangle of her tongue-tip protruding as she concentrates. 'Here's me number. In case he comes back or summat. All right?'

When Melissa goes gratefully back to the kitchen on trembling legs, Tilly is engaged in a phone conversation in the next room. She probably knows she's in trouble and Melissa intends to have some serious words with that girl, inviting random people into the house. What was she thinking?

Her mind buzzes and hums as she begins to clear up the coffee things with shaking hands. Then she spots something pooled on the floor under the table and lets out a frustrated gasp.

It's the muslin cloth that Amber was holding.

Melissa snatches it up and rushes outside into the garden, then through the back gate into the alley where the bins are kept. She's breathing hard; she can't bear the soft feel of it in her fingers. The little girl's face burns into her mind.

She stops in her tracks when she sees that Hester is coming into the alley from the other direction. Her heartbeat begins to gallop again as she goes to her own bin and stuffs the cloth inside, keeping her head down.

But Hester, it seems, isn't going to be denied a conversation. Melissa dimly registers that the other woman is holding a plastic bag that clinks as she places it into her own bin.

'Did you have a nice visit?' Hester's voice is shrill. She looks windswept and pink-cheeked. Her chocolate-button eyes gleam with a sickly shine. 'Lovely little girl, isn't she? Amber?'

'Uh, yes, I suppose so,' Melissa replies, wary. 'How do you know her?'

'We were chatting through the fence,' says Hester. She comes closer and peers up into Melissa's face, so she has to take a step back. 'You never told me that young man had a family!' Her voice is even shriller now and Melissa glances around nervously, willing her to be quiet. 'What were you thinking, letting him into your house? Leading him on, I shouldn't wonder.'

Melissa can't seem to compute what Hester is talking about. 'What?'

Hester barks an outraged laugh.

'If you hadn't encouraged him,' she says, still loudly, 'then he wouldn't have tried it on with you. That's what I think!'

'Tried it on?' she says, feebly.

'Forced himself on you; whatever you want to call it!'

'Oh God, Hester.' Melissa lets out a weary, mirthless laugh. 'He didn't do that at all.'

'But … you said …' Hester's composure slips for the first time. She presses a hand against her chest, whispers now, 'I thought he tried to *rape* you?'

Melissa closes her eyes for a second, trying to gather strength for this conversation. She can't think any of this mess through while Hester is going on at her. 'I never said that,' she says with quiet weariness. 'You made that assumption.'

Hester blinks rapidly and her face flushes a blotchy red. 'I saw him on your landing that morning, you know,' she says shakily. 'In just his *underpants*. Where had he been sleeping, that's what I want to know? What do you think Tilly and Mark would say if I told them everything? All of it?'

Something ignites inside Melissa and she is suddenly filled with strength. She moves quickly, shoving Hester hard against the rough brick wall. She can feel the precise contour of the other woman's scrawny collarbone under her palm.

'Shut up!' she hisses in a hoarse whisper, looking into wide, frightened eyes. 'You should have let me call the police right at the start! I never wanted your help and now it's too late! And don't you dare speak to my family. Don't you even think about it. Do you understand me?'

Hester gazes melodramatically up at the sky, mouth twisting, blinking repeatedly.

Melissa doesn't wait for an answer. She lets Hester go and stalks back down the alleyway on legs shaking with fury and adrenaline. Just before she turns into her own garden, Hester's cracked voice rings out again, wobbly and elderly sounding.

'You think you're so clever, Melissa? You think it's all over and done with?'

Melissa turns. Her scalp tingles unpleasantly and sweat prickles in her armpits. The alleyway seems to expand and shrink before her.

Hester's lips twitch with pleasure.

'What do you mean?' she hisses but then Tilly's voice rings out from the garden.

'Mum? Where are you?'

Melissa gasps and stumbles back to the garden gate.

HESTER

I sag into myself when she has gone. I can't believe she *assaulted* me!

An odd mixture of emotions swirls in my tummy. I can still feel the warm pressure of her touch and her coffee-edged breath on my cheek. She could have done anything.

As I stand there, gathering myself, something catches my eye. Whatever it was she put into her bin is poking out a little. Curious, despite how shaken I am, I open the lid and peer inside.

A scrumpled wodge of grubby yellow cloth sits on top of the bin bag. For a second I can't work out where I've seen it before. And then I remember. Amber was carrying it.

Smiling a little, I whisk it out and study it. It's soft and well-loved by small hands. I put it to my cheek and inhale the milky sweetness as I think things through.

That pestle isn't going anywhere. I have plenty of time to go to the police. Maybe there are other ways to make Melissa pay for how she has treated me first. Maybe I should be a little more … inventive.

It's fair to say I am not a woman with many skills.

But I can bake. I am very good with small children. And I have an excellent memory.

***

Flat 302, Burnside Estate, N9 2HJ

The address is a tube ride and then a bus journey away, but it could be in another city in some ways. I clutch my handbag a little tighter as the main road narrows, lined now with a cluttered mix of fast food shops with names like Chicken Licken and a host of foreign names (Turkish and Middle Eastern, I think) along with charity shops and a plethora of betting establishments. The people have changed too and the population is much more mixed than in my own neighbourhood. There are more coloured people generally, and a lot of women in scarves and burkas, trailing small children in Western dress.

I get off the bus in what I think is generally the right area, feeling very out of place. I'm not totally sure that I know where I'm going and wish I had remembered to bring my *A to Z*. A little flustered, I go into a newsagent to buy some tissues and ask directions. An old Indian man is serving. His eyes are rheumy and yellow-tinged; his beard grey and thin. I ask him if he knows the way to the Burnside Estate and he just shakes his head as he hands me the change. I am about to leave when a young man, possibly his son, pops up from behind the counter, where he must have been bending down to do something, out of sight. He is wearing a white robe sort of thing and has a beard.

He also has the most beautiful brown eyes, and he flashes a friendly smile at me. 'Burnside you want, love?' he says in perfect Cockney.

'Yes,' I say, surprised at his English. But I suspect he grew up here. It seems a shame he has to dress that way. Why can't people like that integrate?

'Easier to show you, come on,' he says lightly and leads me out of the shop onto the busy pavement.

He gives me a series of simple directions and I thank him before going on my way. I am not completely sure about what I intend to say when I get to Amber's flat. I don't even know if they will be at home. But my feet carry me with a sense of purpose

224

that comforts me after the sensation of floating, untethered, in space ever since Melissa betrayed me.

My nerves almost get the better of me when I approach the estate. There is a scrubby patch of wasteland and a path littered with fast food boxes and dog mess leading to it. The buildings are those 1960s brown and white ones that have long balconies. I can see some makeshift washing lines from here and am suddenly longing for my own private, quiet garden. A young man with aggressively gelled hair approaches with a dog on a metal chain. It's one of those Staffordshire terriers, which I'm not fond of since one bit Bertie. The dog is muscled, powerful-looking, and strains against the lead as though it wants to eat me up.

Scanning the numbers of the flats I see that Amber's is on the third floor of the first building and so, clamping my handbag even tighter to my side, I gamely head for the staircase located at the end of the building.

It smells of urine, and I blanch, holding my breath. I am picturing gangs of youths now, with Mohicans, taking drugs and clogging up the stairwell, and my nerve almost fails me. But I only pass a couple of giggling teenage girls clutching mobile phones and a tired-looking woman about my own age with a shopping basket, who surprises me by smiling and saying 'good morning'. I suppose I shouldn't assume everyone in this place would like to mug me.

The walkway along to Amber's house has an array of rubbish along it, from broken children's bikes to an old pram and uncared for pots choked with weeds. Really, I see no reason not to look after the place you live just because it isn't in the most salubrious part of town. It really doesn't seem like the right sort of place to bring up children, especially ones who have additional health challenges. There are a couple though, which look neat and tidy, with plant pots that contain actual flowers.

But when I get to flat number 302, I am not at all surprised to see that the front door could do with a lick of paint. My heart is thumping as I press my thumb to the doorbell, hearing the sharp ring inside the flat. I wait for a few moments, and, nothing happening, I try again. It's no use. No one is in.

Feeling rather like the withered balloons that hang from the letterbox on the house next door, presumably detritus from a long passed party, I turn to trudge my way home again. And then I see two figures coming towards me and my insides jolt.

'Bertie?' says the little girl in her flat voice. It is in marked contrast to the beatific smile that almost splits her face in two.

The pinch-faced woman scans me up and down as she approaches, brandishing keys. 'What are you doing here?' she says.

I take a deep breath and try to hide the nervous wobble in my voice as I reach into my bag for the cloth. Amber squeals when she sees it.

'Mummy! It's my cuddly!'

'You dropped it in my street,' I say gently and then, to her mother. 'Look, I've come to talk to you about Jamie. And, and … about Melissa.'

'Oh, have you now.' Her expression hardens further and her cheeks pink as she wordlessly gestures for me to go inside.

The flat is tidy but strangely cold. There's an ugly black stain of damp behind the enormous television. I've never understood why people with very little money have the need for expensive electronics, but there we are.

I perch on a battered sofa so low my knees sag to the side and glance around at my surroundings. The sitting room is small, with a nylon carpet like something you might find in one of the more run-down doctor's surgeries, and there are a couple of flowery prints in frames on the wall. Glancing around, I jolt at the large framed photograph of mother, child, and … father, all tumbling together and laughing in a photographer's studio.

I won't look at it.

The woman, who reluctantly told me her name is Kerry when I offered mine, would no doubt have simply interrogated me on the doorstep. But little Amber, mistress of her domain, almost dragged me into the flat before her mother could protest. She claimed she wanted to show me what sounded like 'Doggie and Uncle Dave'. I think I may have misheard.

Kerry offers me tea in a flat tone, eyes as dead as a shark's. I accept and try to concentrate on what I intend to say. This seemed like an excellent plan when I initially thought of it. I liked the idea of Melissa's face encountering those false nails. Hell hath no fury, and all that. But I feel rather out of my element in this council flat.

Doggie turns out to be exactly that, a Hush Puppy toy that has been loved into a state of greasy, limp submission. The other toy thrust at me by an eager Amber appears to be, as I believed I'd heard, called 'Uncle Dave'. It's a strange sort of clown toy. Amber is telling me something in a garbled stream of consciousness that I can't follow when Kerry comes into the room holding two mugs of tea. She places them none too gently on a low coffee table next to a couple of hair scrunchies and an ashtray with a single squashed butt.

She hasn't brought milk separately. I only take the smallest splash in a cup (Earl Grey, preferably) brewed very strong. I stare a little queasily at the beige liquid in the chipped mug.

'She calls it that because we once joked its hair was like our Dave's,' says Kerry now, jutting her chin at the ragged headed toy I'm pretending to admire. As if I'm meant to know who 'Our Dave' is without explanation.

'Oh,' I say with a polite smile. I can't think of a suitable response and force myself to sip the tea. I think I may have grimaced involuntarily because, when I meet Kerry's eye, she is looking at me with an expression of disapproval.

She takes a savage sip of her own tea and then bangs it down with a heavy sigh before fumbling in the pocket of her sweatshirt.

'Hey, Amb. Go play in your room while Mummy has a cig.'

The little girl gets up and obediently carries the toys towards the small hallway. Honestly! Surely the adult should smoke outside! But I bite my tongue.

Kerry lights up and I force myself not to waft the sickly smell away with my hand.

'Come on then,' she says, blowing out a thin stream of smoke and closing one eye. Her accent makes me think of *Coronation Street*, pies, and fog. 'Tell me the worst.'

'Well …' Being in control for once tastes cool and sweet on my tongue, like melting ice cream. 'I happen to know that your chap stayed the night at her house. And that they were, I'm sorry dear, but they were, well … intimate.'

Kerry's face folds inwards. 'I knew it. Fucking bastard!' she says. 'Where'd he go then? After?' She blinks hard, several times and I can see she is struggling not to cry in front of me. A shiver of sympathy passes through me, despite it all.

'That I don't know,' I say and clear my throat. 'Maybe you should go and see her again. Really have it out with her and clear the air? After that you can try and move on. For Amber's sake?'

I think this is rather a good little speech, if I say so myself, so it's a surprise when Kerry barks a bitter, contemptuous laugh.

'Oh yeah?' she says. 'You do, do you, Mrs Helpful? You have no fucking idea.'

I don't see any reason for her to be so rude when I am trying to help. 'No idea about what?'

'What it's like!' she says, 'Living in this *shit*hole. He told me he had something on that was going to change everything for us. We had big plans.' Her voice skids at the end of the sentence and she swipes furiously at her face, as though trying to push away the weakness.

Amber saves me from finding something to say by bustling back into the room.

'Mummy finish ciggie,' she says and Kerry, to my surprise, stubs it out.

She is probably much younger than she looks, and I try to picture her at Tilly's age. Did she have the dreams of any young person? Or had her upbringing prepared her for a different, more mundane life?

'I come visit Bertie,' says Amber, pressing her hot, compact body up against my left side and staring at me intently. I turn my face to look at her mother, and Amber grasps my chin and directs my eyes back to her own. It's impossible not to laugh at this sweet, bossy gesture.

'Who's this Bertie, then?' says Kerry, obviously trying to force a friendlier tone into her voice.

'He's my little dog,' I say. 'Amber played with him through the fence.'

'Ah, right,' says Kerry, 'she's mad about her nanna's dog. And she told you the address too, right? She does that. I keep telling her.'

'Yes,' I smile kindly and then give Amber my attention once again.

'You can come anytime you like,' I say.

'Come today,' says Amber. 'Come see Bertie now.'

I laugh, surprised, and Kerry gives an impatient shake of her head.

'Amb, leave it,' she says. 'The lady's too busy.'

I pause. 'Actually, I'm not really busy. I'd be very happy to look after Amber for a few hours to give you a break.'

Kerry tuts. 'I don't even know you!' But her voice betrays weakness.

I nod, trying not to let my excitement show. 'That's true. But I worked in a nursery for many years and I still have an up-to-date CRB certificate.'

This last part is a slight exaggeration. I don't even think they call them that now. But maybe I can help to make things right for this little girl. 'You know where I live. And you look to me like someone who deserves a bit of a break, if you don't mind me saying.'

Have I gone too far?

But Kerry, fraught and exhausted as she clearly is, hesitates just long enough to leave a crack of doubt.

'Pleeeeeeease, Mummy!' whines Amber, almost shouting now and tugging on her mother's sweatshirt so it gapes at the shoulder and reveals a grubby grey bra strap. 'Let me go see Bertie!'

And so it is that, ten minutes later, I am escorting the little girl and her 'cuddly' down the dark stairwell and into the light.

MELISSA

'You don't invite just anyone into the house! What's wrong with you?'

Melissa's raised voice echoes around the kitchen. Tilly stares at her with a shocked, dropped bottom lip. Melissa is aware her daughter is a bit scared of her mad mother but is unable to stop.

'But she knows Jamie,' says Tilly, her voice wobbling. 'And she has a little girl. What harm could it do, letting them come in? Mum!'

Melissa starts to bang and clatter mugs and milk jugs at the sink and when one of the fine china mugs cracks, cutting the meat of her palm, she throws it into the sink viciously so it smashes. She bursts into tears.

Tilly comes over and awkwardly puts an arm around her mother's heaving shoulders. 'What is it? What's wrong? Why are you so upset?'

Melissa cries a little harder. An image comes into her head so seductive she almost gives into it.

She pictures herself turning to her daughter and telling her everything.

All of it. Sex with Jamie. Disposing of the body. The madness of Hester. All of it. And Tilly would say, 'No, really? It's not your fault. Any of it. I love you, Mum. It will be okay,' as though it is no big deal, disposing of a man's body in a river.

As her tears subside, Tilly hands her a piece of kitchen towel for her cut hand and she is at last able to speak.

'I'm sorry, sweetie,' she says thickly. 'It's just that him turning up here brought up a lot of bad memories for me. You know I didn't have a childhood like yours. I didn't want to see him and I was really glad when I got—' She was about to say 'got rid of him' and panic flares. 'When he went away again. I just wish he'd never come here.'

Tilly pats her arm in a clumsy, well-meaning attempt at comfort. 'It's okay, Mum, I understand,' she says, although it is clear to Melissa that she doesn't, not at all. And how could she?

Melissa blows her nose loudly and manages a watery smile. 'Why don't you go and watch some telly,' she says. 'I'd like to get on with cooking.'

'Okay,' says Tilly with clear relief. 'Er, Mum?'

Melissa turns to her, distracted.

'I promise I'm not seeing Nathan,' says Tilly hurriedly. 'But I really need to get something off Chloe. Can I go if I promise to be back for dinner?'

Melissa nods wearily. She doesn't care anymore.

Tilly starts to leave the room before Melissa calls her back.

'Oh and Tils?'

She turns to face her mother, a question on her face.

'Can we not mention any of this to your dad? I just want this evening to be a special family time.'

Tilly frowns doubtfully but nods. Melissa hears the front door closing a few minutes later.

She begins to collect the broken pieces of china and put them into a carrier bag. Her chest feels tight and her head has begun to throb. The lighter feeling she'd had while food shopping earlier feels impossible to recapture now. How can she have been so naive to think this was over? That there were no consequences?

232

Her mind throbs with questions. Was Hester trying to frighten her with the things she said? What does she mean about it not being over? Has Jamie's body turned up?

Chills finger their way up Melissa's arms and she rubs them savagely in an attempt to get her blood circulating. She's so cold. Her lips feels numb, bloodless. As she walks to the sink for water, the doorbell rings.

She heads into the hallway, assuming Tilly has forgotten her keys again, but she can see the outline of two people through the glass door. The doorbell rings, once, twice. Her heart slams against her ribcage again. Something Laurie, the English lecturer in her distant past, used to say comes to her, unbidden. *What fresh hell is this?* The doorbell rings a third time but still she can't move.

Then the letterbox snaps open. Melissa gasps and covers her mouth with her hands. A man's eyes peer through at her.

'Hello? Can you open up? We just want a little word with you.'

Melissa creeps to the front door. Her hands shake as she slots the chain into place before opening it and peering out.

A man and a woman stand on her doorstep. Her childhood radar kicks in and she knows what they are even before the man simultaneously flashes both badge and friendly smile.

He conforms to the cliché perfectly by looking about sixteen, with his fresh face and spiky gelled hair, like some sort of junior estate agent. His suit looks like it was bought for him by his mum. The woman is a little older. Short and pretty, with black hair in a severe bun and intense brown eyes that fix upon Melissa.

'Sorry to bother you, Mrs Fielding,' says the male one. 'It's nothing to worry about at all. Just a routine enquiry. I'm Detective Constable Steve Milner and this is DC Khadijah Abdul. Would it be okay to come in for a moment?'

Melissa can't gather enough saliva to speak. She only manages an awkward sort of cough-laugh as she ushers them over the threshold.

'Sorry!' She lifts her hand to her face, aware of how blotchy she looks. 'I've got hay fever and I was, um, upstairs sneezing my head off. Do come in. Can I ask what this is about?'

Why is she speaking in that high-pitched voice? She broadens her smile as they come into the hallway. She has already forgotten their names. The man watches her with interest. The other one still hasn't opened her mouth. Melissa's question hangs in the air, unanswered.

'Come through, come through!' says Melissa now, unable to control her excessive bonhomie as she gestures for them to walk ahead.

'Can I offer you something to drink?' she says when all three reach the bright, sunny kitchen. *Please say no.*

'That would be lovely. It's a long drive from Dorset,' says the man cheerfully, his voice soft with a West Country burr.

Dorset, Dorset. *Oh God.*

'Tea? Coffee?' It's so hard not to sound shrill and demented. She breathes out through her nose slowly, trying to calm down. 'Sorry, I didn't quite catch your names ...'

'Tea, please. And it's DC Milner.'

'DC Abdul, and the same for me, thanks.' Tiny moles are scattered across her cheeks. Her eyes haven't left Melissa since she opened the door.

Melissa goes to make the tea. With her back to them she says, 'So what is this all about?'

'It's about a young man called Jamie Cox,' says Milner. 'I gather he's an old friend?'

Melissa's stomach twists and dips. How do they *know?* It's over. Is it?

'I wouldn't say that, exactly!' she says with a bright, shrill laugh. 'Why would you think so?'

The kettle has boiled; everything is ready. She can't find any more reasons not to sit down so she does, forcing her gaze to meet theirs.

'He told his Probation Officer all about you,' says Milner,

spooning sugar into his tea and stirring. The sound makes Melissa's teeth ache and reverberates inside her skull. She forces unwanted black tea past her lips and down her throat, nodding foolishly to buy time.

'He told her all about how he was friends with someone off the telly. Or at least, their wife.' He pauses and smiles. 'We like that programme, don't we Khadijah? Remember the couple who had the little boy even though the dad was dying of cancer?'

DS Abdul smiles for the first time. 'That was great, that one. Made me cry.'

I highly doubt that, thinks Melissa. 'Look, why are you here? What's happened to Jamie?'

The two police officers regard her. The cheery vibe has dissipated now. 'That's the thing,' says Milner. 'I'm afraid something *has* happened to him. His body was fished out of a river in Dorset yesterday.'

Melissa puts her hands to her mouth and widens her eyes. Is it too much? Or too little? How should she react?

'That's terrible,' she says, taking another mouthful of tea and forcing it down. 'Was it suicide then?' This is a good question, she thinks. The right one.

'No, we don't think so.' Milner doesn't elaborate. He takes an audible mouthful of tea and shifts position. 'The thing is, we were able to triangulate where his phone was last used and could narrow it down to this street. And what with his boasting about celebrity friends ...' He makes air speech marks at these last two words. 'We were thinking you might have been among the last people to see him alive.'

Melissa nods, buying time, and places her cup carefully on the table. 'Well, I'm very sad to hear that this has happened. But we weren't in any way friends. Jamie and I were in care together as teenagers. I hadn't seen him for twenty odd years until he turned up a couple of weeks ago.' It's starting to feel like a well-worn script.

'What did he want then?' says Abdul, scrutinizing her over the rim of her cup.

'He wanted money,' says Melissa bluntly. No point in pretending otherwise now.

'And did you give him some? Money?' Melissa is sure no double entendre was intended by Milner's open expression, but heat creeps up her cheeks anyway.

'Yes,' she says and meets his eye directly. 'I gave him a hundred pounds and told him to sling his hook. I don't really want my husband to know I did this. He might not understand. I just wanted to get rid of him, you see.' She instantly regrets the words and, flustered again, looks down at the table.

'Did he say where he was going next?' says Milner, saving her.

'I'm afraid not. I wish I could help further.' *Please just go …*

Milner fixes her with a sympathetic smile. 'Well, we will need you to pop down to the station to give us a statement to this effect, I'm afraid.'

Melissa keeps her expression impassive as the walls pulse around her. In this moment she understands that, despite everything she has been through, she hasn't really been tested until now.

Burying her face in her hands, she begins to cry softly. It isn't very difficult to do.

She can feel the police officers' gaze sitting heavily upon her and when she raises her head, she attempts a watery laugh of embarrassment.

'I'm sorry,' she says. 'It just sort of hit me then that he was here *in my house* and now he's dead. God knows I didn't want him here, but he didn't deserve this, did he?' She pauses and hunts for a tissue in her pocket. Dabbing her eyes, she says, 'I wish I'd helped him more. I just wanted him to go away.'

'Look,' says Milner kindly, 'sometimes these things happen, particularly when people keep the sort of company he did, if you see what I mean.'

Melissa's heart jolts at these encouraging words but she nods and lowers her eyes.

'Well …' With a sigh, Milner gets to his feet. 'You can come down to the station and give us a statement any time in the next few days,' he continues and rummages in a pocket for a card, which he deposits on the table. 'If you think of anything at all, can you give us a call? Any time.'

'I will,' she says, relief beginning to trickle through her. 'I hope you have a good drive back.'

'We have to go and see his partner first,' says Abdul. 'You were first on the route from the motorway, you see.' She pauses. 'They have a little girl.'

Melissa swallows. 'Oh no. That's … that's very sad. He never said.'

A few minutes later she closes the door and leans against the hallway wall. The shocks keep coming today, like billiard balls smashing into one another.

Even though she'd sworn to herself that she wouldn't do this again, she stumbles to the kitchen and pulls open the drawer. Greedily sucking on the cigarette by the back door, Melissa tries to rationalize what just took place. What is Kerry going to say to them?

But the police already know Jamie was here. That doesn't mean they know any more than that, does it? No one can know that, beyond her and Hester.

She thinks about what Milner said.

Sometimes these things happen, particularly when people keep the sort of company he did. This is a good thing. This means there may be any number of suspects in his murder.

It will be all right.

She will go down to the station in the next few days and make a statement, saying exactly what she told the two police officers.

237

Shuddering, Melissa forces her feet to move towards the fridge. She has to get a grip. She will get on with the cooking. Tonight she will have a lovely meal with Mark and Tilly. It will all be okay.

HESTER

After a lovely session in the park, feeding ducks and playing on the swings, I ask Amber if she is hungry. She nods so vigorously I fear she will hurt her neck but her eagerness makes me chuckle. She is the sweetest little angel. I keep imagining what it would be like if she were mine.

I decide to take her to one of the cafés in the High Street that I usually avoid. It's always filled with women whose small children climb all over the chairs and beg their mothers to pay them attention as they text on their mobiles and gossip with each other. I do often wonder why some people bother having babies at all when they have so little time for them.

I wish I had more time with Amber. I'm acutely aware of the afternoon ticking by and slipping away. But maybe this could be a regular thing? It doesn't look as though Kerry can manage as a single parent. I won't want her to pay me and I doubt she could anyway ...

I'm musing on all this as we make our way to the café; Amber's soft, slightly sticky little paw in mine.

We're just about to open the door when I hear someone say, 'Hester? Is that you?'

Oh no.

That Binnie woman from the computer course is standing behind me. Her face is tanned and leathery-looking, as though she's been somewhere hot. She jabs me with her curious looks and, as she runs a fat tongue over her lips, I have the oddest instinct that I must keep Amber away. I gently nudge the child closer to me.

'Yes, hello, Binnie,' I say with a sigh. 'It is me, obviously.'

She laughs as though I have made a joke.

'This must be the grandchild you mentioned! Hello sweetie?' She bends over a bit and beams at Amber.

To my immense gratification, Amber shies away and hides her face. I have to contract my cheeks to stop myself from beaming.

Binnie frowns. 'Oh dear,' she says, cheeks darkening further. 'It must be very hard. I take my hat off to you, Hester, I really do.'

'I beg your pardon?' I say frostily.

'Well …' Binnie fusses with her scarf and her eyes go all skittery. 'I can see that she is … well, special. It can't be easy.'

I have to breathe deeply in and out a few times before speaking.

'She certainly *is* special,' I say. 'She's a very special and sweet little girl. Now I really must get on.'

And with that, I bundle Amber into the café, leaving Binnie standing outside.

When we are seated a young woman with a cheerful smile grins at Amber and asks what she would like to eat and drink. Amber responds with 'cake' and 'milkshake' and, after a little further coaxing for specifics, the waitress bustles off.

I must confess to needing a bit of a sit-down. I hadn't realized quite how tiring it would be, looking after a five-year-old. I suppose I am a little out of practice since my days at the nursery.

I am having tea and a bun. Amber tucks messily into her chocolate cake and strawberry milkshake. Perhaps I should have gone for something a little healthier, but isn't that what they say about grannies? That they spoil their grandchildren in the way they never did with the parents?

I stir my tea absent-mindedly, thinking about the awful prospect of taking Amber home. What if Kerry won't let me see her again?

'What you doing, Hester?'

Amber's fluting little voice brings me back to the room, and I look down to discover that I have been pulling the bun into tiny pieces that cover my half of the table in sticky crumbs.

'Messy Hester,' says Amber sternly.

The sound coming from my bag now is so unfamiliar it takes me a moment to register what is happening.

'Is it my mummy calling? Is it my nanna Phyllis?'

'Oh, yes, I'd better …'

I'd given Kerry the number. Had to. She'd insisted. I scowl at the phone now as I see the words 'Unknown Number' flashing up and I somehow know it's her. Who else would be ringing? With a sigh I hold it to my ear.

I can't work out what she's saying at first, her words are so garbled. Then I realize she's crying noisily. I make out 'Jamie' and 'Can't believe it', before she descends into a loud, snotty, nose-blow. Glancing quickly at Amber I get up, mouthing, 'Can't hear! Back in a minute!' cheerfully before hurrying to the door of the café. This isn't a conversation a child needs to hear.

'What is it, Kerry, what's wrong?' I say once I am outside.

Here we go …

I turn back to see Amber twisting in her seat to look. I only have a few moments before she follows me out here.

'It's Jamie!' wails Kerry. 'He's dead! They found him in a river! What am I going to do? How can I tell Amber?'

'Oh dear, dear,' I soothe, 'how dreadful! You poor thing!'

She goes on for a while longer, as I look anxiously back into the café. The waitress is bending down and speaking to Amber

241

now. I make the right noises for a while then interrupt her, trying not to sound impatient.

'Look, why don't you let me have her for a few more hours until you get yourself together? Can someone come and sit with you?'

She tells me her mother is coming from Manchester on a coach that will get in the following morning. Maybe this is the granny that Amber mentioned before; the one with a dog. I continue, 'It won't be good for Amber to see her mummy so upset, will it? Why don't I bring her back in the morning when you've had a proper sleep and time to calm down?'

She protests, but weakly. I almost can't believe it when she agrees. What kind of mother is she to let her little girl go off with a stranger?

I gaze back through the steamy window of the café and see that Amber is now making her way to the door, her face scrunched with imminent tears.

I hurry back in towards her.

'Guess what!' I say, bending down so I am at her height. 'Mummy says we can go to the toy shop and then you can come and spend a whole night with Bertie! What do you think about that?'

She regards me suspiciously for a few moments then slips her hand into mine. 'Toy shop now,' she orders.

'Your wish is my command,' I say, joy expanding in my chest. I almost want to thank Melissa for this gift. Maybe it was part of a grand plan all along. Who am I to say?

MELISSA

The percussion of cutlery against plate, glass against tabletop, fork against teeth crashes against Melissa's eardrums.

The world seems to be entirely composed of sound. Tilly sniffs repeatedly and Mark gives little satisfied 'Mmms', as though the lamb *isn't* grey and acrid, the vegetables shrivelled and tasteless. She feels a powerful urge to throw her empty wine glass across the room and start screaming until her throat bleeds.

Instead, she gets up from the table, aware that Mark and Tilly are both watching her, and retrieves the bottle of Sauvignon Blanc from the fridge. There isn't that much left so she decides to finish the bottle.

'You're knocking it back tonight, sweetheart,' says Mark, gently.

A wave of something close to hatred washes over Melissa. Look at him, she thinks, sitting there in his neat pink polo shirt, so innocent and uncomplicated. Everything has come easy to him, all his life. His parents live in Staffordshire in a nice Victorian house. They play golf and garden and gently bicker with each other in a way that reveals how besotted they remain after forty years of marriage. Nothing has ever come easy to Melissa. Nothing …

But she can't concentrate on any one train of thought right

now. Questions crowd in, demanding attention. How long before the police come back? Maybe she should just come clean. Tell them all about Hester's role in things. But will they believe her?

Tilly clears her throat. 'That was … great, Mum. Is it okay if I go and watch telly? Or shall I wash up?'

Her plate is still half-full and she has rearranged the meat and vegetables as she did as a small child, trying to hide the gaps. Tilly almost never offers to wash up. It's funny. Almost.

'Fine,' says Melissa wearily.

Tilly hurries from the table with her plate, projecting relief from every pore, before emptying the contents into the bin. Each scrape of the fork echoes inside Melissa's skull like a bright blow.

She takes another deep pull of the wine. It's sharp and good, despite the sickly headache forming over her right eye. Maybe she is getting the hangover early, before she has even been allowed to get properly drunk. The wine isn't working tonight. And both Tilly and Mark know something is seriously wrong and she can't seem to do anything about it.

Images keep flashing across the surface of her mind but she can't remember any real light that morning. Hester's face turning to her and saying, 'I bet it's a lovely spot in the daytime.' The silver peaks of the churning water and the dead pallor of Jamie's skin. All of it in shadow.

She is barely aware of Mark's presence until his voice cuts into her thoughts.

'How much longer, Melissa?' His voice is hoarse and when she turns, bewildered, to look at him, she sees her husband's eyes shine with emotion.

'How much longer, what?' she says. 'What are you talking about?'

Mark screeches his chair back over the tiles, making Melissa wince, then rests his elbows on the table. He presses his face into his hands so that his words are muffled when they come.

'How much longer will you go on punishing me?'

His shoulders start to shake and it seems to take a disproportionate amount of time for Melissa to understand that he is … *crying?*

She has only seen him cry once before, when Tilly was tiny and had to go to hospital with a serious attack of croup. All medical training deserted him as their baby daughter barked and struggled for breath and it struck Melissa, as it would many times over the years, that he simply wasn't as tough as she was. He was somehow made of weaker materials.

She can't think of what she should say or do now and simply watches him until he gets up to hunt for kitchen roll. Tearing off two sheets, he blows his nose loudly and blinks at her. His eyes are puffy and his nose crimson around the nostrils.

She swallows.

'I'm not punishing you,' she says quietly, moving to the kitchen door and pressing it closed in an attempt to seal this conversation inside the room, away from Tilly's ears. 'Why do you think that?'

Mark laughs humourlessly.

'Oh come on, Melissa,' he says. 'For fuck's sake! You're like a walking zombie. Look at you! You've cut all your hair off. You barely look at me. Tilly might as well be a lodger for all the attention you pay her.' He pauses. 'And I know all about that ex-boyfriend. I've got a pretty good idea what happened at that party.'

Frigid shock explodes in her stomach and her hands start to shake so hard she has to press them to the table as she sits down.

Mark regards her and then laughs again, equally without mirth.

'Tilly told me all about him staying the night. And your reaction now pretty much confirms everything I thought.'

Melissa stares at the table. She clenches her hands together until her knuckles whiten. The weight of Mark's gaze upon her feels intolerably heavy.

'I get it, okay?' he says and his voice cracks again.

She looks up at him, sharply. It is only now that she notices the puffiness of his face. His hair needs a cut and he looks his age for the first time she can remember. 'I don't blame you, after what I did. I just don't want you to leave me. To leave us.'

He bends his head and he starts to cry again. Melissa stares at him and feels something rupture inside her. She loves this man. He used to make her laugh so hard she couldn't breathe. He felt like the only home she'd ever had once. He didn't know everything about her, but he knew enough and he still loved her.

He looks up now, his face twisted by grief. 'I promise you, it was the only time I've ever done anything like that. It's the last too. I'm going to leave the programme. I've had enough of it. All I do is work and work and in the meantime my family is—' He gives a sob and doesn't finish his sentence.

Melissa is up and around the table, where she takes hold of his hands and pulls him until they are standing. They clutch each other, both crying now until they hear the kitchen door open and then close again, softly.

'Mark,' says Melissa thickly after a few moments. 'There's something I have to tell you. Something else.'

She can't tell him everything. Not about the biggest thing. But keeping the toxic burden of her past inside is what started it all.

It's time to let it out.

She'd had a stupid, jealous tantrum. That was the worst thing. The temper constantly smouldering inside during her years in care was largely under control these days.

But she hadn't slept properly for a while and her nerve endings were zinging with the wrong kind of energy.

Sticky summer heat and a constant topping up of vodka and weed over the weekend had muddied her thoughts and spiked her mood. When Jez suggested going to the party in Holloway, she should have said no. But she never said no anymore. And she was starting to trust him. He had been all over her when he first moved into the squat, this private school boy who liked to party and whose hands and body had made her finally get the whole sex thing.

So they'd gone to the party, and as she drank and then took the E offered by God knows who, the evening started to take on a sinister feel. Flashcards of scenes made her head spin and her stomach roil:

Jez dancing with a tiny blonde-haired girl dressed in a striped dress.

Jez kissing the girl, her arms wrapped around his neck, and their faces grinding together.

Music, so loud, and everyone laughing.

There was no air.

She'd stumbled outside and seen the car parked there, keys in the ignition. It felt like a sign. A benediction.

Later, she discovered that the owner was simply helping his elderly mother through her front door. But Melanie had so badly wanted to go home. To get to the squat and pull her duvet over her head until it all went away.

As she had roared down the road and turned into the next one, she had been aware of the thump of something against the car. When the police car pulled her over, less than ten minutes later, she had pitifully pretended she didn't know she'd hit someone. But it was a lie.

He didn't die. But for a time, it looked as though he might.

'He's called Thomas Pinkerton,' she says now, keeping her head dipped and her voice low. 'He was a student on his way back from the pub. He lost … lost a leg and was in a coma, but he survived.' She sucks in a drag of air audibly and then begins to speak too fast. 'I sometimes look him up online and I see that he has a good life now. He has kids! He works for a charity. He hasn't made his Facebook profile private. They were on holiday in the Seychelles the last time I checked.'

Shame burns brighter and harder. Why is she telling him that? As if it makes everything okay; the act itself. The lies since.

Mark lets out a long hiss of air. 'Jesus,' he says at last.

Melissa knows she has to press on through to the end, however bitter the taste in her mouth right now. She can't bear to look up and see disgust in Mark's eyes.

'And I got six months in Holloway,' she says quietly. 'I don't want to talk about that. I did it and it's over. But you must understand why I could never tell you. Why I don't want to share your limelight.'

His silence is so absolute she looks up at last.

He is staring down at the table, his expression stony.

'Mark?' she says as fear begins to flicker inside her. 'Can't you say anything?'

He gets up from the table.

'I'm glad you told me,' he says quietly. 'But I don't know what to say. I don't feel like I know who you are.'

'Okay,' she replies in a tiny voice.

He holds the sides of his head and then lets out a strange barking laugh.

'Christ! I need ...', he swallows. His eyes are wide. 'I need to think. I'm taking Tilly and going to see my parents,' he says in a harder tone. 'Maybe we both need some thinking time.'

He doesn't look at her as he walks out of the kitchen, his head down.

HESTER

All my kitchen surfaces are covered in a floury residue and the floor is gritty with sugar.

I don't want to wake Amber by hoovering though, so I must make do with dustpan and brush.

I never expected to have that little girl sleeping here, yet there she is, curled up on my bed in her new jammies, with the dragon toy she has named, 'Toofless', for some reason, clutched against her rosy, hot cheek. She cried a little bit and asked for Mummy but I reassured her that all was well and that Mummy would see her soon.

It did take a lot of cajoling, and only the promise that she could bathe Bertie tomorrow and tie ribbons around his ears eventually calmed her enough to sleep. I can't imagine what Bertie will make of this indignity but hopefully she will have forgotten all about it come the morning.

Once the kitchen is back in some semblance of order, I look around with an appraising eye.

I'm quite exhausted, but I want everything to be tidy.

I still can't really believe Amber is sleeping upstairs.

All I can think is that my prayers have been answered, after all these years. I waited for a very long time, but finally it is *my* time. I can do the things I've always longed to do.

When the kitchen is spick and span I unwrap the bright blue plastic bowl that I picked up in Asda and give it a good wash in hot soapy water. In the morning I will make porridge and scatter blueberries on the top for Amber's breakfast.

There were too many cakes and sugary treats today, but that's only because it was a special kind of holiday. Tomorrow will be healthier.

We have such an exciting day ahead of us. I can hardly wait for the morning to come around!

The idea came to me on the bus as I bore Amber's sweet weight against my arm.

Kerry clearly isn't fit to be a mother and, even if she has good intentions, it isn't a healthy environment for a small child, what with the damp and the smoking. I am doing her a service. Maybe she won't even bother to come looking for us. It's the right thing to do. I feel it deep in my bones.

It is a long time since I have used the old computer in what was Terry's office but once I finally got online, I was able to find what I was looking for quickly enough.

All those years when we visited Carbis Bay, Terry and I, I felt as though there was someone missing. What fun is there, sitting on a beach without a child to make sandcastles with, or to splash with in the waves? He would suggest playing Crazy Golf or going on a boat trip and it made me want to brain him. Couldn't he see how pointless and banal it all was?

Anyway, the Four Keys Guesthouse looks so pretty, with its blue and white nautical banner. They told me they had plenty of rooms free and they looked forward to greeting me and my granddaughter some time tomorrow afternoon.

I used my maiden name, Strickland, and, although I don't have a bank card with that name on it, I do have my old passport. I am going to claim that my handbag has recently been stolen; I am much bolder about this sort of thing than I was just a couple of weeks ago.

I drew out £2,000 from the bank on the way home earlier and that should keep us in fish and chip suppers and buckets and spades for at least a short amount of time. After that ... well.

We'll cross that bridge when we come to it.

Amber is star-fished across my bed when I finally get upstairs. Bertie has snuck in so he is lying by one of her outstretched arms. I am filled with love as I look at them – my little family! – and will suffer any amount of discomfort in order not to disturb their innocent slumber.

She enjoyed her pre-bedtime Ovaltine (a drink I loved as a girl), and I don't think there was any bitter aftertaste to it at all. She actually smacked her lips, in fact.

I have a stockpile of medicines from Terry's last few months and, although I have never resorted to sleeping medication myself (it gives me severe indigestion), I don't think there is any harm in helping a little girl who has had a very long and exciting day to sleep peacefully. No doubt the political correctness brigade – like that Irena at the nursery – would disapprove. But well, they're not here to question my choices, are they?

Taking a spare eiderdown and pillow carefully from the top of my wardrobe, I try to make myself as comfortable as I can on the floor next to the bed. I think it may be a long night but I want to get as much sleep as I can before the long journey tomorrow I am not in the slightest bit nervous about the drive this time. I know that I am capable of a great deal more than perhaps people give me credit for.

As I lie here, I try to climb inside the cuddle of my own childhood memories. Sunday afternoons with *Family Favourites* on the radio; the Laughing Policeman always made Mum quite giddy with giggling. Roast dinners in the winter and picnics on the Heath in the summer. Those boiled eggs with a twist of salt in silver foil; I've never been able to replicate the taste.

They said I was their 'little miracle', coming as I did when they were both in their forties.

So why couldn't I have had the same?

And now he's here again, Terry, invading my thoughts. I seem to fall into the memory more and more these days.

Amber snores in her sleep – a surprisingly loud gust of sound for such a small girl. A smile curls at my lips and around my heart.

Tomorrow will be a fresh start.

MELISSA

Sleep had come, swallowing her into a black, dreamless void at about 4 a.m.. She is still on the sofa, fully dressed. Her back and shoulders ache. She is chilled and her mouth feels fuzzy and foul from a half-bottle of vodka.

Tilly had refused to pack her things at first when Mark demanded it. But it wasn't out of loyalty to her mother. It transpired it was more to do with a cinema arrangement she'd made with friends for the next day. Then Mark had started bellowing in a way she had never experienced before. Visibly stunned, Tilly had hurriedly thrown some clothes into a bag.

Melissa hid in the upstairs bathroom until they had gone. She was too shocked to cry.

This was it, then.

The thing she had always dreaded. Letting it all out was a huge mistake after all.

She'd spent the evening getting drunk in front of the television and now, as she stretched her aching body, the awful parallel hit her with the force of a fist smashing into her stomach.

Falling asleep, drunk, on the sofa.

Like mother, like daughter?

Melissa runs to the shower and washes herself until her skin is raw and pink. Trembling, shaky, and still breathing vodka fumes, she forces coffee and breakfast down but not before she's poured the last of the Stolichnaya down the sink.

Now she's in the hallway, holding the flyer that came from Kerry's cheap Primark handbag. With shaking fingers, she taps the number onto the screen of her mobile.

It's answered straight away.

'Yes, what is it?' the gravelly northern voice isn't Kerry's. It's someone older.

'I need ...' she says and then clears her throat. 'Is Kerry there please?'

'This is her mother,' says the woman. 'She's very upset. She can't talk. She's just had a tragedy.'

'Um, yes ... I know,' Melissa swallows. 'But can you tell her it's ... Melissa?'

There are muffled background voices and then Kerry's voice rings out clear in her ear.

'What the fuck do you want? Do you know what's happened? Do you?'

Melissa closes her eyes in an attempt to absorb the hostility blasting from the earpiece.

'Yes, the police asked me some questions. Kerry, I ...' What can she say? What can she possibly do to make anything better? 'Look,' she continues, 'I just wanted to know if I could help. You know, with the cost of things ...' Her voice peters out, small and inadequate. She feels ashamed in so many different ways.

Kerry laughs aggressively. 'Yes you can, lady! Because if you had helped him out, then he'd have been able to pay his debts and this wouldn't have happened. Daft bugger. Always making enemies.' She breaks off into a sob and the phone is once more handed back to her mother.

Melissa feels more alert now. Enemies? That makes sense.

Maybe the blackmail attempt wasn't just about greed, but self-preservation too? Guilt corkscrews deeper into her guts.

'So Kerry says your neighbour is minding our Amber,' the mother is saying. 'One or other of you can bring her back now. She needs her mum and her nanna.'

At first she can't make sense of the words. Hester has Amber? Why?

She manages to squeak, 'I'll go and get her right now. What's your address?'

She writes it down hurriedly and then says a barked goodbye before running out of the front door.

Next door the house feels as still and silent as a mausoleum. The net curtains turn the windows into opaque sightless eyes and, when she looks through the letterbox, she can see a tidy, empty hallway.

'Hester!' she shouts. 'Are you there?'

There is only silence. Melissa can't explain why this feels so wrong. But she knows now that the woman living next door to her all these years is one of the strangest people she has ever met. She can make the darkest things sound entirely reasonable. It's possible that she thinks she is helping by looking after Amber but it all feels skewed. Something is wrong.

She has an idea.

'Bertie!' she calls in a singsong voice. 'Here boy!'

Melissa silently prays for the sound of skittering claws on tiles … but there's nothing. She lets the letterbox fall back with a loud snap.

If the dog isn't there, she's gone away and taken Amber with her.

And Melissa has the strangest feeling she knows where.

HESTER

The journey will take five hours from Paddington to St Erth, then it's a short hop to Carbis Bay. I know that travelling so far with a young child and a dog is not going to be easy by train, but I cannot face getting on that motorway again. And for Amber to sit in the van when it has transported ...

Well, it just wouldn't be right.

But we are still only at Paddington and Amber is already grizzly. I have told her that her mummy needs a rest and that we are going to take Bertie to the seaside for a few days. At first she seemed to embrace the idea. However, as the tube train rumbled through the depths of the city towards Paddington, she started to fidget and whine. She said she was hungry. Then that she needed a wee. Then came the universal signifier of an anxious child the world over: she had a 'tummy ache'.

So when we got to Paddington, finally, after what seemed such a long period of travelling when we've only just begun the journey, I crouched down to her level and asked her to look at me.

Warily, she turned her beautiful blue eyes towards me and I could see that her bottom lip was starting to jut. I told her, very quietly, that Bertie needed a holiday because he had been sad and that a little holiday with Amber was what he wanted most in the whole world.

She'd frowned and chewed her bottom lip for a moment, then glanced at Bertie, who was sitting nicely and looking around at the busy station.

'So will you come and make him happy, just as a special favour?' I'd cajoled. 'I can't do it without you, you see.'

She tried to pick him up then and he'd scrabbled free and scratched her a little bit with his claws. This prompted the tears that had been steadily brimming to start falling from her eyes and I almost gave up on the whole enterprise.

Then I had a brainwave. There was a branch of Claire's Accessories across the concourse. The day before, Amber had tried to dress Bertie up with one of her hairclips, much to the poor dog's distress.

'Hey!' I said. 'Shall we go and buy some pretty things in there for Bertie to have on his holiday? We can buy a scarf to tie around his collar. What do you think?'

Amber's face was still grumpy but she nodded and meekly took my hand.

And so it is that we have been on this train for three hours. We are not far from Plymouth, I think. Amber has looked at all the comics I brought with me and eaten all the sweets, despite my assertion that today would be a little kinder on the teeth.

She has endlessly walked Bertie up and down the train until he got so tired he simply sat down by my feet and wouldn't move any further.

I am a little worried about the toilet issue. When we got to Exeter St David's, I tried to persuade Amber to hold our seats while Bertie did a widdle but she created quite a fuss. I had to risk losing our seats and bring everything with us. As it was, Bertie was too overwhelmed by the noises and smells of the station to go.

We had just managed to get back onto the train as the whistle went and the doors locked. It was a very close thing. I am telling myself that Bertie is able to go all night without going to the toilet so, hopefully, my boy won't let me down now.

I keep looking around at other families on the train and almost wishing I had some sort of iPad thing, just for this one time. It seems to be how most other parents are keeping their offspring occupied. A frazzled-looking woman across the way, who has a boisterous boy of about six (who Amber is fascinated by, naturally) and a tiny sleeping baby, gives me a sympathetic look now.

The boy is engrossed in something on her device, his eyes glassy and round, his bottom lip hanging open and shining. I don't approve of using screens as babysitters for children but I can finally see the attraction of those things.

The woman blows her cheeks out and grins at me. It is a moment of parental camaraderie that pierces me with such happiness that I feel my eyes prickle with tears.

I hurriedly look away, blinking hard.

Thank you, I say inside my own head.

Amber starts to kick the seat with her heels, a rhythmic, metallic thumping sound that is instantly intolerable. A young man, who appears to be surgically attached to his laptop, glances up sharply and even the woman opposite frowns and looks a bit irritated.

'Amber, darling, do please stop that,' I say.

She continues, even harder. The little minx is really testing me now.

'Amber! Stop that!' I didn't mean for it to come out quite as loud as it did, and she starts to cry.

I have no idea what to do. I can feel the disapproval of the carriage coming at me like gusts of stormy wind and my cheeks catch fire. In a minute we will be kicked off the train and then what will we do?

'Would your granddaughter like to play with this?'

The woman across from us is leaning over and holding some sort of plastic toy in bright primary colours.

Amber is immediately distracted from her bad behaviour and snatches the toy from the woman's hand.

'Amber!' I admonish. I am becoming quite exasperated.

But the woman just laughs and says, 'It's no problem. My sister's little boy has Down's and he likes things like this. It's the baby's, really, but if it helps, you're welcome to play with it for a while.'

I could hug her.

'Thank you so much,' I say sincerely and she just smiles and turns back to her baby, who has woken up and is starting to grizzle.

The toy is some sort of caterpillar with various parts to it. Some are magnetic and some must be jammed together to stick. Amber's little brow is fiercely scrunched as she concentrates on putting pieces together and then taking them apart again. The tiny pink tip of her tongue pokes out the side of her mouth and I am flooded with love once again.

Bertie is asleep at my feet and countryside is flashing by outside the window.

I am journeying to a new land. A new phase of my life. I don't know what will even happen tomorrow. Maybe today will be all I have. So I make a decision there and then to try and relax and enjoy the journey.

I settle a little more comfortably into my seat and think about the moment when we scrunch our bare toes into golden sand. We will have fish and chips on the seafront tonight in St Ives.

And maybe an ice cream afterwards. I wonder if some of the same cafés will be there?

Contentment warms me through as the West Country pulls us deeper into its heart.

MELISSA

Melissa stares down at her mobile on the kitchen table and pictures herself calling the police. Her hands begin to tremble from the poisonous mix of hangover and shock.

What is Hester *doing?*

She gets up and begins to pace the kitchen, trying to tick off points in her head.

Is Amber in actual danger? No. Hester is nuts about children. She'd never harm one.

But it's entirely possible she won't come back. She will disappear off somewhere with the little girl and twist the logic so that it seems like entirely the right thing to do.

And then everything might come out in the open about Jamie.

Melissa begins to reach for the phone and then hesitates.

Maybe there is another way. Maybe Melissa can confront her, persuade her to hand Amber over. Then the police won't have to be involved at all?

Melissa's fingers are slick with sweat as she fumbles the laptop open and on and begins searching for flights to Cornwall. Driving isn't an option. There is no time and, anyway, she is far too shaken up and hung-over to drive.

She and Mark had almost flown for that anniversary weekend,

then decided that first class train travel would be more fun. But this will take half the time. Clicking onto the suggested airline's website, she sees there is a flight leaving at 12.50 from Gatwick. It is 10 a.m. now. She might be able to get there for the early afternoon. She buys the ticket, leaving the return open, and prints off her boarding pass.

Melissa doesn't know what she will do when she gets to Carbis Bay. Will she even find them? Her instincts tell her to curl up in a corner and stay out of this, but doing nothing is not an option.

It has taken until now for her to understand there is something seriously wrong with Hester. This fussy, buttoned-up woman is able to mould the most grotesque realities into shapes that seem acceptable and even logical to her. But whatever her justification for taking Amber away, Melissa needs to stop her. She owes this to Kerry. And to Jamie.

Half an hour later she is in a cab travelling to King's Cross. She hides her puffy, wild eyes behind sunglasses. The driver, a small, bespectacled Indian man, has shot more than one curious glance at her. She is aware that she crackles with tension, stress sparking off her like an electrical discharge. He doesn't attempt to make conversation.

Pushing through the crowds of slow-moving tourists and forests of wheeled cases at the station, she manages to catch the Gatwick Express and it is only when she settles into her seat that she begins to shake. She sends Kerry a text message.

I am going to bring Amber back to you by this evening. Please don't worry. She is safe and well and happy. Melissa

She doesn't really know if any of this is true.

Then she turns off her phone and buries it deep in her handbag. Kerry will ring as soon as she gets the message. It feels now as though the phone glows radioactively inside the leather bag. Kerry's fury and terror will be funnelling towards her like a mini tornado and she bites her lips in distress before quickly looking around the carriage. But no one is looking at her.

The train is busy. A good-looking Italian group in their twenties chatter and take endless pictures with their mobiles. The women wave their hands expressively; colourful bangles tinkle up and down slim, tanned arms.

Elsewhere businessmen and women hunch over laptops or peck confidently at their phones with busy fingers. Everyone else's life is easy and uncomplicated, it seems.

Melissa suddenly pictures getting to Gatwick and taking the first flight out of the UK.

No. She has to see this through, wherever, however, it ends.

HESTER

Why should I expect things to go right for me? It's not as if they ever do. As if *I* ever get what I want.

I had it all planned out. We would check in and then head for the beach. I thought we could buy what we needed here and then while away the afternoon building sandcastles.

First of all, we couldn't find the guest house. Carbis Bay is much bigger than I remembered and in trying to follow the directions I had written down, we ended up in a complicated warren of houses on a very steep hill. Amber began to complain within a few minutes of walking. I tried to cajole and coax her with soft words but there was a resolute set to her little jaw and before long she began to wail. The pitch and volume of it was quite extraordinary.

I knelt down before her and tried to get her to pick up Bertie, even though he was frightened by the noise and straining away from me. Her face was turning a deep red and she kept running on the spot, her small feet pounding against the pavement so hard it must hurt.

It seemed to go on and on and several people passing by stared at us, muttering in disapproval.

And then, just to make it even worse, a light rain began to

fall. The weather changes so quickly here; I remember this. I looked up at the glowering darkness of the clouds rolling in from the sea and actually prayed for a bit of luck.

Amber stopped crying so abruptly I thought maybe my prayers had been answered. Then I saw that her attention had been snagged by a couple walking by with a toddler in tow and a gigantic white dog that was staring at us with a haughty manner. Some sort of husky, I think. I had a flash of inspiration then and said, gently, 'Can you see the wolf, Amber? They have friendly wolves here. Did you know?'

She gazed up at me with those blue eyes, clouded by tears now, and shook her head. Her tongue was slightly protruding but she had stopped crying at least.

'Let's go and quickly find where we are staying and we can go and see if we can find anymore, okay?'

I held out my hand and she took it with hers, which was warm and sticky. A clear trail of snot ran from her nose to her lip and I got out a tissue to clean her up.

But our troubles weren't over. When we got to the guest house I was told that they only took pets during the winter season, between October and April.

'But it didn't say that on your website!' I protested, quelling the sudden urge to cry.

The man on reception, who was young and sort of scruffy with a small beard, sighed and tapped away at his screen before turning it to show me. I could see then that the words 'Off Season Only' appeared in red next to the words 'Pet friendly'.

Blinking back tears, I asked him whether he could suggest another place we could stay. He wrote down a few names on a piece of paper and then, at my insistence, rang them to see if they had rooms. The first two were full and despair was really beginning to nip at my ankles, but thankfully, the third, a place called Hope House, had a large room available. He called us a taxi and good job too. It is about as far away from the sea as you can get and I would never have found it.

We are sitting here now. The room is not what I had hoped for. It smells very doggy and there are visible extension cables for the bedside lamps. The glass shades of these are thickly embedded with sticky dust. I think someone has been smoking in this room too.

Still, we are here.

Amber is sleeping on the bed, worn out by the travelling.

I have managed not to think too far ahead yet. It's amazing what you can put out of your mind if you really make the effort. But for some reason I keep hearing blasted Terry in my head today. I can just imagine what he would make of all this. 'Oh Hester, what on earth have you gone and done?' he'd say. Or, 'Well this is a bit of a mess, old girl. You're going to have your work cut out sorting this.'

Shut up, Terry, shut *up*. Wittering on inside my head all the time. Am I never to be free?

I hear a small sound and realize Amber is looking at me. She has her cheek pressed to the duvet, her mouth squished open. One eye regards me and for a horrible moment it feels as though she can see right into my soul. See all the things I've done.

I swallow nervously and then force a bright smile.

'Shall we take Bertie to the beach?'

Bertie, who is curled up in a tatty tartan dog bed by the window looks up at his name. I can't help thinking there is hope in his eyes that we will go home. I look away from him.

'I'm hungry. I want Mummy,' says Amber, as though the two phrases are intrinsically connected. Her voice has that low dangerous quality again, as though she is building herself up for another tantrum. I sag inside.

Why did I think this would be easy?

'Let's go and find something nice to eat, shall we?' I say

265

desperately, attempting to sound chipper. But it doesn't really wash. This little girl may have special needs but she isn't stupid. She knows something isn't right about all this. She knows I'm flailing.

'Want MUMMY, want MUMMY, want MUMMY,' she begins to chant and my head feels like it is ballooning inside and I just want her to—

'BE QUIET!' I yell and she gasps.

I wrap my hands across my mouth, wishing I could pull the words back inside. I have frightened her.

I have a sense that things are spinning out of my control.

But there's no going back now.

Things have gone too far. I won't go back to my life the way it was before. I've done too much in these last few weeks to allow that.

I'm in this now and the only way is forward. And I won't be alone again.

Wherever that takes me. And wherever it takes Amber.

MELISSA

Newquay airport was too small for a cab rank, Melissa found to her irritation. She had to search online for a local service, then wait ten interminable minutes for one to arrive.

The driver was a frowsy blonde woman, middle-aged, and squeezed into a bright red and white spotted top. Scarlet lips grinned wide over slightly yellowing horsey teeth.

She had attempted to engage Melissa in conversation for the first fifteen minutes of the drive before lapsing into humming along to a CD of country and western songs.

Melissa barely notices the scenery showcasing itself outside the car now. They travel along stretches of coastal road; the sea sparkling like green-blue silk to the left when blades of sun occasionally spear from the heavy cloud.

She is only dimly aware of her surroundings. Instead she mentally replays scenes in her head. Jamie at her front door. Jamie in her bed.

Jamie dead.

And then she sees the look on Mark's face when she finally passed on the burden she had been carrying for twenty years and told him about Thomas Pinkerton. Disgust. And a wariness that makes her insides shrivel with shame.

'Hello?'

The driver is looking at her in the rear-view mirror and frowning.

'Where is it in Carbis Bay that you're wanting, Lover?'

Melissa swallows and blinks. She has been in a half-trance during this drive and now her eyes throb and her mouth feels stale and woolly.

'Oh, I ...'

Coming here suddenly seems monumentally stupid.

They are on a winding road through a village. Grey stone buildings would be touching distance away if she opened the window and reached out. She sees a sign saying Lelant.

She has no real plan.

'Um, can you take me to where the hotels and B & Bs are?' she says.

The driver flashes her a tolerant look and lets out a low laugh. 'They're spread out all over, my love,' she says. 'Is there a particular one you're wanting?'

Hopelessness washes over Melissa now and she feels herself sag inwards.

'Are you all right?'

She blinks hard and forces a weak smile at the woman, who is now turning round from the front to look at her in a rather reckless way.

'I'm fine,' says Melissa hurriedly. 'Maybe you can drop me off in the centre of the town.'

The driver sighs. 'Well, it isn't Newquay you know. There isn't really a centre of the town as you call it. Tell you what, I'll drop you off by the big Tesco. There's a few B & Bs along there. And you can walk into St Ives in no time if you keep going—'

'Stop the car!' Melissa's voice is so shrill she shocks herself.

'I can't just stop here, it's—'

'Please!' Melissa turns and cranes her neck to get another look at the distinctive helmet hair shape of the small woman just emerging onto the main road, a little girl with a sulky set to her shoulders being pulled along next to her, and a small dog on a lead trotting along behind.

Swearing, the driver indicates and then, with agonizing slowness, pulls to a stop at the side of the road. A car bibs its horn as it passes. Hester and Amber are now out of sight around the bend.

'Look, I'm sure this is enough.' Melissa has already torn off her seatbelt and throws five twenty pound notes into the front seat now. 'I'm sorry!' she says breathlessly. 'And thank you!'

And then she is pounding along the pavement.

HESTER

It was the promise of seeing the 'friendly wolves' that got things moving in the end. I feel sluggish and a bit grubby as we make our endless way down towards the coast road. There's a path here somewhere, which I have been promised will lead to the sea.

Amber is silent now and I wish I could coax one of her beautiful giggles. When I take her hand to cross the road, she shrinks from me in a way that breaks my heart. It's as though she is a little frightened of me. I should never have shouted. But her ghastly mother seems to shout all the time and it's apparently water off a duck's back. One rule for me and one for everyone else, as usual.

The school holidays haven't begun yet and the sky is grey and oppressive. But there are still a few individuals and families walking along the main road in wetsuits and sarongs, sandy feet in flip-flops and sandals. I scrunch my toes inside my tights and court shoes and think about treating myself to some pretty sandals. But the thought doesn't feel as pleasurable as it did when I pictured it all from home. None of this is quite as I'd hoped it would be.

We find the entrance to the coastal path and my goodness it's steep. We start to walk downwards and I almost have to jog in order to stay upright. Small stones skid under my feet. There is a wire fence separating us from the drop on the other side. A tunnel of dark green trees seems to enclose us and I can see patches of sea through gaps below.

When someone shouts my name, I half-imagine my silly Terry thoughts are getting out of hand, and I turn, in an almost dreamlike state.

I can't believe what I see. I touch my cheek, just to be certain and then Melissa ... *Melissa* ... is running and stumbling down the path towards us. She almost trips, just managing to grab the wire fence to right herself. She is breathing hard; her cheeks bright with spots of colour and her eyes wide.

'Hester! Oh thank God!' she says and stops, placing a hand on her chest to get her breath back.

I reach for Amber and pull her toward me. She doesn't resist and leans her dense, warm weight against my hip. I stand tall, protecting her.

'What on earth are you doing here?' I say. I have never wanted to see someone less and distaste curdles in my mouth. 'This is none of your business. Go away and leave us alone.'

A blonde-haired family dressed in wetsuits pulled to their hips comes into view and regard us warily as they pass. The mother has a pink bikini top on and the father and son are bare-chested and tanned. The teenage boy is all gangly limbs and glasses. Their curiosity is almost palpable and I have to glare until they look away. Melissa seems oblivious and starts shouting.

'You can't just snatch her!' she cries. 'The police are probably looking for you; don't you understand what you've done?'

I glance in alarm at the family, who are hurrying away, heads bowed in towards each other in furtive conversation.

We have to get away from this witch who has brought me only pain.

'Come on, Amber,' I say and take her hand, pulling her with me. Bertie, frustratingly, has stopped to do a wee and I have to yank his lead to get him to move.

But Melissa won't be shaken off so easily.

'Hester!' she shouts. 'Haven't we done enough? Don't you think we need to put things right now?'

Anger rises like mercury then and I let go of Amber, marching back to Melissa. I thrust my face towards hers. Because I am lower on the incline, I feel even smaller in size than usual but my frustration and fury are a mighty thing and I see something nervous flash, gratifyingly, in her eyes.

'That's what I'm doing!' I hiss. I don't even care that a little drop of spit hits her face. She doesn't seem to notice. 'You can just let it go, Melissa!' I say and wave my hand like a magician producing a dove from a handkerchief. 'Poof! There! All your guilt is absolved! It was all me! I did it! I was the one! Now will you leave us alone? And anyway, that's what I'm doing, can't you see? Making it right?'

Melissa's mouth opens and closes like a fish. I've never seen her look less appealing than she does now, and I realize I don't even hate her anymore. She is nothing to me at all.

'What do you mean?' she whispers. Her skin looks wan and almost greenish in this odd light.

Reaching up on my tiptoes, I whisper into her ear. Her hair tickles my face and it feels unpleasant and smells dirty.

'I killed him,' I say. 'Not you! So why don't you leave us alone and get on with your life!'

She makes a sound that is neither a gasp nor a groan but something in-between. Her hands fly to her cheeks and tears begin to squeeze out over her lids and run down her pale, bony cheeks.

'You're a fucking monster,' she whispers but then her attention is snagged by something beyond me. She yells, 'No!' and shoves me out of the way.

I turn to see Bertie's tail disappear through a gap in the fence that leads to the open cliff. And then Amber, moving faster than I have ever seen, is squeezing through after him.

MELISSA

'Amber!' she shrieks, 'Come back! It's dangerous! Oh fuck, please! Amber!'

She is on her hands and knees, body half through the hole. The cliff surface comprises clumps of vegetation, knotted and dense as chainmail, but with clear patches that show sky and the deadly drop below. The dog is standing on a sandy outcrop, whining, paws scrabbling for purchase. Melissa can see a fine grain of sand falling below his feet.

Amber has become lodged on one of the twisted thickets, her hands bunched into the thorny mass. A thin line of blood runs down her wrist and she is making a terrible moaning sound, guttural and raw.

Hester screams; immobilized, it seems. She has been reduced to something useless.

'Oh fuck!'

Melissa knows that if she puts too much weight onto the area above Amber, she could cause more sand to fall and it might frighten her enough to let go. She carefully pulls her body through the gap, thorns tearing at her hands, until she is belly down on the ground, feet higher than her head. If she reaches out a hand she can just touch Amber, but the little girl has gone to a place of terror and won't be able to follow instructions; she knows this.

'Amber, sweetie,' she says, and the effort of trying to sound gentle is immense. 'You're going to be okay, but I need you to reach back and take my hand, okay?'

There is no response at first and then Amber murmurs a small sound. Melissa realizes she is saying, 'Help Bertie.'

'Bertie is going to be fine!' She sounds hysterical and can't do anything about it. 'But there isn't room for everyone here so we must get you first, okay? Okay, Amber? Shit!'

Tears break through and she lets them run down her cheeks and into her mouth. She is scared to move her hand but knows she must.

Hester is still wailing, saying something over and over again that Melissa can't make out. Melissa wants to *hit* her. Make her shut up.

'Amber, sweetheart, your mummy really needs you right now. We have to make sure you get back home to Mummy today. Do you understand?'

The little girl doesn't respond but there is a stillness as though she is finally listening.

'Come on,' says Melissa, encouraged enough to inject some fake control into her trembling voice. 'Just reach out and take my hand and then we can worry about getting Bertie out. Come on … Amber? Please sweetie?'

The little girl moves with agonizing slowness and, at last, turns a little, holding out her small pale hand. Melissa grabs it, but in her relief she snatches too hard and frightens her. Amber wails and tries to pull back. Sand and stones dislodge beneath her as they engage in a tug of war. And then Melissa has her in both hands and is pulling her back through the hole.

It's only then that she notices the ledge holding the dog has entirely disappeared.

HESTER

When Melissa comes back through the hole with Amber, I experience a moment of pure, sweet relief. Then I see her face and understand what has happened.

I can't control my weeping as I try to claw through the hole after him, but strong hands pull me back and then a male voice says, 'Come on, love, it's all right, it's all right!'

Through the mist of my tears I see a tall blond-haired man, a policeman, is holding me and there are other people standing around. A couple of gawkers watch from up the path, and another policeman is approaching us at speed. Through the trees above I can just see the yellow and blue squares of a panda car parked on the road.

'It's my dog!' I cry. 'Please help him!'

Melissa grips Amber, whose face is turned towards her. Melissa's eyes are cold and I can't bear to look at them.

It all comes rushing in. That Jamie man. Taking Amber. And poor Bertie …

Am I being paid back? I sink to the grass verge, not caring how damp and scratchy it is through my skirt, and I cry and cry, wishing I could turn the clock back and make it all right. My poor little Bertie is to pay the price for the acts I have committed.

And just as I feel that my chest is breaking in pieces with grief, the blond policeman is suddenly in my line of vision and he's holding …

'Oh thank God!'

I grasp Bertie to me and he wriggles, claws scratching my chest but I don't care. He's shaking violently, covered in sandy mud. But he's alive.

'He'd just fallen down to the next outcrop below,' says the policeman and he looks pleased, but I suddenly wonder why he appeared so conveniently. And then I remember the family who passed us and heard us fighting. Who heard Melissa say I had snatched Amber.

My joy at having Bertie back turns into a cold realization. And a weary acceptance. Terry was right. I do bring things on myself. I nearly caused Amber to be hurt and Bertie too.

I'm not a good woman. I've messed it all up. I've done some terrible things and the time has come to let it all go.

'So would you like to tell me exactly what has been going on here?' says the policeman now, getting out a notebook from his pocket.

Despite my tear-streaked face and sandy, filthy clothes, I have a moment where the chaos inside has truly calmed. I feel strong and full of acceptance.

'Officer,' I say, in a clear, confident voice, 'I would like to report a murder.'

PART FOUR

MELISSA

Melissa gazes from the back of the police car at the neon slashes of motorway flashing by outside. She is numb with exhaustion and the hangover of shock. The two policewomen in the front talk in low murmurs.

Amber lies with her head on Melissa's lap, the seat belt awkwardly around her soft middle. Melissa wants to stroke her hair, as much for her own comfort as anything else. But she doesn't want to wake the little girl. Not after such a traumatic day.

When Hester came out with those heart-stopping words, the ground seemed to rise up sickeningly before righting itself. She thought she would faint. The two police officers exchanged glances; one of them actually smirked and Melissa vaguely registered a thought. Maybe people should take Hester a bit more seriously. Herself included.

They were all taken down to the police station. Melissa watched Hester be led to an interview room while she was taken into a small back office. A policewoman distracted Amber with hot chocolate and an iPad while she was questioned.

Not knowing what Hester would say was a torture. But Melissa repeated basic facts several times over: Amber's father was an old friend who had visited and then disappeared. He had turned up, dead, and her neighbour somehow took it upon herself to take Amber away. No, she had no idea what Hester had meant about a murder. And please could she go home? She had promised Amber's mother she would return her.

It all felt like one of the most arduous things she had ever done. Physically hard, like there was a weight above her head; an avalanche she must hold back with her weak arms.

She longed to know what Hester was saying, how much she was implicating her. The fear felt it was injuring her inside, corroding her soft tissues. Somewhere along the line she'd agreed to take Bertie home. Perhaps if Hester heard about it, she might not mention Melissa? It was too good to hope for …

Then, incredibly, she was told she could leave. There would probably be some questions when she was home and she shouldn't stray too far but, yes, she was free to go and did she want a lift back to London?

The dog makes an odd sound now like a series of popping bubbles. It shakes all over and stretches out a back leg before pulling it back in again. She looks at it lying there in the footwell and wonders if dogs have nightmares. Is it – is *he* – reliving the mortal terror of that moment. The sickening free fall into nothingness?

She knows nothing about dogs. Has no desire to know anything further. The dog is a problem she isn't able to deal with right now. Melissa gnaws at her finger, nipping at the skin around her nail until blood oozes from her finger. Sucking the blood away, she tries to imagine, yet again, what Hester is doing right now. It is an impossible thing to picture: Hester in an interview room at a police station. *What is she saying? What is she telling them?*

Melissa closes her eyes in agony. She hasn't had the time to process what Hester told her on that path before everything went crazy.

Could it be true that she really didn't murder him? It means she must once again paint her world in new colours.

She starts to weep softly now. If only she had called the police that night. If only she hadn't gone along with the insane plan to bury his body.

Before long, they are passing Heathrow.

Melissa knows she should go with the police to return Amber. But seeing Kerry's grief up close will destroy her. She is too cowardly.

She will ask that she be taken home.

Back to her empty house and her nightmares and whatever comes next.

HESTER

'Hester,' I say out loud. 'You have a lot to answer for.'

Shivering a little, I regard the thin green blanket on the bed and wonder how bad it smells. I suppose beggars can't be choosers.

They didn't really want to put me in here but they tell me there is no one to take me to London, where local officers will be taking over my investigation, until the morning.

The cell really is as mean and cold and desperate as I would have imagined. In other respects though, it's funny how different it all is compared to the television. It's the speed of things more than anything. It's all so very *slow* in real life. On screen, criminals get processed and questioned in no time and then lickety-split, it's time for the trial.

Whereas I feel as though I have been here since last Wednesday at least.

Might as well get used to it, Hester, I tell myself. Your time is no longer your own, old girl.

I don't think they exactly know what to do with me. For quite a while they behaved as though I were a harmless old woman with delusions. That rankled, I can tell you. Just because I am a quiet person past the first flush of youth, must I be endlessly patronized?

When I arrived they put me in an interview room and left me for such a long time. My poor hips ached horribly on that plastic bucket seat.

A policewoman with a sharp nose and rather greasy-looking fair hair offered me tea but there had been no sign of it. I felt as though I could deal with the next bit, if only they would do this one thing.

I looked around at the interview room, imagining all the horrible things that had been confessed to here. The walls were a sickly green colour and there was a large mirror, two way, I'm sure, on the wall opposite. I suddenly got the urge to wave at it, just in case anyone was looking in. That would certainly have given them a surprise.

My thoughts jumped back to Amber being taken away, crying noisily. I don't think I have ever felt worse than I did at that moment. I will never see that sweet child again. I took on the task of keeping her safe and I failed in that one thing. This knowledge was a knife to my heart and I began to moan softly.

'Are you all right?'

I hadn't even heard the door opening but they were back, Greasy Hair and a man I immediately called Baldie. They stared at me as though I was quite the oddest thing they had ever come across. If so, they have led very sheltered lives for representatives of the law.

'Still waiting for my cup of tea, since you ask,' I said crisply and was gratified to see a slight colouring in the policewoman's cheeks.

'Oh, I'm sorry, let me just …'

A cup of tea arrived a few minutes later, in a mug, rather than from a machine, to my surprise.

They sat opposite me. She had a tired face and carried weight around the midriff. Her blue suit jacket was shiny and cheap and there was a small stain on the lapel, which I was certain was baby sick. I knew in that moment that a woman like her would never understand a woman like me.

Him, the man, was quite good-looking, if you like that sort of thing, with his dark eyes and rather effeminate eyelashes.

He met my gaze directly and I found myself glancing away. I expect he gets all sorts out of people with that penetrating stare.

They did that thing with the tape recorder then and I got to hear their names: Detective Constable Maggie Donovan and Detective Constable Ian Rivers. They asked me if I would like them to arrange a lawyer, and I gave a loud bark of laughter that I think surprised all three of us.

'I think it is a little late for that,' I said, taking a sip of the tea, which was foul and milky. I grimaced and swallowed it anyway, needing the meagre sustenance it provided.

'Okay Hester,' said Donovan, 'so you say you would like to report a crime?'

'I would,' I said patiently. 'This is my confession. It shouldn't take too long.'

They did it again, exchanging glances. He, Rivers, looked like he might laugh.

It enraged me, I can tell you.

I leaned forward and looked very deliberately into both their faces. I could almost feel the energy in the room becoming more focused. It was quite thrilling in a way.

'I will make this very easy for you,' I said carefully. 'I should be charged with abducting that child. But I am also guilty of the murder of my husband, Terence David Morgan, in 1999. He was very sick and I drowned him in the bath. It wasn't one of those situations where he'd begged me to do it. I don't imagine he wanted to die at all. There,' my cheeks feel flushed and I am exhilarated by my own speech, 'is that clear enough for you?'

It had been a sticky, unpleasant week. The sort that frays tempers. Dust motes danced in the slash of sunlight coming through the bedroom curtains and the smell of sickness pervaded the house, however much I opened the windows or sprayed Airwick around the place. Terry'd had this blessed stomach thing for a few days.

Well, that was just the final straw.

The dementia had started slowly. A lost wallet here, a forgotten appointment there. Then he started to forget my name and then his own name. The doctors said he was very unlucky to get it at only 68. *He* was unlucky? What about me?

Terry had only ever let me down. He wasn't a father. He wasn't a businessman. I needed the patience of a saint, that final year. Caring for him and having to be his memory and his chaperone and his *everything*.

So when I'd had to clean up his mess for the third time in two days, I decided enough was enough. He took the sleeping tablets without complaint and was docile as a lamb as I encouraged him into the bath. He even smiled like a little boy being given a treat when I placed the full glass of whisky on the side of the bath. He always liked a drink and hadn't been allowed one for such a long time that he drank it as though it were squash. It wasn't long before his eyelids began to slip and his face slacken into sleep.

Then all it took was the gentlest push. He struggled a tiny bit and the bubbles rising to the surface were a little distressing. But it didn't take long and that added to the feeling that it was all meant to be, if you see what I mean.

I was hoping I might have been able to share this, the deepest of my secrets, with Melissa after that night we spent together. But now I know that she wouldn't understand.

In a way, all of this is Terry's fault. If we'd had a child, I may have been a grandmother by now. (Yes, a grandma Jamie!) I would have been far too busy to get mixed up in Melissa's nonsense. Why couldn't he have just done that one thing for me?

So I've been formally charged, and now I sit here in this dingy, oddly quiet, cell, I can almost sense Terry finally leaving me.

I suppose I could have told them about the other thing. But

I think this is quite enough to be going on with. Terry has been the albatross hung around my neck for so long.

Jamie can stay as our little secret. And I need someone to look after Bertie, don't I?

I'm sure Melissa will grow to love him in time.

Five months later

MELISSA

She must have muddled her times because the estate agent is still here. Melissa experiences a blast of panic and has an urge to hide behind a car or simply turn the other way. She didn't want any part in this process.

But it's too late. They have all seen her. She tries to smile. Bertie tugs at the lead and gets twisted around her leg and she irritably untangles him until she is free again.

The estate agent looks like a schoolboy in his work experience clothes. His cheeks, so newly free of acne, have a scrubbed, almost boiled look. His shoes are shiny and pointed. A young couple are coming out behind him. Indian, she thinks. The woman is small with a prominent pregnancy bump and quick brown eyes. She looks like she would be fun. He is tall and bespectacled, serious and suited.

'Here's the lady of the house right now!' says the agent. She can never remember his name. Kev or Keith or Kelvin. Something like that.

'You have a beautiful home,' says the man, very formally. The woman nods, too enthusiastically, and Melissa feels tired.

'Thank you,' she says. 'I was just going to …' but she doesn't finish the sentence. What was she going to do?

'We actually had a question about the boiler,' says the man now, leaning his head forward, brow furrowed. He begins explaining something she doesn't really understand. She tries to answer the question, and he doesn't seem satisfied but is too polite to say.

'And the neighbours?' says his partner before leaning in conspiratorially, still grinning. 'Anything we should know? Any nosy parkers or party animals?' She laughs as she says it, as though it isn't important, but there is a sharp intelligence about her.

For a second, Melissa flounders and then manages to say, 'We've never had anything like that, no. It's a very good neighbourhood.'

Inside the house she rests her hand against the hall table and breathes deeply. She wonders what they would have done if she'd said, 'Actually the woman next door is currently serving a life sentence for murder. But you can rely on her in a crisis and she makes decent cakes.'

She starts to laugh, deep from her belly but it feels unnatural in the quiet house, tidy as a show home. She stops and goes into the kitchen where the dog is waiting to go outside.

Opening the back door, she notices that his back legs seem to sag. An unexpected sadness washes over her.

'Stupid animal,' she murmurs and swallows a lump of grief back inside herself. That won't be easy, when it comes. She's grown quite attached to the smelly little beast. And Tilly loves him.

Melissa gets a glass and fills it from the filter before taking a long sip. She wonders if that couple will make an offer. The thought scares her a little.

They still haven't made a final decision about whether they will buy two properties, possibly outside the M25. One for Melissa, one for Mark and Tilly. Or one for Mark, one for Tilly and Melissa. Nothing has been decided.

Tilly is studying for her A levels at a local FE college. They don't have the money for boarding school anymore. Mark has had to take on extra shifts to try and recoup some of their losses. He turned down the offer of a new contract on *BBB*. He looks much older than he did a few months ago.

Melissa had stayed up all night when she got back from Cornwall, slumped at the kitchen table. She'd tried to get drunk but the vodka tasted bad and her stomach wouldn't accept it.

By five the following morning she began repeatedly ringing Kerry's number until the very groggy and bad-tempered mother answered. At first she hadn't taken Melissa's demand to know Kerry's bank details seriously.

Melissa kept saying that she wanted to do this. That she should have helped Jamie when they were young and she should have helped him more recently. That she felt responsible for what had happened to him. She wanted to make it up to Kerry and to Amber. Suspiciously, the woman, Phyllis, found her daughter's chequebook and recited the details Melissa needed.

It was then the work of a few keystrokes to transfer £20,000 – to Kerry. After this she looked up the charity Thomas Pinkerton worked for – an environmental group, it transpired – and made a donation of another £20,000. The rest of the money she donated to The Down's Syndrome Association and the NSPCC.

Then she went upstairs and took the remaining diazepam in the bottle before lying down on the sofa and waiting to die.

They said afterwards that she hadn't taken enough. But when Saskia called round the next morning on the way to work and heard the dog barking inside, she got Nathan to break a window and climb inside.

The police had been interested when they learned of this. There were too many strange conflicts swirling together over these two properties like a mini tornado. Dead men. Snatched children. Suicides and large bank payments, because, oh yes, they knew about that.

But there was no real evidence that Melissa had taken part in any crime. And there were only so many resources available to Dorset Police. The high-profile murder of a young mother in Dorchester a few weeks later was deemed a higher priority. So, after a handful of interviews that started next to her hospital bed, the case was left unsolved.

Melissa no longer wants to confess. She has done enough to her family, she knows that. Mark is like a ghost these days, and Tilly seems to have shrunk into herself. She constantly sneaks looks at her mother as though she is a stranger. Melissa knows how she feels. She is like a stranger even to herself.

She picks up the pile of post from the kitchen surface now and goes to the table, catching a flash of red from her hair reflected in the side of the microwave. She isn't used to it yet. She has kept her hair short and let her natural colour grow through.

Mark hasn't said whether he likes it and she supposes she shouldn't care. But she does. It's so exhausting, tiptoeing around his anger and grief. Throwing all their money away as she did is unforgivable. Inexplicable. But she doesn't regret it for a second.

She has told him the same story so often she half believes it now: Jamie stirred up bad emotions from her past; she feels guilty that he was murdered and that Hester became involved. She only wanted to help.

Kerry wrote to her, not long after. She was moving to Manchester to be with her mother. She said if Melissa thought she was forgiven for not helping Jamie when he needed it, she had 'another thing coming'. Then she had awkwardly included something about Amber sending her love to the dog.

No, she doesn't regret it.

But she's sick of them looking at her like she is a stranger.

Last week at Couples Counselling, she had told Mark all about her childhood for the first time. He'd been shocked enough to cry a little but she remained dry-eyed. Afterwards, he had moved to hold her, but she had stepped to one side. She didn't know how to be forgiven. It seemed like a coat that was too big or too small to wear.

As Melissa stares down at the pile of junk mail on the table, a thought seems to gain weight and form until it is a thing that slithers and twists inside her.

I could just leave, she thinks. *Let them get on with their lives without me.*

What is to stop her? None of them would really miss her. She's nothing but trouble.

Melissa stands still for a few moments and then she is hurrying up the stairs and into her bedroom. She goes into her walk-in wardrobe and begins pulling out clothes and throwing them into a pile on the floor. She doesn't need much. Just a few tops and some jeans. One decent jacket. She can't seem to care about that stuff anymore. Scooping it all up in her arms she flings it onto the bed and goes to get her wheelie case from its place on top of the extra wardrobe in her bedroom. She tries to remember how this felt before, the specific dimensions of those moments, but they're like a half-remembered dream and she can't seem to grasp them.

As she stuffs clothes messily into the case, downstairs, her phone chimes with a text. Distractedly she goes to the bottom of the stairs and reaches for her bag, which she dropped in the hallway when she got home.

Melissa frowns when she sees it's from Mark. This is such a rare occurrence now that she briefly wonders if something is wrong.

The message says:

Let's me, you, and Tils go out for dinner together at the weekend. Somewhere nice as a family. She needs you and so do I. I miss you. Mx

Melissa slumps down onto the bottom stair, gazing at the screen. She begins to cry.

She cries for Jamie and she cries for Tilly. She cries for Mark. He isn't the only cheat and she has done far worse things in the grand scheme of things. Then she cries for young Melanie with her hard, pretty little face and her broken heart.

Lastly she cries for the here and now and what has gone.

When she finishes she sits for a few moments longer and then begins to climb back up the stairs to unpack her case.

HESTER

I do miss Bertie. I will say that.

But I know Melissa will be taking good care of him. Apart from that, I miss oddly little about my old life.

I suppose I just wanted someone to need me. The irony of it all is that now I have no shortage of young women who need my care. Oh yes, I was frightened at first of all these girls with their hard hollowed-out eyes and their sallow complexions. I kept myself to myself and barely looked at anyone for the first few months.

It was Charly who first brought me out of my shell.

She is twenty-nine years old and here because of drugs and prostitution, like so many of them. She can't help having a silly name. I tried to call her Charlotte, as she was christened, but she wasn't having it!

The fact is that prison has been the making of her, although she misses her little boy, Tyler. We got talking one day while we were working in the laundry room and she poured out some of her worries. I was able to give her advice based on my consider-able experience with small children and she was so grateful it brought tears to my eyes.

Soon she would share news with me: how he had been praised

for a picture he had done at school; how he wanted to start karate lessons. He lives with Charly's mum in South London for now but she is full of plans about what she will do when she leaves here.

I will miss her.

But there are others now who ask my advice. I think I have become a bit of a mother figure to these young women.

And then there is Sandra.

She's older than the rest, although still a good few years younger than me. She murdered her husband. He was a drunk who hit her sometimes but her lawyer was not able to argue self-defence. It was because she killed him in his sleep, you see. Stabbed him with a bread knife while he lay drunkenly on the sofa.

I have no doubt that he deserved it.

Sandra is an educated woman, unlike almost everyone else here in Holloway. She has a Bachelor of Arts from Birmingham University, in English, grade 2:1. She is always reading books from the (admittedly meagre) library and has encouraged me to do the same. I never felt that I had time for reading in the past. But I am getting a great deal of pleasure from the quiet companionship we enjoy on an evening in my room or hers.

I try not to call it a cell. Living with a toilet in the room is something I never thought I would be able to tolerate but I simply cover it with a throw I stitched in one of the needlecraft sessions and you would never be the wiser about it. I have made some samplers that I have hung up around the place just to make it a little more homely. I never had time to do that before either but I find it very relaxing.

One of my creations says, 'Home is where the heart is' and, yes, you could argue that I am stuck in a terrible place, filled with murderers, drug addicts, and worse, and will probably be here for a good ten years.

But what is the point in complaining?

I had nothing to live for out there. Bertie, maybe. But no one loved me or wanted me to be in their life. No one *needed* me.

Well. Plenty of people need me here.

It's funny, the things you find out about yourself, isn't it, in extreme situations? Sandra won't be going anywhere for many years either and this thought fills me with a quiet pleasure.

She won't be able to leave me, like others have done.

We can be together for ever, if I want it.

And sometimes, late at night, if I feel frightened or lonely, I picture myself telling the police everything about Jamie. Why not? I have nothing to lose. It wouldn't take long for them to look in Melissa's kitchen and find what they were looking for. But what would be the point? I think it is best that we put all that behind us. Anyway, she has Bertie.

I hear a sharp rap on my door and look up.

Sandra stands there, holding up a battered copy of *Emma* with a smile. She has been reading it to me. I'm not sure I understand it, but I find her voice very soothing.

My heart floods with a sense of peace.

I can put up with the discomforts of being here.

It really isn't so bad at all.

ACKNOWLEDGEMENTS

First of all, I'd like to thank my brilliant agent Mark Stanton (Stan) for taking the initial chance on me and then putting up with my endless questions and needy emails. I feel very lucky to have an agent who is such a talented editor (as well as being huge fun to hang out with).

I had several early readers of *The Woman Next Door* and am enormously grateful to Lee Weatherly, Emma Haughton, Susannah Rickards, Ruth Warburton and Emily Gale for their incisive comments, which helped to make the book a better read. My beloved sister Helenanne Hansen has read every bit of fiction I've ever written and her input is always hugely appreciated. Thanks also to my lovely brother in law Pete Hansen, who helped with some of my questions about cars (and never let on how stupid they were).

The Woman Next Door is my first book as Cass Green and I hope it will be the first of many. I have written four books for the Young Adult market and always felt lucky to have worked with wonderful editors in the past. I didn't think I could strike gold again but it seems that I have, with Sarah Hodgson at HarperCollins. Not only did she pick up this book for the Killer Reads imprint in the first place, but she has been a real pleasure to work with during the editing process.

My dad, George Green, died while I was writing this. He was such a big cheerleader for my writing it was like having the publicity budgets of all the biggest publishers put together at my disposal. He would have been so excited to see me branching out into adult fiction and, let's face it, would no doubt have bored everyone senseless within a five-mile radius.

I miss him every day.

Thanks always have to go to the three gorgeous chaps in my life for putting up with the neurotic writer who lives amongst them. Love you, Pete, Joe and Harry. Pete never quite gets the thanks he deserves for his support in this writing process. Sometimes words aren't enough.

I hope you enjoyed reading *The Woman Next Door*.

And that you will always be lucky with your neighbours...

Caroline Green (Cass Green) June 2016.

KILLER READS

DISCOVER THE BEST
IN CRIME AND THRILLER

Follow us on social media to get to know the team behind the books, enter exclusive giveaways, learn about the latest competitions, hear from our authors, and lots more:

 /KillerReads   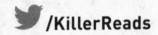 /KillerReads